DARK CITY

Sarah Kay Moll

A NineStar Press Publication

Published by NineStar Press
P.O. Box 91792,
Albuquerque, New Mexico, 87199 USA.
www.ninestarpress.com

Dark City

Printed in the USA
First Edition
July, 2018

Print ISBN: 978-1-949340-28-0

Also available in eBook, ISBN: 978-1-949340-24-2

Warning: This book contains depictions of prostitution, drug use, addiction, murder, torture, cutting, knife play, patricide, graphic violence, and gore, and mentions of childhood molestation and spousal abuse. Allusion to death of an animal.

Jude has a tender heart. Yet he was born into a criminal empire and groomed from childhood to step into his father's violent footsteps. To survive, he created a second personality. Ras is everything Jude isn't—cruel, remorseless, and utterly without fear, as incapable of love as Jude is of malice.

But when Ras meets a ruthless socialite, he begins to feel a strange stirring of emotion, a brush of Jude's passion against his own dark heart. Meanwhile, Jude finds himself with a knife in his hand, the evil in Ras's soul bleeding into his own.

As the walls between them crumble, they could lose everything—their lovers, their family, and their hold on the dark city itself.

Coming together could break them...or make them whole.

To my Dr. Jekyll, with love

Prologue

ALTHOUGH THERE ARE fuzzy, incomplete reminders of his time in Russia, Jude's first real memory is of the city. Of the crowded harbor, which had once been a military fort, a bleak concrete space surrounded by gray stone walls that had stood for hundreds of years. He walked with his mother and brother through the throng of people, who all spoke different languages and smelled of faraway places, the spices and sweat mingling with the tang of salt in the air.

Entranced, he let go of his mother's hand and slipped away, darting among the many legs striding purposefully around him. He followed the length of one wall, his palm pressed to the weary gray stone, until it came to a corner where a circular tower spired upward. It seemed immense as he craned his neck to see the top, and he—barely having to duck—walked under the yellow tape strung across the entrance and into a cool, dim space. But he was unafraid. His mother had told him so many things about the city, the size of it and all the places that would be within, green parks with leafy trees, stores with toys and candies and books. A big house that would always be warm, where he would have his own room. It only occurred to him much later how fictional these accounts were, as Mama had never been to the city herself.

He climbed the stairs, six spiraling flights, and with each flight his excitement grew, as he knew that something magnificent must lie at the top. This was the magical city, his promised land.

He arrived at a flat area, roofless, surrounded by a mesh fence through which he could see in all directions. The city lay before him like a map come to life. It had its own topography, manmade mountains of rooftops and valleys of asphalt roads stretching as far as he could see.

"Jude." A low, gravelly voice came from behind him, and he turned.

He didn't recognize the man standing there, squatting down so they were level. He was blond and clean-shaven, with a strong jaw and a warm smile.

"Do you live in the city?" Jude asked, tilting his head curiously. He spoke only Russian then, and it never occurred to him that this stranger might not. "Do you like it? I'm going to live here now."

The man chuckled. "Jude, don't you remember me?"

Jude shook his head.

The man didn't seem upset, smiling widely at the little boy. "I'm your papa."

His mother had told him Papa would be here at the harbor, and they had been searching for him. She would be proud that Jude had found his father, and all by himself.

"Do you want to see the city?" the man said. Papa. He must start thinking of this stranger as Papa now. "Let me pick you up so you can see better."

Jude nodded eagerly and held his arms up. He was lifted as though he weighed nothing, even though his mother always said he was too heavy to be carried. They looked out at the city together.

The city's a lot bigger than this," his father said. "Someday, I'll take you somewhere where you can see every part of it."

"When?" Jude demanded.

"Tomorrow, maybe. I'll take you to my office. You can see everything from there."

"Is that where you help people buy and sell things?" Jude asked. This was all his mother would say when he asked what his father did for a living.

"Is that what she told you?" Papa sounded amused, but not unkind. "Do you want to know what I really do?"

Jude nodded.

"There are two cities here," Papa said. "There is the city in the day and the city at night. In the daytime, there's a man called a mayor in charge of the city. Do you know what a mayor is?"

"Yes."

"But in the night," Papa said, "I'm in charge." He spread his free arm, as though to embrace every building they could see and all the space between. "This whole city is mine. And maybe someday, it will be yours. Would you like that?"

Jude looked out over the rooftops and imagined the people beneath each one, imagined them looking up at his papa, and at him.

"Yes," he said, and grinned. He couldn't imagine ever wanting anything more.

Part I

1: Jack of Spades

AROUND ME, THE hallway is silent. No soft brushes of footsteps on the dark green carpet, no huff of breath, no rustle of clothing. But a fragment of a second before he strikes, I know he's there.

I raise my hand, grazing my fingers over a thin metal wire but failing to stop it from circling my neck. My attacker jerks my head toward him with the noose, the cold wire digging into my skin. Like any trained Special Forces soldier, he's turned his back to mine, intending to yank me over his shoulder like a duffel bag and strangle me with my own weight. I have only a single second before my feet leave the ground, and I use it well, launching myself into the air. I backflip over him, turning through the still, stale air to land on cat feet facing him. The wire, made long to give better leverage, loosens enough for me to pull it over my head.

I throw a kick, a downward thrust toward his knee. Graceful as always, he steps easily aside. He answers it with a quick punch, fist flying toward my jaw, but my arm is already there, deflecting the blow harmlessly away.

I barely dodge another jab, a decoy strike before he grabs my arm, twisting it behind me and pushing me up against the wall. A picturesque landscape in a gilt frame crashes to the floor by my feet.

He jerks the captive limb once and pain shoots up and down my arm like sharp splinters of bamboo. He's always believed pain to be an excellent teacher, so it's become a frequent companion.

When he releases me, I turn to face him, shrugging my right arm a few times to work the pins and needles out.

"You heard me," he says, approval softening his stern features, the crooked nose—broken three times over his forty-five years—the steely line of his mouth, the sharp angle to his jaw.

"It wasn't exactly that, sir," I say. "It was more like I sensed you. I didn't hear much but I knew you were there."

"Even better. Go get something to eat. I'll be there in a few."

"Yes, sir."

I continue down a hallway lined with dim lights encased in stained-glass sconces. Narrow latticed windows let the deep blue of twilight fall over me.

The kitchen I step into at the end of the long hall is brighter, cheery white-yellow light over dark wooden counters. My mother stands at the stove. Beside her, sausages in a cast iron skillet hiss and spit.

"It smells good," I say. On rare nights, Mom lets the housekeeper go home early and cooks something herself—the rich, salty flavors of her homeland.

"Hello, Jude," she says in her faint voice, delicate as a flower's petal and rarely louder than a murmur. Her soft smile fades as she walks toward me and runs a gentle finger across my neck where there must be a red line from the garrote. "Your father needs to be more careful."

"My father knows what he's doing." I trust him, and I don't want her to talk like that when he might overhear.

She sighs, turning back to the stove as my brother Eli walks in. He's wearing his date-night clothes, groomed and stylish as someone on a magazine. He hates to hear how alike we look, but we do both have thick black hair, a striking contrast to our pale skin, and the same high cheekbones.

We take after our mother, who looks a little like Snow White, gazing wistfully out into the dark gardens. They're January-dead right now, brown and crumbling, but flourish in the summers; rows and rows of blushing rosebushes, a pale cobblestone path laced between.

"Mom." Eli puts his hands on her shoulders and says something in Russian.

She turns to face him with a smile, responding in kind. I listen to their murmured words, but only understand a few. I wasn't allowed to speak Mom's native language since we came to the city, and somehow I've managed to forget almost everything I knew. It means Mom is close to Eli in a way she can't be with me. She reaches up to pat him gently on the cheek, affectionate as always.

While they talk, I get a beer out of the fridge for him so he'll have to look at me for at least a few seconds. His hostile green-eyed gaze doesn't linger as he takes the cold bottle from me.

"I thought we could take the horses out tomorrow," I say.

"No."

"But you haven't ridden Sun in months."

He glances at the stove, but Mom has stepped out of the kitchen. "Fuck off, Jude. I'm busy." He turns and walks to the table. I follow and he sighs, setting his beer on the wooden surface with a clunk.

"Do you always have to look at me like that?" he says.

"Like what?"

"Like so sad. You look like a fucking puppy I kicked into the bay."

I cross my arms, as though I could block his stinging words and hide the part of me that feels just like a puppy he kicked into cold water.

"You're an asshole," I say. "I just wanted to spend time with you."

"You want to step into the gym and say that?" He walks toward me, an intimidating frown on his face, taking full advantage of the six inches he has on me, his bulky frame. By now, I've given up the hope I'll ever be as big or as strong as he is. But I'm faster, darting like quicksilver, elusive as water when we spar. As we've grown up, I've become his equal.

I hold my ground, looking up at him. "Yes. Let's do that."

"Fucking waste of my time." He steps away and turns back to the table. It's my victory, but I don't feel any triumph, just the usual weary guilt.

Mom sighs, standing in the doorway. She doesn't say a word, so used to our fighting she only tries to stop us if we're actually hitting each other. I should be more careful to keep it from her.

Dad comes in. He catches my eye with a warm, proud smile that makes me feel a little better. My mother turns her face up toward him, and he kisses her on the cheek. Her features are angular but beautiful, her slender neck clad in a gray turtleneck that doesn't quite cover the bruise at the base of her jaw. Dad must have been drinking last night. He doesn't mean to hurt her, but he can't always help himself. I should have been here to stop him.

"Smells good, Nadya," he says.

She gives him a timid smile. "For you, Vance. Mama used to make it when you visited us. You remember?"

"Of course I do, honey," he says.

Mom puts plates on the table in the breakfast nook, a small alcove surrounded by tall windows edged with lacy curtains. They let the darkness encroach on us, stars absent in the overcast sky.

"Do you have plans for tonight?" Dad asks. Eli and I both know he's talking only to me, Eli beneath his notice as always.

"Brienne's throwing a party," I say.

"Oh, Jude," Mom murmurs. "Shouldn't you stay and study? Have you studied one time since you were suspended?"

"That's right," Dad says. "You're back to school on Monday. Fucking shame. I had something pretty interesting planned."

"I don't have to go." I'd much rather work with Dad, like I've been doing since I was thirteen. Now that I'm eighteen, I'm an expert in everything from smuggling illegal drugs to running protection rackets.

"You do have to go," Dad says. "I had to pull a lot of strings to get them to take you back, so don't fuck it up again, hear me?" A cold, steely wire is threaded through his words, and I know I'll have to be careful.

"I don't know why you care," Eli says. "Jude doesn't learn anything. He doesn't even try. When I was—"

"He's learning plenty," Dad says, talking over Eli as usual. "You're not there to learn calculus or some shit. You're there because that's where the mayor and city councilmen and CEOs of major corporations send their kids. When they run this city, you'll be glad you know their names."

"They're not going to run this city," I say, grinning. "We are."

Dad chuckles. "Don't get cocky. But I do have the feeling that someday soon, we'll be able to do a lot of expanding." He stands. "You can't go to the party tonight. I need you boys with me. We have work to do."

DAD, ELI, AND I walk along a concrete path beside the dirty shore. The bay's gently lapping waters wash up pale plastic bags and soda cans that glint in the darkness. To our other side, solid squat warehouses in dull grays and browns. Dad's carrying a briefcase full of cash, a bribe for an important witness in a case we'd rather not lose.

Dad hands the money to me. "You take point, Jude."

I smile, though, out of the corner of my eye, I catch Eli's angry glare.

The woman we're bribing stands in the distance, in front of a car still running, casting a flood of light so all we can see is her silhouette.

I approach her, Dad and Eli flanking me.

"It's good to see you, Ms. Linders," I say. "I take it this means we have an agreement."

She nods, eyes downcast, the long straight line of her nose pointing to the ground. "My kid is really sick. I just…"

"I understand," I say gently, holding out the briefcase. "The syndicate looks out for its own. Remember that."

She looks up at me, startled, then takes the briefcase. "Thank you." She hurries back to her car.

As we watch her drive away, my father's phone buzzes. He answers it with his usual gruff hello.

"You're fucking kidding me," he says into the phone. He listens for a moment, scowling intently. "Jude did what?"

I take a cautious step back, his face darkening while the person on the other end of the line talks. I meant to tell him about this, I really did. I was just waiting for the right moment, and I didn't think he would find out so soon.

Dad lets out an exasperated sigh as he says goodbye, then turns to glare at me.

"I can explain, sir," I say.

"You'd better," he growls.

"What?" Eli asks, looking from Dad to me. "What did Jude do this time?"

"He killed his fucking boss," Dad says.

It's mostly true. Ras was the one who actually broke Kevin's hand and cut his throat, but only because I let him do it.

"You're the boss, sir," I remind him, though Kevin was my immediate superior, the man who oversaw all the crime in the Warrens, the ancient labyrinthine slums west of the river. I've been working for him for a year. While I'm technically a contractor, little more than hired muscle, Kevin saw my ambition as an opportunity to sit back and let me take care of everything from prostitution to protection rackets.

"Seriously?" Eli says. "I know you can be a sick little sadist, Jude, but you can't just kill because you feel like it."

"I'm not a fucking sadist," I snap, though it will do me no good to argue the point because Ras is, and I take credit for every one of his bloody kills. Still, I hate that Eli thinks of me that way. I know it's part of why he doesn't respect me. He thinks that violence for the sake of violence is childish and irresponsible. I agree, of course, but Ras doesn't, and it's not like Eli can see much of a difference between us.

"Then why did you do it?" Eli asks. "Did he piss you off?"

"He raped a woman. One of the whores. She wanted out so he beat her and raped her."

"And you thought this was a good enough reason to go behind my back, break one of my most important rules, and kill your direct superior?" Dad's shouting now, shoulders set and fists clenched. I hate the way that he and Eli can draw themselves up to their full height when they're angry so it feels like they're towering over me.

"Yes, sir," I say, holding his gaze. "I'd do it again."

"And not only did you kill one of my people, one of my fucking supervisors," Dad bellows, "but you broke his fingers and put a note on him telling people why he was killed. You know what Jenny just told me about? A fucking news story. This is going to be all over the fucking city, Jude."

"What Kevin did isn't unusual. I wanted to make an example of him."

"Jesus fucking Christ," Dad mutters. "I'm going to have to put out so many fucking fires." He turns to me, raising his voice again. "You know if you were anyone else, I'd have you killed. No trial, just shot in the head. Do you realize that?"

"If you think you can take me down, sir, you're welcome to try." I hold my breath through a long tense silence, until he makes a small noise that might be a chuckle and then starts to laugh.

"What am I going to do with you, Jude?" he asks, his anger fading. "You probably think you're going to get his job now, don't you?"

I look past a single dock, jutting like a lone wooden tooth into the bay, and imagine the black waters rising and rising, a dark tide to drown the city.

"Yes, sir." It's another rung on the ladder for me, another step closer to his office on the top floor of the skyscraper downtown, where he runs his empire and someday I'll be his consul, his right-hand man.

"I'll take it under consideration," he says, but I know from his tone he's already decided.

"You've got to be fucking kidding me," Eli says, scowling. "He kills someone without permission and you're giving him a fucking promotion?"

The fondness disappears from Dad's face, and he casts a harsh glance at Eli. "I said I'd think about it."

Dad starts walking with me by his side and Eli lagging a few feet behind us. I tell Dad about all the work I've been doing for Kevin, the contacts I've made, the secrets I've learned, the seedy underworld I've gained entry to.

"You like what you do," he says. "I'm glad. It's going to be more of the same, just on a bigger scale, when you're my consul."

I smile, though some small lonely part of me wishes he wouldn't so much as say that word in front of my brother. We spent our childhood in vicious competition for that opportunity, but now that I've won, it's easier for me to see the damage it's done to Eli—the oldest but the second son, the spare. He's Dad's most effective hitman, but that's all he does, and probably all he'll ever do. He gets all the money he wants—Dad has more than enough—while I have to earn my own way, but I don't envy him that. It's more than worth it to stand by Dad's side, to look out over the city and know that every back alley, every seedy bar, every dangerous dark place belongs to us.

"It's a long drive out to the Warrens, sir," I say. From our mansion in the Rise, I have to cross the river and drive through Ghost Town, which in bad traffic can take more than two hours, and I need to be there almost every day.

Dad glances at me. "You having second thoughts?"

"No, sir. I was just thinking maybe I should get an apartment of my own out there." The Victorian mansion, dark and stuffy and oppressive, has never felt like home, and when I think of my room—forest green, shadowy corners, door to the balcony boarded up—I'm eager to find somewhere else.

Dad's quiet for a few moments, then, to my surprise, he nods. "I think that's a good idea. I'll miss you, but it'll be good for you to get away from your mother's apron strings. You're young, but not too young to get started on your life."

"Will you—" I hesitate. "Will you look out for her when I'm not there?" I know that Dad doesn't mean to hurt her, and I know that deep down he doesn't want to, but I'm still afraid of leaving her alone with him. Eli will be there sometimes, but...

"Your mother will be fine." Dad's voice, flat and annoyed, cuts through my anxious thoughts. "So quit worrying. You've always been such a fucking momma's boy. It's time for you to grow up."

I clench my jaw and look away. Sometimes, I can't tell if I'm angry at him for the things he says, or at myself for deserving them.

Dad sighs. "You know I love your mother. And I love you. Nothing means more to me than our family. I just hate to see her hold you back."

"You really think she holds me back, sir?"

"Your mother can't deal with the real world. That's why she never leaves the house. If it were up to her, you'd spend the rest of your life in the kitchen with her like a fucking sissy. I know you're strong enough and smart enough to do better than that."

I turn the words over in my head and wonder if there's truth to them. If she is making me weak.

"Do you have enough money to get started on your own?" Dad asks.

I force a smile, a playful tone. "No. You should give me some."

He laughs. "Nice try. Do you have enough?"

"Yes, sir. I should be fine."

"That's my boy." The pride in his voice makes me feel a little better. "I got you a little something." He pulls a black switchblade out of his pocket and hands it to me.

I press the little button on the side and a shining blade clicks into place. I turn it to let the steel glint the cold white of the moon.

"Thank you, sir," I say, folding the blade back in so I can watch it jump into place again. Ras is going to love this.

When we get back to the car, Dad puts a hand on my shoulder. "Okay. The gig's yours. For a trial period. We'll see if you're ready for it."

I grin. "Yes, sir."

Behind him, Eli says nothing but gives me a cold, flat, snakelike stare. At times like this, I can't shake the idea, so strong it feels like a premonition, that someday we're going to fight and only one of us will walk away.

2: Monster

BREATHING DEEP THE salty air, Ras grins up at the sliver of moon hiding coyly in the sky. Tonight will be a good night. Dark and good for hunting.

Across a stretch of black water, standing atop the deck of a yacht, a wealthy playboy gazes at the shore. Ras is huddled beside a large shed with corroded metal siding, concealed in the shadows gathered between two weak industrial lights. Behind him, the Stacks stretches for desolate miles, modern boxy warehouses and crumbling remains from the Industrial Revolution sitting side by side. A skyline made distinctive by smokestacks, old and new.

This is no place for a man like the one aboard the luxury ship, and Ras imagines that the playboy, Damien Chase, is eager to unload the goods he stole from the syndicate and be done with this transaction.

Beside him, he senses rather than hears Vance moving through the shadows like a wraith. For all his bulk—broad shoulders, solidly built frame—he's impossible to catch when he wants to be.

"I had plans, you know," Ras says.

Vance's stern mouth turns in a fond smile, slight wrinkles just beginning to show at the edges. "By all means go. It's not that late."

Ras huffs a soft laugh. Vance is joking; they both know there's no place he would rather be.

"What did you see?" Vance gestures to the boat.

"Two guys. One there, the other walked to the back of the ship."

"Two hours and that's the best you've got?" Vance asks with a stern glance Ras ignores. He doesn't give a fuck what his father has to say. "Tell me what you saw."

Ras rolls his eyes, their vibrant green dimmed to colorlessness in the low light. Vance, a Special Forces soldier turned crime boss, insists upon constant awareness and keen observation of one's surroundings at all times, no exceptions.

"That's Damien." Ras gestures to the man now anxiously leaning over the railing. "He's not used to places like this, and he's nervous."

"And with good reason."

"One security guard who knows what he's doing. He's got an assault rifle and he gave Damien a pistol. But I doubt that idiot is going to shoot it." The playboy held the weapon delicately at arm's length, then set it aside near the cabin. He keeps casting brief glances at it, but it's unlikely he'll pick it up.

"Good." Vance's approving nod, which would have warmed Jude's heart, makes no difference at all to Ras.

"Can I have his yacht?"

Vance shakes his head with an amused smile. "Nice try. But no."

"Why not?"

"Because you're learning the value of a dollar. Let's go. You take Damien and get him restrained. Do it quietly. I'll tackle security and meet you on the deck."

"Fine." Ras scowls, still thinking of the yacht he really does deserve as he moves through the darkness beside his father, stepping silently over the warped boards of the dock and climbing onto the boat.

They part ways and Ras sneaks along the edge of the deck. Were he a cat, his ears would be perked and tall, listening intently to the soft lap of water against the sides of the boat. Limbs both tense and graceful as he crouches, moving slowly over the hardwood. Damien stands before him, shoulders slumped and hands pressed to the railing.

Ras lunges across the five feet between them, hitting Damien hard in the back of the head with the butt of his gun. The playboy's body goes limp, landing on the deck with a thud, limbs sprawled beneath him. Ras ties the unconscious man to the railing, then stands, looking out over the water.

His appearance is one of stark contrasts; pale skin against a shock of black hair. Deceptively lithe, remarkably strong. Cheerful, charming, but with a constant hint of danger, like the almost imperceptible crackle in the air that lingers before a storm.

Waiting is not among his many talents, and he fidgets, pacing the deck. He's just about to go downstairs and hunt for the security guard himself when Vance emerges from the lower part of the ship.

Damien has come to, and beneath the yellow light he's sickly pale, shadows like inky thumbprints beneath his eyes. Sitting silently, staring at his two captors.

"You better be wearing your gloves," Vance says, eyeing Ras's hands resting on the railing in the darkness.

"Of course I'm wearing my gloves." Ras sighs, raising his hands so Vance can see them clearly. "Can I take them off now?" He dislikes the feel of the thin black material between his fingers.

"No. Stay focused."

Vance kicks their prone prisoner in the ribs and tells him to get the fuck up. Damien has fair hair, blond enough to shine golden under the light, and a runner's slender build.

"Look," he whimpers, struggling to his feet with his arms bound. "I don't know what you want. You've got the wrong guy, you—"

"Don't bullshit me," Vance says with a menacing step forward.

"Look, whatever the boss is paying you, I'll double it. Triple it. I swear I—"

"I am the boss."

Damien gasps in comical surprise.

Ras suppresses a smile.

"Jesus Christ," their prisoner whimpers, "I'm so fucking sorry. You have to understand I was just the messenger. I didn't even know the syndicate was mixed up in it."

"You're a pawn," Vance says.

"That's right." Damien eagerly bobs his head. "I didn't plan anything. I just did what they told me."

"Who?"

Damien stands straight like an ice cube was just run down his spine. Ras watches him curiously, the tremble in his fine pianist's fingers, the wide eyes and half-open mouth that make him look like a pale fish. This is the thing they call fear. Everyone feels it. He even saw Vance feel it once, when a desperate junkie held a pistol to Ras's head and made wild, nonsensical threats. Even in that moment—fourteen years old, the barrel of the gun a cool metal kiss on the side of his head—Ras felt no fear. Fear fascinates him, as do all things he doesn't understand and has never experienced, like the inner workings of the human mind, like death, like the elusive thing Jude calls love.

"No way," Damien says. "I'm not going to sell them out. No fucking way."

Vance glances at his son and nods.

Ras steps forward with a wide smile, drawing the long knife he keeps strapped to his thigh. He likes this part.

"Tell me," he says, running his finger down the flat side of the blade. "What do you think will happen to you if you don't tell my father what he wants to know?"

Damien thrusts forward an unsteady chin, a pretense at defiance. "You'll kill me and throw me in the bay no matter what I do. I'm not telling you anything."

"This is true. But. If you don't tell my father what he wants to know, he'll let me play with you first."

Ras meets those blue eyes, winking before he traces Damien's pronounced Adam's apple with the blade of the knife, not quite breaking the skin. Drawing the moment out. Deciding where to make the first cut.

He's about to press the knife into the tender flesh of Damien's chest when the playboy gasps and says, "I'll tell you. Jesus Christ, just stop."

At a slight shake of his father's head, Ras lowers the knife.

Vance must see his disappointment. "You look like I just took away your favorite toy," he says, chuckling. "Be patient."

He turns back to Damien, warm fondness for his son replaced by cold wrath. "Who hired you?"

"I—I don't really know. I just had one contact. I never talked to the others."

"Who was your contact?"

Damien gulps a deep breath. "I don't know if it was his real name, but he told me to call him Nikita."

Vance balls his fists and hits Damien hard across the face. "Don't fuck with me, you piece of shit."

"I'm not," Damien whimpers. "I don't even know who he is."

"Was he tall?" Vance steps closer, towering over Damien, who cringes away. "Did he have dark hair? Did he have an accent?"

"He was tall, yeah. D-dark hair. He had an accent. The other guys too. They sounded Russian or something."

"You said there were others," Ras says, stepping forward again with his knife.

"Yeah." Damien swallows hard like something is stuck in his throat. "Yeah. I never talked to them. They only talked to Nikita, and not in English."

Nikita. The name stirs the barest hint of recognition each time it's spoken, an echo from a long time ago. A frustrating mystery. Ras doesn't dwell on it.

"Tell me where you got the passcode to get in our warehouse," Vance says.

Damien talks, telling them everything, but by this point Ras's short attention span is spent, and he fidgets through the rest of the interrogation. The boring details are for Jude to sort out later anyway.

He wants to get up and explore the ship. There's bound to be things to steal. But a stern glance from his father keeps him still. He's come to learn that there are benefits to doing Vance's bidding. When beatings and threats proved ineffective, Vance devised new ways to train his son. Gifts, privileges, and of course the opportunity for games like the one he was about to play with the unlucky Damien.

"I want you to take care of this," Vance says.

Ras's attention snaps back to the prisoner edging as far away from the pair of criminals as his bonds will allow. Without hesitation, he draws his knife across the side of Damien's throat, slashing the artery. The playboy opens and closes his mouth, forming silent words that bounce senselessly off his killer, who watches with a wide-eyed and not-at-all-hostile curiosity.

Ras pulls his knife away and runs a fingertip up the side of the bloody blade. The dark inside him singing, as it always does. What power could be more absolute? This sanguine victory, what triumph could be more complete?

He grins at his father, grateful for the opportunity to play after all. But even the hardened crime boss is sometimes unsettled by Ras's enthusiasm for this work, and now seems to be one of those times, Vance turning away with a nod.

Ras looks over at the lighted windows, wondering what good things might be hidden inside. Jewelry perhaps or cash or, if he's lucky, drugs.

"I'm going to check the rest of the ship," he tells Vance.

"Make it quick. Cleaners will be here in half an hour. I'll see you at home."

Ras makes his way down from the deck into pleasantly lit, opulently decorated rooms.

"Hey." A low voice, with a slight huskiness to it, like coarse fur, comes from a corner of the room. A beautiful woman, maybe twenty years old, smiles at him, a curve of full, luscious lips. She holds her chin high, arrogant and unafraid, and her feet barely seem to touch the ground as she walks toward him. With every step, her hips sway, her silky black dress rippling and flowing over her like an unbroken stream of water. She reminds him of one of those ancient Egyptian statues, queens with long, slender necks set to rule the world.

"You're syndicate, aren't you?" she says, stopping her approach only when they're close enough he could kiss her if he leaned forward. Now he can see the color of her eyes, brown like sugar cooked to a crystalline crisp, with the same shine. She watches him distantly, her composure icy and flawless.

"Yes," he says. "And I never leave any witnesses."

"You should reconsider," she says, and just when he thinks she's going to kiss him, something sharp scratches against his stomach, a little paring knife pressed to his side.

"Let me off this fucking boat," she whispers, "or I will gut you."

It takes some time before he can focus on anything besides the cold turn of her lips, her calculating gaze, like he's nothing more than a chess piece held between her fingers, hovering above the board as she considers her move. But finally he gets his shit together and strikes, a hand as quick as a cobra, catching her wrist in its bite. He twists hard, instinct and training replacing thought, until she drops the knife onto the carpet beneath them. She doesn't make a sound.

The next moment seems to stretch and linger, her wrist still in his hand, her eyes cold and fearless as a winter night, as though she could match him, darkness for darkness.

He, who feels nothing, is unsettled by the stirring within him, by the way her every last detail seems fraught with meaning. The bones of her slender arm beneath the heavy press of his fingertips, the steady firm shape of her mouth, the curves of her body beneath a black satin dress that falls soft as a negligee.

She is dangerous, to him, to his father, to the syndicate. And yet...

He lifts the hand that holds her wrist. "Move your hand in a circle."

She obeys, her hand moving gracefully, delicate fingers, long nails painted wine red. There's no wince of pain, no hesitation or difficulty. Nothing is broken or sprained, and, for some reason, he's glad.

"Let me go," she says, as though her force of will alone could save her.

"Will you keep your mouth shut?" he asks, the words a surprise to himself the moment they leave him.

The corner of her mouth turns up in a cold smile, like she knows she's won. "I'm not an idiot."

"How can I trust you?"

"My name is Scarlett Bancroft," she says. "If I tell anyone, it won't be hard to find me."

The last name, at least, is familiar to him; one of the city's oldest, richest families. The Bancrofts built this city, or so one of the more prominent members of the family liked to say until his campaign for mayor was cut short by a bullet.

"Why aren't you afraid of me?" he asks, fingers still on her wrist, reluctant to break the current he can feel flowing between them, two circuits feeding into each other a blue-white arc of electricity.

"I have nothing to lose," she says indifferently. Not a cry of desperation or a plea for pity, just the simple statement of a fact.

"People will be here to take care of the body in fifteen minutes. Be gone by then."

She nods, and where he expects relief, gratitude, there's only a kind of determined fatigue, a long march through a cold night not yet over.

"My name is Ras." He lifts her hand to his lips, kissing her palm, then releases her and turns all at once, walking quickly into the night without looking back.

The First Fracture

BY THE TIME he was six years old, Jude had mostly forgotten Moscow. His life in the city was far better than it had been in Russia. The house they lived in now was massive and old, with secret passageways and tucked away stairwells, and he and Eli could chase each other through it for hours. His mother sang as she worked in the garden or in the kitchen, insistent on running her own household even though his father had hired a staff to do it for her.

Sometimes, Dad would take Jude and Eli to his office atop the skyscraper, where they would look out at the city or run around the spacious room pretending to be soldiers fighting a war. Their father would put his work aside and join them, dying dramatically—arms flailing, a slow collapse to the floor—when their fake gunfire hit him. He took them to the bay and taught Jude to swim and float in the saltwater.

The first time Dad hit him, Jude was more surprised than anything else. He was six years old and no one had hit him before, no matter how bad he was.

"Speak English," Dad told him for what seemed like the hundredth time. And he tried, not because he was an obedient child—he was in fact terribly disobedient where his mother was concerned—but because he loved his dad and was in awe of him, his physical strength, his imposing, powerful presence. But when Dad got angry, it scared him, and he would trip over the English words he knew perfectly well.

"I'm sorry," he said, but somehow it came out in Russian. And his father hit him, a slap on the cheek that made him step backward, as much out of shock as pain.

"Try harder," Dad said.

He started to cry. He didn't know what to feel. Anger, shame, and fear all tumbled within him like a dryer spinning the clothes too fast and out of control.

Warm, sturdy arms wrapped around him and held him close to cry against a broad, hard chest. Dad didn't apologize—he would in fact never apologize—but he held him anyway, rocking him back and forth, murmuring soothing, gentle things. And another bright, overwhelming feeling was added to those tangled inside him. Love.

When he was hit, when he was beaten with a belt, when he was thrown into the deep end of the pool, and then always, always comforted after, he was pulled apart. Fear and love drove his obedience. He learned everything Dad wanted him to, because he was afraid not to, but more than that, much more than that, because he wanted to make Dad happy.

But there was another part of him, the part he thought of as his shadow, something dark that clung to him and followed him wherever he went. The brighter a light he became, with his capacity for love and kindness, the bolder and more malevolent his shadow got, soaking up the violence he witnessed and the violence he experienced until it became thick as fog. To this part of him, he assigned the anger, the kind of cold, cold anger that eventually accumulates into hatred.

He often felt that his shadow was pulling him downward, and his heart was pulling him upward, and the two halves of him would soon be torn apart. And, like a pane of shattered glass, he could never truly be put back together again. Even if he found a way to repair himself, there would always be shards missing and an ugly jagged seam down the middle.

3: Living Arrangements

RAS FINDS A place with a vacancy on the edge of Ghost Town in a brick building ten stories high, narrow and so weary it seems to sag toward the street.

A fire escape crawls down one side. He lifts himself onto it, testing its integrity. Rusty and a little unstable, but sturdy enough to trust. If necessary, the windows are close enough together he could climb from windowsill to windowsill, either up or down. A little chalk on his fingers and the uneven bricks, jutting out here and there by a few inches, would also be suitable.

He doesn't have any particular plans for trouble, but he likes to be ready.

He knocks on the door to the manager's office and a rough voice invites him in. A portly middle-aged man sits behind a small desk, his feet in brown moccasins resting on the surface by the telephone. Thinning hair stretches over his head, a failed attempt at disguising a hairline receded so far it's almost disappeared.

Cigarette smoke hangs thick around them. Chubby fingers tap the cigarette once against a glass ashtray.

"Nice watch." His gaze lingers on Ras's thousand-dollar timepiece, then over the quality fabric of his coat. "I'm Artie."

"I hear you have a vacancy," Ras says.

Artie takes a long drag, smoke billowing from the corners of his mouth as he taps the cigarette on the ashtray again. "I might. What are you doing out here?"

The patronizing tone makes his meaning clear: what's a rich brat like you doing in a place like this?

"Looking for somewhere to stay. How much?"

Artie leans back, studying a water stain on the ceiling. "Thousand dollars a month. Five hundred deposit, up front."

An absurd price for a run-down tenement at the edge of the Warrens. And more than Ras can afford.

"That's very funny," he says. "How much?"

"Thousand a month. Take it or leave it."

Ras narrows his eyes, fingers on the handle of the switchblade in his coat pocket. "Four hundred a month. No deposit."

The landlord's bushy eyebrows jump upward. "I don't barter, punk."

"Three fifty. You're lucky I'm willing to pay anything at all."

"You'd better run back to your rich daddy because money ain't gonna protect you here." Artie's nasally voice dips condescendingly. "You're in Ghost Town now. Ain't no law but the syndicate law. And the syndicate don't give a fuck about assholes like you."

Ras readies for a fight, the tension through his body imperceptible except to those who know him well. "I know where I am."

Artie very deliberately opens a drawer and takes out a black nightstick. He taps it against his palm like a stern police officer, stepping toward the teenager. "You think I'm bluffing, boy?"

"Boy?" Ras says, scowling. "You're going to pay for that."

"Fuckin' kids." Artie swings the nightstick, eyes narrowed with annoyance. He opens them wide when the weapon flies through the air where the young man had been standing just a half second ago. The black stick swings again, sideways. Ras ducks. As the momentum ends, he grabs the landlord's wrist with unyielding fingers and jerks hard enough to make him yelp in surprise and pain, dropping the poor excuse for a weapon on the floor.

A single punch to the side of the jaw and he's laid out beside his nightstick. Ras kicks the weapon away.

There's a cold, clinical precision to the violence that follows. Enough to hurt, but not enough to leave a permanent injury. Artie should be grateful he can stagger to his feet after, an eye swollen shut, blood trickling from his lower lip.

His other eye, however, is dark with fury, and even as he hands over a key and agrees to an absurdly low rent, Ras knows he'll have to be on his guard. Artie surely knows better than to call the police—they don't come to Ghost Town for anything less than a murder or a substantial bribe, and a syndicate contractor like Ras is untouchable on his own turf. But the landlord may plot a different sort of revenge. He may want to play another game.

Ras already likes his new home. Things won't be boring here.

IN THE EARLY afternoon, I find my mother by the sink. A wet plate glistens in her hand as she stands perfectly still, head tilted upward to let the sunlight fall over her face.

"Hey," I say.

She startles like a doe, a graceful jolt of her body. "Oh. You are so quiet. Like your father." Lines fine as hair gather at the corners of her eyes, dark circles sagging beneath. She doesn't wear makeup unless she's leaving the house, and she hasn't left the house in months.

I take the dish from her and dry it.

"Where were you last night?" she asks. "I heard you come home very late."

I ignore the disapproval in her voice. "I was with Dad."

"And after that?"

"I'm eighteen now, remember? Pretty much an adult. I can go wherever I want."

"Fine. Let your poor mother worry until her hair all is gray." She keeps a straight face, but her eyes sparkle with mischief when she glances at me.

"I was at the library," I say, smirking. "Studying."

She snorts and playfully shoves me. "At two in the morning, Jude?"

"It's quiet then," I say. She gives me a stern look, and I can tell she's not going to let this go. "I went for a run. Dad dropped me off near the bridge and I ran home. That's all."

She frowns, a worried line appearing between her brows. "In the middle of night?"

"Are you giving the boy a hard time, Nadya?" Dad asks, stepping into the kitchen. "Bet you're eager to get your own place, Jude."

"You're moving out?" Mom asks. The line between her brows gets deeper, her eyes weary and distraught.

"I was about to tell you." I turn toward her. "I already found a place. I'm just here to pack up a few things."

"Today?" she asks softly. "You're leaving today?"

"Yes." I hope she can hear the apology I can't voice in front of my father.

Dad's phone rings and he stands, glancing at it. "Gotta get this. Jude, don't take off just yet. I'll be back in a few."

I nod, and he answers the phone with a gruff "Hey," walking off down the hallway.

Mom watches him go, and then she takes my hands, holding them tightly, her own still wet and soapy from the dishwater. "Now is your chance. Now that you leave here, you can do anything you want. You don't have to follow your father's footsteps. You can become someone else. A good man."

"Mom," I say, helplessly. "You know I—"

"I want you to go to college," she whispers. "I want you to have future where no one will point gun at you, where you won't hurt anyone or..."

"I don't..." I want to tell her I don't hurt anyone, that Ras is the one who applies violence when my attempts at diplomacy have failed. But she wouldn't understand.

"Please, Jude. Try. For me. This path will lead only to death."

"I'm sorry," I say, and she lets my hands go, like she can tell how final an answer it is. Tears shimmer in her eyes as she turns back to the sink, reaching into the water for another dish.

"Okay," she says.

"I just need to pack up my stuff," I say, feeling guilty and hollow, and somehow adrift, like I've lost an anchor and am now at the mercy of the sea. "And then I'm going to take off."

"Okay." The word is as brisk and final as shutting a door. Her shadow stretches over the wooden floor behind her as she stares out at the garden, crossing the kitchen where she taught me to cook in the late nights after I went out to work with my father.

I wait by the sink for something. An absolution, a blessing, or maybe just a farewell. But she just stares out into the sunshine, her hands still in the soapy water.

I FOLLOW RAS'S directions through Ghost Town to a tall brick apartment building. On the tenth floor, down a linoleum hallway that smells of cigarette smoke, I find a door with *1010* hanging on it in large tarnished metal letters. The doorknob rattles as I unlock and turn it, the door groaning in protest as it opens. Good. No one will be able to enter silently.

The beige paint peels in a few places along the baseboards to show some kind of hideous green and yellow wallpaper beneath. The hardwood floors, aged and rough, will creak under the heavy footfalls of anyone who hasn't been trained as we have.

The most important thing is that the apartment is secure. The window is a close second. I open it and the chill January air rushes in. I put my hands on the windowsill, lean out, and take a deep breath. Up this high, the smell of exhaust and trash and people is more of an undertone to the fresh scent of the sky. Distant figures walk along the streets. Only a few people brave the sunlight, but the district comes to life at night.

I set my duffel bag on the bed. Ras's clothes are already hanging up in the closet, casual white button-down shirts and black pants, stylish and expensive, mostly stolen. A marked contrast to the black, slightly worn clothes a friend once described as "hipster grunge." But I like black, and out here Ras's usual attire makes him stand out, while mine lets me blend in.

On the kitchen table, the notebook Ras and I sometimes use to communicate is open to a message in his aggressive angular handwriting.

What do you think, Judy? $250 a month not bad, right? Sometimes my way <u>does</u> work. Can you buy some food and booze? I have things to do tonight, so you have to visit the supplier this afternoon instead. Bring me a present. Cocaine would be nice. Love, R.

I sigh, running my hand through my hair. He never does his share of the work. And I'm not sure what he means by "my way", but I know it can't be good.

I set up my laptop beside his on the desk, tapping my fingers lightly on the Cyrillic keyboard he sometimes uses to type in Russian. I wish I still knew the language, and not just so I could keep an eye on what he's up to.

Another note is sitting beside my keyboard.

A girl saw me kill Damien, but I let her go. Her name is Scarlett Bancroft. Can you find her for me?

"You let her go?" I pick up the note and turn it in my fingers, sighing. "You fucking moron." And just like that, I have to clean up yet another one of his messes.

I spend a few hours rigging up elaborate hiding places for my guns, drugs, and cash, and then I sit down at the computer and start searching for everything I can find about Scarlett Bancroft.

4: The Syndicate Law

WHENEVER I'M ABLE, I spend the evening walking around the Warrens. This is the oldest and seediest part of the city, with narrow stone streets, two and three-story buildings hundreds of years old curling up around them to form canyons marked with graffiti and dismal with grime.

At this time of night, First Street resembles a bazaar, if a desperate, gritty one. People have spread blankets or set up card tables to display stolen or counterfeited goods: an array of shining watches, faux-leather purses. Gleaming knives and, beneath the table that holds them, a box that I know contains cheap handguns.

I pause at one of the blankets spread before the sidewalk, off-brand tennis shoes arranged on it. The gamine girl sitting at one edge looks up at me, eyes drooping with fatigue. In her lap, a toddler fusses, and her little brother Aiden, maybe seven years old, leans against her side with his head on her shoulder. All three children have hair so blonde it's almost white, shining beneath the streetlights.

The girl, Molly, climbs to her feet, hefting the toddler on her hip, and digs in her pocket for a cell phone. I take it from her and flip through the texts until I find the one I want, the one naming the time and location of my next shipment of heroin. It's in code, of course, and now that I've read it, Molly's friends will wipe the phone and sell it on the thriving black market here.

"A cop came but didn't talk to me," she says. "Just drove by. I stayed quiet."

It's rare to see law enforcement down here, but it does happen, and I'm glad to know she can keep her cool.

"You have nerves of steel," I say with a warm smile. "I hope you'll want to work for me someday." And because I don't want her to think she has to do what her mother does for the syndicate, I add, "There are lots of different things you'd be good at."

She gives me a shy smile that gets wider when I hand over three folded twenties. The toddler on her hip grabs for the money, mewling like a cat.

"Why are your brothers out here?" I ask, as Aiden shivers in his jean jacket. "It's late." Past midnight, in fact.

Her shrug is so weary it seems like there's a tangible weight pressing down on her shoulders. "Mom said go play. She's got a guy there."

"It's too cold for these two," I say, taking off my coat. I put it over Aiden's shoulders and he looks up at me, startled, before pulling it tight around himself.

The toddler's fussing gets louder, and he begins to squirm.

"Here." I hold out my arms, and, after a pause, Molly lets me take him. I lift him above my head and his whimpers turn to giggles for a moment, tiny hands reaching for my face.

"Let's go home," I say. "I'll talk to your mom when we get there."

Molly leads us several blocks east, to a motel, a slumping L-shaped building around a courtyard with dead grass and an empty pool. I knock on a door with a faded six on it, and Rita answers. She ushers the kids inside and shuts the door behind them, standing with me under the little awning, a bare bulb casting a sallow yellow light over us.

"Thanks for bringing them back," she murmurs, eyes on the ground. "I didn't wanna kick 'em out. I was just tryin' to make your quota. Been a slow week."

"If you don't make it once in a while, I'll understand."

She gives me a skeptical glance. "Bullshit. You just want an excuse so when Thursday comes you get to do whatever you want to me."

"You're new," I say gently. She's only worked for me for about a month, and, in that time, she's never come up short. "You don't know me."

She folds her arms. "I know pimps."

"Two hundred dollars. That's all you owe this week."

She takes out a cigarette, her hands fumbling nervously with the lighter. "Two hundred and what else?"

"Nothing else. You make it up to me when you can."

She takes a drag and eyes me skeptically. "Not gonna fuck you with my kids here."

"I don't fuck people who work for me. It's bad business."

She snorts and then starts giggling, and it's a few moments before she can compose herself. The laughter seems to be as much relief as amusement. "What kinda pimp are you, anyway?"

"I'm easy to work with," I say, and that inspires a few more giggles. "Two hundred dollars on Thursday. Don't forget."

"Yes, sir." She gives me a mock salute—sloppy compared to the real thing, which Dad made me practice over and over as a kid.

"Don't call me sir. And say good night to the kids for me."

"Sure thing." She pauses. "Thanks, Jude."

Ras is right, I think as I walk away. I have a soft fucking heart. I go too easy on everyone who works for me—Dad would be disappointed. But Rita has kids to worry about, and she was so desperate she left them out in the cold in the Warrens in the middle of the night. I don't know how I can ignore that. So what if we come up a few hundred dollars short this week? Ras will just have to deal with it.

BY THE TIME I get back to First Street, an hour has passed. I continue through the marketplace, nodding at a few of my drug dealers. One of them stops me to let me know some college kids had a big party and now he's short on weed. I make a mental note to have someone bring some out tomorrow.

A right turn through a dark alley leads me to Third Street. Four lanes wide, the outer two are occupied by cars skulking slowly by, taking stock of the prostitutes standing along the sidewalk, most of whom look bored and cold.

Two of them come up to me with minor disputes and complaints. I wasn't lying to Rita—I do have a good professional relationship with her and all of the other women who work for me. I don't pretend that I'm doing them any favors, or that I'm some kind of benefactor, but I am a lot nicer than most of the pimps here.

One block down, a narrow pathway twisting beneath crumbling stone arches leads me to Birch Street. A pink neon flamingo glows in the small dirty window of a bar with no sign. I push open the door and step into the interior; murmured conversations, drunken laughter, shadows thick as smoke.

"Jude!" Quinn gives me a grin that stretches her top lip upward in a way that makes it look like she's baring fangs, although she's only being friendly. Sallow yellow light shines on the bald half of her head, accentuating her tattoos—vines that crawl from below the line of her shirt over her neck to blossom on her skull.

I sit on a barstool and she pours me a whiskey, a rare and expensive one that she's put into a cheap-looking bottle so it won't get stolen. She bought it for me as a gesture of gratitude shortly after Ras and I saved her bar, and probably her life as well. The bloodstains she's been unable to get out of the wooden floor serve as a permanent reminder of that night. Most of it belonged to the gang members; only a little is ours.

"What's happening, Quinn?" I ask.

She fills me in on every detail she's heard in the last week, the minor conflicts and comings and goings of pimps and drug dealers and thieves, most concerning of which is the news that two syndicate drug runners have been recently arrested.

"And that's not the weirdest part," she says. "After Pablo and Danny were both busted, this guy comes into the bar. He's older, forty or fifty maybe, and he looks out of place here. I don't know why, but something about him just didn't fit in, like he was too good for all of us. He ordered a drink, and, when he finished it, he said he wanted me to give a message to the syndicate boss. I told him it's not like I talk with Vance de Haven on a regular basis, or like, ever, but he insisted on telling me anyway."

I raise an eyebrow. "What was the message?"

"My name is Nikita Fyodorov," she says in an atrocious Russian accent. "Tell Vance de Haven I am coming to settle debt. He will know what this means."

Nikita. I knew a Nikita, a long time ago, when we lived in Russia, but my memories of him are vague and fuzzy. I was only five when we came to the city, and most of my life before that is a haze of impressions and barely remembered voices. But Nikita—the name makes me think of warm hugs and a fond smile, laughter and a gentle voice speaking Russian. This can't be the same man, can it?

"You know him?" she asks.

I laugh, to cover the strange emotional turmoil all this has dug up. "Not all Russians know each other. And please don't do that accent ever again."

She snorts good-naturedly. "It was pretty bad, wasn't it?"

"I'll make sure the boss gets the message. He'll be grateful to you for passing it along."

"Thanks, Jude," she says, grinning. She knows the boss's gratitude is priceless.

I down the rest of my whiskey. "I'd better go," I say, sliding my glass back across the bar. "If you hear anything else about Nikita, call me right away."

"Will do," Quinn says.

I walk out of the smoky bar onto Lispard Avenue, a long, thin stretch of road curving lazily southwest. It turns out onto a larger street like a tributary meeting a river, and, at that intersection, a diner's friendly glow shines through great glass windows. I step inside, the fluorescent light dazzling after the darkness. Among the grime and graffiti of the Warrens, it's almost too wholesome, speckled Formica, red vinyl seats, posters with blonde women from the 1950s holding plates of breakfast food.

"Two coffees to go?" Miri asks, looking up from the salt and pepper shakers she's refilling. She wipes her hands on her apron and walks over to me.

"Yes," I say.

She pours me two cups of coffee and hands them over, along with two little bags, one with a handful of OxyContin, one with a few Valium. I thank her with a kiss on the cheek and walk back out into the night.

Coffee in hand, I hurry south until I reach Bancroft Square. Named for one of the oldest and richest families in the city, it features a small circular park, and, at the center, a statue of a tall, proud man, once pristine white stone, now covered with graffiti scribbles—most of which read "Fuck you Joe". Notes left for Joseph Bancroft, our unpopular mayor of five years ago. Many of our elected officials are Bancrofts, running the city more like a dynasty than a democracy. Some are corrupt, but most are natural enemies of the syndicate. And Scarlett, the girl Ras asked me to find, is one of them. He couldn't have picked a worse person to show mercy to.

Despite its lofty origins, Bancroft Square is where the male prostitutes work, lingering at the edge of the street or in the darkness of the park, waiting to be propositioned. I don't work with them—men rarely have pimps—and I really have no reason to come out here, no business, anyway. But lately I've found myself here almost every night I do this circuit.

I see Ash before he sees me, and I slow my pace for a moment to watch him. He's leaning against a lamppost, an oasis of yellow light in the darkness. He holds a book in his right hand, his face tilted down toward it. I study his profile—proud, regal nose, full lips, curly black hair falling over his forehead—so that I can remember it later, on the nights when he's not here.

He's too engrossed in his book to notice my approach, but he looks up when I call his name and smiles at me, marking the page with a scrap of paper. He sings the first few bars of "Hey Jude," like he often does when he sees me, his voice soft but clear and beautiful as the chiming of bells. He takes the cup of coffee I hold out toward him.

"What are you reading?" I ask.

He hands me the book, a battered paperback, and I turn it over in my hands. *"The Odyssey?"*

"Not what you'd expect someone like me to read, I know." He shrugs. "I get that a lot."

"I don't expect anyone to read a book like this. Unless you're like me and get it assigned at school."

"So you read it?"

"No. I got bored so I looked it up online."

He laughs, the sound both jaded and joyful. He's like a precious gem, an emerald or sapphire or diamond, all hard, smooth edges and sharp angles, catching and trapping light.

I press the drugs into his hand, too aware of the short moment when my fingertips brush his warm palm.

"I don't have any cash," he says, which is what he almost always tells me, these days. He used to pay on time, but I think he's realized he doesn't have to.

"Don't worry about it," I say. "You can pay me when you've got the money."

"Thanks." A car pulls to the curb and he gives me an apologetic smile. "Friend of mine," he says, jerking his head at it. "I better go. Thanks for the coffee."

It feels like something in him goes blank when he turns from me, as it always does in these moments, and I want to call his name, bring him back to himself, to me. But I don't. It's just business, and I understand that as well as anyone else out here.

I asked him once if he wanted to work for me. I think that offended him, though he laughed. Ash is tall, but delicate and slender, and I worry he won't be able to take care of himself. I would protect you, I promised him. I would make sure you get paid.

But he just smiled at me. "Jude, baby," he said, and something in me melted, to hear the endearment. "You'll look out for me anyway, won't you?"

He's probably right.

Because I have nothing pressing to do, I sit with my coffee and my phone and wait on a bench nearby. He's rarely busy for more than a half hour.

We met when I was dealing drugs on the street for pocket money, before Dad let me officially start working for the syndicate. His drugs of choice are opiates and benzos, all pills except the occasional weed or blow. He's an addict—dealing drugs you learn to tell the difference between people who want to party on the weekend and people who are truly addicted—and something of a drifter too. But I wasn't surprised to see him reading *The Odyssey*, not after I told him I was half Russian and he launched into a monologue about how Tolstoy is one of the greatest writers of all time.

After about twenty minutes, the car drops him back on the curb, and he walks toward me.

"Cool. You're still here." He's smiling, sitting on the bench beside me, his torn-cover copy of *The Odyssey* in his lap. "How's the business?"

"Good. I got a promotion."

"Nice. You gonna do something crazy to celebrate?"

"I hadn't thought about it." All of my energy has gone to getting things shifted over to my control, making sure I have phone numbers and contacts and that everyone knows my name.

"You hadn't thought about it?" he says, with exaggerated outrage. "Seriously?"

"Seriously."

He shakes his head and then slouches in the bench and leans against me, the warm line of his arm pressed to mine, his head on my shoulder. "Where would you be if you could be anywhere, doing anything, right now?"

"I don't know," I say, though I do. I'd be right here, the weight of his head on my shoulder, his low smoky voice in my ear.

5: Falling Stars

SCARLETT WAKES AT six, a habit impossible to shake, eyes open wide the moment the clock ticks over. After a few seconds lying back against the Egyptian-cotton sheets, the golden shade of pollen—no more little girl's pink for her—she gets up.

A year ago, she would have showered, fixed her hair, sat at her vanity applying makeup just how he liked it, and dressed in something sexy and playful, short skirt, V-neck top. She would have fastened her choker around her neck, a noose of black velvet and diamonds, and gone downstairs to the kitchen to retrieve his breakfast. Carrying the tray carefully, mindful still of the time she spilled it and the punishment that followed, she would make her graceful way on high heels down the hall to his bedroom and bring it inside.

Now, she lets her long hair hang down her back, unwashed, as she gets up to sit at the black grand piano in the parlor that marks the entrance to her wing of the mansion. She feels a memory starting to unfurl, with its attendant shame and despair. Her mother's wedding night; her first time in her stepfather's bed. She spreads her fingers over the keys and tries to play it away.

Downstairs in the sprawling kitchen, her mother sits at the counter. A mug and an open container of yogurt, a spoon in her hand, pausing on the journey to her mouth so she can look Scarlett up and down.

"Would it kill you to wash your hair and put on something nice?" she says. "You look like a hobo."

Scarlett gives her a good-natured smile, lifting her mother's mug and swallowing the gin inside. "Morning, Mama."

"I've set up a date for you," her mother says. "The Cothson boy. He's nice. Not bad looking either. And the family's loaded."

"Mama." Scarlett tips the bottle of gin sitting on the counter, the clear liquid trickling into the coffee cup. "You're not my pimp anymore. Quit it."

"You're not a whore, honey. Whores get paid."

Scarlett drinks the alcohol in a single tip of the mug. "Careful, or you'll be back in the Warrens before you know it."

"I don't know how in hell you got the old bastard to leave everything to you." Her mother scowls, grabbing the bottle of gin.

"I'm persuasive," Scarlett purrs, though in the end it hadn't been Chris, her stepfather, who she persuaded, but Vance de Haven. Chris had once been a friend of Vance's, and he'd introduced Scarlett to the crime boss as well. But he had fallen out of favor after running for office on an anti-crime platform. Scarlett had asked for Vance's help, and he had given it, and more. He set up the hit, arranged the cover-up, tampered with the will—all schemes that worked to his benefit as well as hers. But he didn't have to let her be the one to pull the trigger. And when she sank to her knees in the alley after firing the shot, covering her face with her hands, he didn't have to lean down and place a warm, fatherly hand on her shoulder. She was grateful, then, for his touch and for his silence.

"Scarlett." Her mother puts a hand on her arm, frowning. "Are you having one of your episodes?"

"I'm fine." She jerks her arm away and steps back. Sometimes, randomly and without warning, she'll have flashbacks, moments where she's immersed completely in the past, whether it's the days they lived on the streets, her year in juvenile detention, or her time with Chris. The present simply ceases to be, as though it never was, and the memories overwhelm her.

"You think too much," her mother says. "That's your problem."

Scarlett smiles, pouring a third shot of gin. "You don't think enough. That's your problem. Think about where you'd be without your whore daughter. You'd be back on the streets. If you didn't have me to sell, what would you do?"

"Scarlett. Babygirl. You know everything I did, I did for you and your sister." Scarlett's mother grabs her hand. "I—"

"Morning." Amber walks into the kitchen in sweats, rubbing her eyes.

"Morning, honey." Their mother's cigarette-coarsened voice is sweeter for her youngest child, a pretty, soft-featured girl, fourteen years old. "You have a late night?"

Amber gives them an enigmatic smile, settling on one of the barstools. "You won't believe it. Kaylee actually asked me to a party. And she was super nice to me the whole time, and her friends were too."

"I told you that you'd win them over," their mother says.

Amber's smile fades as she grabs the bottle of gin, screwing on the cap more forcefully than necessary and putting it away in a liquor cabinet.

The three have breakfast, Amber chattering away about the party in a determined effort to fill the silence left by Scarlett's cold anger and their mother's inebriated indifference. When they're done, Scarlett walks back up the stairs and down the long hallway to her room, lost again in memory.

A year ago, she would have eaten breakfast with her stepfather, fucked him, and helped him get dressed. After that, her time was her own for a half hour until her first tutor arrived. In that half hour, she used to sit in the back of her closet, among the beautiful clothes she'd earned by spreading her legs, reading books like *Anna Karenina* or *Pride and Prejudice*. Love stories, whether bitter or sweet, as long as the love was so deep and rich you could almost drown in it, like a great pool of chocolate.

Now, all of her time is her own, and yet unassigned hours cause her great anxiety, so she fills each one, with luncheons and dates, with tutors coming to teach her French and Spanish and ballroom dancing, with school, with her charity work.

Today is mostly the latter, a brunch with potential donors, arranging for the silent auction that will be held at the charity gala she's planning. She has lunch with her step-aunt, the district attorney, and listens patiently and sweetly as her aunt breaks confidentiality in several cases to give Scarlett the most interesting details. She knows that she's being groomed to follow in those footsteps, and she barely minds. Although she yearns for more, aches for it, she can't yet fathom what shape her future might someday take. For now, this is enough.

The Bancroft family legacy rests on her shoulders, an unlikely fate for a woman born in the Ghost Town slums. There were whispers of dissent when Chris married Scarlett's mother, but Chris's parents were smart enough to realize this was the closest they would come to having grandchildren. They lavished attention on Scarlett and Amber, introduced them to high society, and saw to it that the rest of the family welcomed them, polite, at least, on the surface. They died shortly before Chris—a car crash that took them both at once—but by then, Scarlett was well integrated into the fabric of the Bancroft dynasty.

She had cried at her grandparents' funeral, but, when their cold bodies lay below the earth, she planned for Chris to join them.

NO MATTER HOW frenetic her days, a schedule can only run so late, and it is the evening and night that are the most dangerous. She has parties, she has her men, she has friends, but still, the hours between midnight and six in the morning remain open as a gaping mouth, full of minutes sharp as teeth.

Tonight, she would be with Damien, except that he's been sunk to the bottom of the bay or dissolved in acid or disposed of however the syndicate typically handles bodies. Poor Damien. There's no one so reckless as a man who thinks he's smarter than he really is. She told him it was a bad idea to double-cross the syndicate, but he didn't listen, and she, drawn by the promise of conflict and excitement, hadn't left.

It was a close call—if Vance de Haven had found she was helping Damien, she would certainly be dead, their past collusion aside. It was only by chance that the man with him turned out to be such a soft touch.

She barely escaped with her life, and yet, she can't bring herself to care, about Damien's death or the proximity of her own. She knows how love can trap you, how relationships become sticky as spiderwebs and render you helpless. She loves her mother and she loves her sister, and she will never allow anyone else to catch her.

Tonight, like so many nights, she lies in her bed and tries to sleep, although she knows from the hyper-alert tension, the clench to her muscles, the wideness of her own eyes, that it's impossible, at least until the sun comes up. As the moon falls in through the great glass window, she wonders why she chose this room, his room. I am the master of the house now, she said, and I should get the master bedroom. A showy way of demonstrating her bravery, like a child running up to touch the front door of a haunted house.

She walked into this room that first night on trembling legs, though she too had agreed to the deal her mother had made: my daughter, your money. She'd hidden her fear well, and he had been pleased. From then on, there had always been enough for them to eat, braces and private school for her beloved sister, a string of doctors for her mother's back and anxiety attacks. And for Scarlett—diamonds, a Mercedes. A walk-in closet full of designer clothes.

In his opulent bedroom, upon a large bed with ivory sheets, she would lie on her back and stare at the chandelier above her, fragmented like falling stars. As he fucked her, she would imagine herself one of them, a single point of light across a cold, cold distance.

At fourteen, her mother taught her the place where love ends and pragmatism begins. But she need draw no such line in herself. There is no heart to woo or to break.

Yet she lies there, beneath the falling stars, heartbroken. Hoping the syndicate killer with the green eyes will come for her after all so she won't have to do this anymore.

6: The Ice Queen

RAS WALKS INTO the foyer of a house grand enough to have its own ballroom, elaborately ornamented white staircases curving down toward him on either side, ending their graceful sweep at the base of a round fountain. Just past it, a butler standing at attention by the entrance to the house proper eyes him cautiously.

As he approaches the door, the butler steps into his path. Ras reaches into his pocket and lets his fingers brush the cool handle of his new switchblade, but even he knows better than to cause such a scene here.

"The caterer is set up out back," the butler says stiffly.

Ras grins, cheerful and eerie as a jack-o'-lantern. In his white shirt and black slacks—the closest he comes to black-tie attire—he does look like he should be serving drinks.

"My name is Jude de Haven. I'm not with the help."

The butler's eyes widen for a second, and then he bobs his head. "Of course. Of course. You look just like your brother; I don't know how I missed it." From his eager, placating tone, Ras knows he's heard and believes the rumors about the de Haven family, their syndicate ties, their roots in the Russian mafia.

He gives the butler a polite nod and brushes past him through the door, ignoring his timid protests: proper attire, black tie, at least let me lend you a coat.

Inside, it's very pleasant. Pleasant music drifts from a string quartet in the corner, pleasant ivory tablecloths drape the tables, pleasant conversation fills the room. It's not what he would have expected from the cold, calculating woman on the yacht. Scarlett Bancroft: socialite, model, philanthropist. Heir to the Bancroft fortune, scion of one of the oldest and most respected families in the city. Her stepfather, once a vocal member of city council, was shot dead in an alley close to a year ago, leaving everything to her.

This ritzy gala is largely her doing, as the highest profile member of a charity organization dedicated to helping exploited and abused children.

She's also a student at the city's exclusive private college, and a model. He's seen (and rather likes) the ads she's done for an upscale jewelry store, black-and-white photos where she wears diamonds and little else, the only color the red of her lips, or maybe a ruby at her throat.

But, although he's glad to know more of her, none of it matters as much as what he learned from their confrontation: that she is heartless, that she is unafraid. She hasn't said a word to anyone about what she's seen, even though one of her aunts is the district attorney. He would know; the syndicate has a plant in the DA's office and corrupt police officers across the city are kept on retainer. She hasn't pursued justice for the man she saw Ras kill, and he knows it isn't cowardice staying her hand, but rather a ruthless indifference he could sense the first time she met his eyes, the yacht rocking gently on the dark water beneath their feet.

Gideon Reed steps into his path with a smile. Born into the family that once owned the quarry in the heart of the city, he wears old money like a second skin: platinum watch, silk tie, diamonds twinkling in his cufflinks. But he's always up for something fun—snorting lines of cocaine off their textbooks in the bathroom at the exclusive private school they attended together, running illegal games of blackjack during homeroom, selling the answers to the final exams.

Gideon graduated two years ahead of Ras and, in addition to getting his MBA, has been working for the syndicate as one of their many accountants, creatively shuffling numbers to stay ahead of the tax collectors. He's helped Ras launder and invest the modest amount of money he's made since he started dealing drugs in the ninth grade.

"Hey, man." Gideon slings his arm over Ras's shoulders. "What are you doing here? You hate stuff like this."

Ras catches sight of Scarlett across the room, her long, silvery evening gown shimmering over her body, a diamond choker at her throat. And everything in him is still for a moment, watching her cross the floor.

She is for me. She is mine.

"Oh," Gideon says, his voice low and knowing. "Scarlett Bancroft, huh?"

"Yes," he says. Across the room, Scarlett catches his eye, and instead of an eyelash flutter and a coy glance away, she holds his gaze, raising an eyebrow.

"Be careful." Gideon claps him on the back. "Sleeping with the enemy can be a hell of a lot of fun, but it's risky too."

"She's not the enemy," Ras says, and the two men fall silent as she approaches them.

Ras gives her his wide, wicked grin, the toothy smile that has gotten many beautiful girls into his bed. He himself is not handsome, his features too angular, his jawline too sharp, but his effortless confidence and aura of danger make up the difference.

"You look beautiful," he says.

She looks him up and down with icy amusement. "You look like a waiter. A lazy one."

She likes me, he thinks gleefully. *She likes me, and she is not afraid of me.*

Gideon makes a gracious exit, which Ras hardly notices, his focus entirely on Scarlett.

"Have you missed me?" he asks her.

"Have you changed your mind?" she says, the corner of her lip quirking upward. As though she's asking him whether he likes the opera, instead of wondering if her life is in danger.

"If I wanted you dead, you'd be dead." He speaks carelessly, not menacingly. A fact, not a threat.

She laughs, low and husky and cynical, and he's delighted by the sound, that he was the one to bring it forth.

"You're a little arrogant, aren't you?" she says. "What makes you think you could get to me?"

"Because I'm Ras. There's no one in this city I can't get to."

"I was wrong. You're very arrogant."

"Aren't you going to introduce us?" Eli asks, approaching them. For all his bulk, he has the uncanny knack for making himself invisible, then appearing as though from nowhere. Ras narrows his eyes at his brother, and resists the childish urge to shove him away.

"*Fuck off*," he says in Russian.

"I don't think she speaks the mother tongue, Jude," Eli says, laughing, then smiles at Scarlett. "Eli de Haven, at your service. I see you've already met my little brother."

She looks them over with a sly smile. "It's good to meet you. I'm Scarlett Bancroft."

"I know. You've done an amazing job with all this." Eli spreads his arms to indicate the ballroom. "I'll be making a generous donation."

"It's strange," Ras says, studying Scarlett. "You don't seem like the charitable type."

Again she laughs, and again he is delighted, giddy with it. "What makes you say that?"

"Because you're like me," he replies, oddly earnest. This is not how he would usually seduce a woman, not by telling her the truth. "You're cold. And heartless."

Eli raises his eyebrows, stifling a laugh at what he perceives as Ras's clumsiness, but Scarlett's lips turn up, so plush and full that for a moment her mouth seems as sensual as the curve of her breasts above the low silver neckline of her dress.

"I don't think you're cold at all. And I think the work you do is really important." Eli smiles graciously at Scarlett, the protector, swooping in to defend her honor.

Ras rolls his eyes. If there is anyone who doesn't need defending, it's this woman. "*Go away*," Ras says, switching back to Russian. "*She's mine.*"

Eli laughs, replying in kind. "*Does she think that?*"

"What language is that?" Scarlett asks.

"I'm sorry." Eli gives her a sheepish smile. "That was really rude. We're speaking Russian. We were both born in Moscow."

"This is boring," Ras says. "I want to take you somewhere fun."

"This isn't boring," Eli interjects. "Scarlett put a lot of work into making this happen."

She catches Eli's eye with a sly smile. "I did. But he's right. It's boring as fuck."

"Then let's go," Ras insists.

"Where?" she asks, and, when she catches his eye, Eli and the rest of the room disappear for a moment, so enthralling is she.

"A surprise."

She tilts her head, considering it, like she's doing him a favor, even though she owes him her life. Finally, she agrees.

VANCE'S OFFICE SITS on the top floor of a skyscraper downtown, a sheer building of glass so dark and reflective it obscures rather than reveals the interior. A smooth black pillar, holding up the sky.

Ras leads Scarlett inside, leaving the lights off. Ample moonlight falls through the floor-to-ceiling windows that line one wall, the city a glowing sea of yellow lights, spread before them.

"This is beautiful," Scarlett says, her dress catching the pale light, sparkles clinging to her body as she moves, gazelle graceful, across the floor.

He hangs back to take it in, the sight of her at the window. The woman, the city. Both will someday be his.

"I've never been up here at night," she continues. "The city seems like it goes on forever."

"You've been here before?" he asks, tilting his head like a curious cat.

Her lips turn up in a cold, cynical smile. "Your father and I have met a few times. Don't tell him I was on that yacht, though. I'm sure he would have killed me."

"You know that if you do tell anyone what you saw—"

"Yeah, yeah." She waves dismissively at him. "You'll kill me. I know."

"Yes." He thinks if he was betrayed by her, he's not sure what he would do, but it would likely be bloody. The first sweet stirrings of whatever this is turned inside out, turned to brutality. To banish the thought, he flicks on the lights and walks to the well-stocked bar in the corner to mix her a drink. Something elegant, but not sweet or fruity. *A martini.* He reaches for a bottle of gin. For himself he pours a whiskey, which is Jude's drink, but there aren't any bottles of red wine up here.

"Jude de Haven," she says, still by the window. "Why didn't you tell me your real name?"

"Ras is my real name." He hands her the martini glass. "Jude is the name my father gave me, but I think the truest name is the one you choose yourself."

"What does it mean?"

"Ras? It doesn't mean anything. It just is." The moment he was created, a fully formed teenager, no longer a whisper in Jude's subconscious but a person all his own, he'd known his name. No one had given it to him. It had always been his.

"Ras," she says, as though tasting the word. She says it right, something like: "Rahs," an exhalation soft as a sigh, as a shadow, as a curtain drawn. Almost everyone calls him Jude, and most of the people who know him as Ras die soon after meeting him. Hearing his name from her lips, full as plums and red as fresh, still-hot blood, gives him an almost sexual thrill.

Between a large glass conference table and an imposing oak desk, two short sofas sit facing each other, a black coffee table in the center. Scarlett sits on one, Ras beside her, and she starts to ask about the syndicate. Smart questions that trace the veins and arteries of the operation until she's asking about the heart, following the lines of money that flow like blood in and out of the center. She asks questions he's never thought to wonder about, questions he sometimes can't answer, although Jude might be able to. And he responds without hesitation, eager to give her anything she wants.

"It's set up to sound like a corporation," he says. "You have the boss—the CEO. His second-in-command is the executive consul. Beneath him is a board of directors. The lieutenants on the board each oversee several supervisors, who are in charge of all the crime in a small portion of the city. The supervisors are the ones on the streets actually doing the work. And that"—he grins, leaning toward her—

"that is what I do. But soon, I'm going to be the consul. And someday, I'll be the boss."

"You'll inherit it, you mean," she says, sipping her drink. "What about your brother? Isn't he older?"

"It's not a question of inheritance," Ras says, annoyed at the assumption. "I earned my place."

"I think I'm in the wrong business." She gets up to look out the window. "This sounds like so much fun."

He joins her, standing close enough to breathe her scent, fresh and almost sweet, like a rose just beginning to blossom. "What business are you in?"

She turns to face him, the corner of her lip quirking upward in a smirk that makes his heart race and his fingers itch with the desire to touch her skin. If she were a siren, he would drown.

"I'm interning at the DA's office this summer. I was thinking of going into criminal law."

"That makes us enemies, then," Ras warns her, stepping closer, trapping her against the window. "You should be careful."

She toys with the buttons on his shirt, still smiling. "I'm doing it because I'm bored. Maybe you could help me find something I like better. Something with the syndicate."

"I will," he says, thinking that Jude can sort out the details.

She starts to unbutton his shirt, taking her time with each button while he watches her, enthralled. Desperate to claim her, to reach past her cold exterior, to make that aloof smirk into a real smile.

This is not how it usually goes, with her cool fingertips running down his chest while he stands paralyzed with want. He is the one who leads, the predator, not the prey. And yet. For the moment all he can do is stand as she pushes his shirt off his shoulders and he lets it fall to the floor.

She meets his eyes, both distant and hotly, achingly near. "Fuck me, Ras," she says. Giving him not just permission, but an order.

He growls, pushing her back against the window and pinning her there. She answers his rough kisses eagerly, her soft body melting against his. Yielding, pliable, moaning with pleasure as he bites at the smooth skin of her shoulder, determined to leave a mark, as he lifts her so she can wrap her legs around his waist, his fingertips digging hard into her hips.

He holds her against the window, whispering sweet, filthy nothings in her ear, her body shuddering against him as he talks, as he fucks. As submissive as he could want a woman to be, but, in the back of his mind, he has the distinct feeling that she owns this, that she owns him. Without her command, he would be powerless to touch her.

For the sweet moment just after he finishes, he holds her in his arms, the woman and past her the lights of the city like so many diamonds glittering on black velvet, and someday, he'll steal every one. And he will give them to her.

7: The Gentleman

I WAKE IN a strange place, too bright, too cold, and even before I open my eyes, I'm on edge. Then a soft sigh comes from beside me, and I sit up abruptly. When the room comes into focus, I realize I'm in our new apartment, and that, lying naked beside me, is the most beautiful woman I've ever seen. She shifts in her sleep, full lips turned down, but doesn't wake as I get out of bed.

It takes me a moment to recognize her, and when I do, I shake my head at Ras's recklessness. He should know better than to have anything to do with her. When he disappears from her life, like he always does after he sleeps with a woman once or twice, she might be vindictive enough to go to the police with what she saw on that yacht.

I pull on a pair of pants, moving silently as a ghost over the creaky floors. In the next room, I put a coat over my bare torso and sneak out the door.

The air outside is so cold it seems to crystallize against my face the moment I step onto the fire escape, the metal creaking softly beneath my weight. I close my eyes and try to sink into that calm, meditative place where I can summon my other half. If he's willing. I have very little control over when Ras comes and goes; he's sometimes with me, watching through my eyes, and sometimes dormant.

"Scarlett Bancroft is in our bed," I say.

Waking, he joins my consciousness, a dark presence like a heavy shadow in the back of my mind.

I know. In my head, his melodic voice sounds as clear as my own. *I want you to make her breakfast.*

I rub my forehead. "She's your date. You make her breakfast."

You know I don't cook.

"What did you do last night?" The time he spends out in the world is always a blank in my mind, like a dreamless sleep.

I fucked the most beautiful woman in the world. He sounds a little smug.

"She saw you kill someone, and so you brought her to our home? How do you know you can trust her?"

I know.

"You should have killed her, Ras. You know that." Even as I say it, I regret it, but I know it's true, and that I shouldn't back down from things like this, things that need to be done.

If you think it's necessary, why don't you go do that? She's there right now, sleeping. She probably won't even put up a fight.

I don't have an answer for that, and I can sense his smug satisfaction at my silence. He knows I won't, knows I can barely bring myself to hurt the spiders that make their webs in the corners of our apartment.

"Maybe I'll sleep with her," I say, looking out over the thin layer of white covering the sidewalks. "Did you think of that?"

A dark laugh echoes in my mind. Ras knew I was gay well before I was able to admit it to myself.

What about your hustler? Are you going to forget about him?

"I'm not going to sleep with Ash. He's just a friend."

You love him. And you could have him, if you let yourself.

"For fifty bucks, anyone can have him. I don't want it to be like that. And anyway, can you imagine what Dad would think if he found out?"

Vance can go fuck himself.

"Don't talk about our dad like that," I say, wishing, not for the first time, that Ras was another person so I could hit him.

Why not? he murmurs, sulky as a child. *Vance has fucked with you for eighteen years now. He doesn't deserve your love or even your respect.*

"Ras," I say, rubbing my forehead as though I could dispel the splitting headache threatening, the one I often get when we fight. "Please. Just don't."

I think I love her, Judy. I think she's the love of my life.

I roll my eyes. "You just met her."

Make her breakfast. I will do something nice for you.

I sigh. She is already in our apartment, and it's not like I'm going to tell her the truth about us. "Fine. You better do something really fucking nice."

WHEN I STEP back into the apartment, Scarlett is sitting on the couch, thumbing through the hardback copy of *The Iliad* I bought. I meant to give it to Ash, but I'm not sure if I should. I'd intend it to be a friendly gift, nothing more, but I could see how he might think otherwise. He probably already knows how I feel, but even so, I don't want to make it glaringly obvious.

Scarlett looks up at me. Even with her messy hair and wearing one of Ras's white shirts, she's elegant and composed. Her legs are bare, stretched out across the couch cushions, but there's nothing vulnerable or approachable about her. She might as well be wearing armor.

"Good morning," I say. "Would you like some pancakes?"

She raises an eyebrow. "You cook?"

"I've been known to." Cooking is actually one of the things I do best, a gift from my mother, who spent countless patient hours teaching me. Here, in my own apartment, there will be no one to get angry at me for spending too much time in the kitchen like a "fucking girl", and there are some things I'm eager to try with my newfound freedom.

She sets *The Iliad* aside and walks toward me, long, lean legs beneath the white shirt that barely covers her hips.

"You're beautiful," I say, but it's not a compliment, not exactly. She's beautiful like the sun setting over the bay, casting its trail of shimmering light down the water, beautiful like the city at night, yellow gems suspended in darkness, beautiful like the light glinting silver off the blade of Ras's knife. Her beauty is a fact, not an attribute; something she is, not something she has.

She smiles wearily. "Thanks."

"You probably hear that all the time," I say, recognizing my mistake.

She shrugs.

"I should say you're reckless."

"Right back atcha," she says, smirking as she points her finger at me like a mock gun and mimes shooting. The spark of playfulness tugs at my heart, something deeply hidden peeking cautiously at the surface, to see if it's safe to come up into the clear, fresh air.

"Not likely. I'm a very light sleeper."

"I noticed. I got up to go to the bathroom and you freaked out."

I blink at her. "I did?"

"Yeah. You held me down for a few moments, then woke up the rest of the way, apologized, and went back to sleep." Her eyes sparkle with amusement, but she doesn't seem to think our paranoid, hair-trigger reflexes are something to be afraid of or mock.

"I remember," I say, though of course I don't. "My brother and I used to play a lot of games. For one of them—we called it Killer—we'd take turns trying to assassinate each other. It was pretend, mostly. Eli liked to sneak up on me in my sleep."

"That's cute," she replies. I think back to the beatings Eli used to dish out when he won, or the kitchen knife he once buried an inch into my thigh. Cute.

"Tell me about you," she says, leaning against the counter and watching me as I stir batter to make pancakes.

"What do you want to know?" I ask, because I don't know what Ras has already told her.

"Do you go to school?"

"Yes." I pour batter onto the skillet. "I graduate in May."

"Wait." She giggles and I find the sound incredibly endearing, a sign that beneath all the poise and grooming is an impossible sweetness. "Do you mean you're still in high school?"

"Yes."

"Please tell me you're at least eighteen."

"As of September."

She reaches a hand toward my face and I startle, catching her wrist. "It's okay," she says softly, like she's talking to a spooked horse. I force myself to hold still as she brushes a lock of hair out of my eyes.

"I'm sorry. I'm not used to being around people who touch me."

Ras has been sleeping with his mentor for years and has plenty of one-night stands on the side. He's used to being touched. But not me. And especially not in the face.

Scarlett studies me carefully, and I get the uncanny feeling she can see right through to my core. "You're a little different this morning."

"I don't know what you mean." I try to hide the anxiety that starts bubbling in my chest.

She shrugs. "Just a feeling."

As we eat our pancakes, I reassure myself that there's no way she can see the difference between Ras and me. Not even Mom and Dad can tell us apart, though sometimes I think it's because they only see what they want to see when they look at me.

As we eat and talk, I start to relax. She smiles more and more, and those smiles feel genuine, like very small cracks in the flawless wall of ice. I realize I like her, her cold composure, the way her mouth quirks up at one corner when she's amused, how smart she is, how elegant. I've never met anyone who was so ladylike, and yet her posture and manners and perfect diction have a ruthless edge, like she herself is a weapon, as carefully trained and disciplined as I am, just in a different arena.

And yet there's more to her, a depth I can somehow sense, despite her attempts to hide it. Like the dark blue waters of a lake, trapped beneath a perfect sheet of ice.

AFTER BREAKFAST, I drive her home, to a mansion built to look like a Greek temple, with a row of white columns two stories high.

She laughs as I give her a chaste kiss on the cheek. "You don't have to be a gentleman just because we're in front of my house," she says, looping her arms around my neck.

"I'm a gentleman because you deserve it." I carefully remove her arms before she can try to kiss me. "I'll call you."

She smiles as we say goodbye, like she knows as well as I do Ras is going to make good on that promise.

Do you think tonight is too soon to see her again? Ras asks me as I drive away.

It's hard not to laugh. I've never seen him like this over a girl. But Scarlett is special. Something about her tugs at me, like a fishhook caught on something precious buried beneath the river mud. It seems like she's an answer I've been searching for, if only I could figure out the question.

"I want to see her again too." I expect a fight over it—he hates to share his toys. But he agrees without hesitation.

8: Scar Tissue

RAS STEPS OUT of the February cold and into a strip club on the bottom floor of an upscale hotel and brothel. It obviously caters to a wealthy clientele, leather-lined booths set back in cozy shadows. Beautiful women in G-strings gyrate slowly on the wide stage, leaning down to pay particular attention to this client or that. Suit coats are stripped off and thrown over chairs, ties loosened and cuffs undone.

Ras walks toward the bar where Vance stands with a tumbler of whiskey in his hand, looking out over the room.

Vance greets his son with a fond smile and they make their way to a discreet door in the back. A barrel-chested man in a black suit stands beside it, arms crossed.

"No weapons," he says.

To Ras's surprise, Vance surrenders his gun and boot knife. Ras does the same, reluctantly. The man sets their weapons in a black box and pushes open the door.

They step into an atrium with a wall of windows, compact squares of glass, overlooking a snow-covered garden. The antique furniture is a pale green in the light filtering through the heavy clouds. A chessboard sits at the ready, pieces arrayed upon it as though someone left in the middle of a game.

Vance walks over to the well-stocked bar and picks up a bottle, examining the label before he pours himself a drink.

"You gave up your gun," Ras says. "Why?"

"This is neutral territory," Vance says. "I'd like it to stay that way. The Russians won't be bringing any weapons either. I'm hoping we won't have to kill anyone. But if we have to, we have to. I assume you have a knife?"

Ras nods. Of course, he does.

The door swings open, and Elena Nikitichna walks into the room, flanked by two bodyguards. They puff up their chests and dangle their hands awkwardly by their sides, obviously missing their firearms. She's taller than both of them, her platinum-blonde hair falling to her waist in a shining sheet. She wears tight jeans and a white turtleneck, her body slender and languid as a snake on a warm day, sunning itself on a rock. And, like a snake, she's both venomous and cold-blooded, the woman who manages the Russian mafia's business interests here in the city.

"Vance de Haven," she says in a sweet, even voice. "It's good to see you."

Vance returns the greeting with an equally solemn insincerity, and they shake hands.

"And Jude," she says, a hint of a smile playing on her lips as she takes his hand. "How are you?"

Ras hates being called Jude, though he's pragmatic enough to understand the necessity for the disguise. He knows that if their parents realized the broken state of their son's mind, there would be doctors and therapists and possibly mental hospitals and almost certainly their guns and knives would be taken away, as well as the opportunities to use them. Not even Elena, with whom he's shared many violent moments and an equal number of intimate ones, knows who he really is.

"I'm good," he says, holding her hand for a little longer than necessary. She winks at him when Vance's attention lands elsewhere, gently scraping her long fake nails down his palm as she lets go.

She and Vance sit at the chessboard, clearing it as they exchange pleasantries. When the black and white pieces stand in neat rows, Elena lifts a pawn and moves it two spaces forward.

"What brings the great Vance de Haven out from his castle today?" she asks, a sardonic smile playing on her face.

Vance considers the board for a moment, making his move before he looks up. "Nikita Fyodorov stole something from me."

"Why come to me?" Her delicate fingers carefully lift another pawn. "My father and I haven't spoken in years."

"You expect me to believe you had nothing to do with this?"

Elena shrugs her skinny shoulders. "Believe whatever you want, Vance. It's not going to change anything."

Vance and Elena make several moves in silence and Ras tries not to fidget, bored and restless. Judging by how many pieces they've captured, the players seem to be evenly matched. Ras doesn't know enough about chess to tell in any other way. His father tried to teach them a few times, and Jude took to it quickly, but Ras has never had the patience.

Vance knocks over a pawn with his bishop and collects the toppled piece to add to his small collection. "So Nikita came to the city and didn't even think to contact you?"

"You think that Papa would kick the hornets' nest, and then come running to me to protect him?" A cold smile plays on Elena's features. "You underestimate us. Someday, it's going to get you killed."

"We'll see." Vance studies the board, his mouth pressed into a narrow line. Beside him, Ras suppresses a sigh.

"Is chess not your game, Jude?" Elena asks, smirking. She knows very well it isn't.

"It's boring," Ras says.

She laughs, leaning back in her chair. "Honesty. From a de Haven, no less. I might die of shock."

"I'll be honest with you when you're honest with me," Vance says in Russian. Ras pretends not to understand, studying the chessboard. Neither Vance nor Elena know that he can speak the language.

"And why should I be?" Elena asks. *"You have spilled the blood of my family. You are hunting my father like a dog. If you showed yourself in Moscow, you would be torn apart."*

"This is not Moscow, and you do not have the Bratva to protect you, girl. Be careful what you say."

Ras carefully maintains a neutral expression, his head down as Elena and Vance glare at each other. He reaches out and casually slides Vance's queen one space backward, into the path of Elena's knight.

"Why do you keep Nikita's secrets?" Vance asks in a more reasonable tone. "He's done nothing for you."

"There is no love lost between my father and me," Elena says, "but even if I wanted to help you, I wouldn't be able to. He hasn't contacted me. If you know so much about our relationship, you shouldn't be surprised."

She studies the chessboard, one eyebrow slightly raised, then picks up her knight and gently knocks aside Vance's queen. After that, it only takes a few moves before she looks up from the board with a slight smile of satisfaction. "Check."

"Nikita stole from me," Vance says. "I can't tolerate that. If you really have nothing to do with this, you'll help me find him."

Elena watches Vance's move with cold amusement. "Of course. If I hear so much as a whisper, you will be the first to know." She slides her bishop into place. "Checkmate."

"YOUR KNOTS NEED work," Ras says, tugging on the rope binding his left wrist to one of the bedposts on Elena's big canopy bed. Her sheets are a crisp white beneath him, the canopy strung with fairy lights and gauze so it looks like stars in mist.

"You're mouthy today," she says, but she attends to the loose knot anyway. She's never been any good at tying secure ones.

"Why is your father attacking the syndicate?" Ras asks as she moves to secure his right wrist, looking deceptively angelic in a satiny white robe.

"You don't know?" She finishes off the knot and glances at him. "It's kind of a long story."

"Well..." Ras tugs at his right wrist and finds it satisfactorily restrained. "You have a captive audience."

She laughs, moving to tie down his legs. "Fair enough. You know your dad was a spy, right? He went to Russia to spy on the Russian mafia. Well, my dad was his Russian contact, a cop who had infiltrated the mafia."

"So when Vance double-crossed the mafia, he betrayed Nikita too? And now he's back in the city to get revenge?"

"There's more to it than that." Elena steps back, admiring her handiwork. "If you're good, maybe I'll tell you."

Ras smirks, raising an eyebrow. "Do you really want me to be good?"

"As if you could." She picks up one of several knives lying on her nightstand, the blade glinting in the light as she twirls it in her fingers. It's long and thin, and, Ras knows, sharp as a scalpel. She studies him for a moment, baby-blue eyes dark with lust, then takes the blade and runs the dull edge down his chest, the metal cold against his skin. A quick taste before she flips it and starts to trace the contours of his body with the sharp side, applying the perfect light pressure, almost but not quite enough to break the skin—as long as he remains perfectly still, that is.

For years, Ras has watched Elena, as she taught him to use his knives on some unfortunate soul who'd wronged her, as she gave him a very different sort of anatomy lesson in the bedroom. Studying her rare interactions with his father, or the moments when he got to watch her conduct business. He learned to mimic her arrogant, commanding demeanor so smoothly it became his own. At sixteen, when they met, she was what he wanted to grow up to be—ruthless and untethered. Now, his ideas about himself are a little more sophisticated, but he still learns from her, in the bedroom and out of it.

He has a few scars from these games, but not many, and none that were unintentional. Elena is an artist with a blade, and, even now, she can make him feel like an apprentice.

"Let me cut you," she says, biting the corner of her lip like the blushing schoolgirl she definitely is not. He's about to refuse—he doesn't let her do it often, because Jude complains bitterly about the scars—but then she says, "I'll let you do me."

He grins at her and agrees. And when it's his turn to tangle her in the ropes, he whispers his real name in her ear, a shock of heat crashing through him when she repeats it.

"I SHOULD HAVE known you were Ras the first time I heard about him," she says afterward, lighting a cigarette.

He takes it from her and reaches past her to put it out in the ashtray on her nightstand. He hates the smell of cigarette smoke. It reminds him too much of his father's study and the many times he's been beaten there. Vance has never inspired fear—not in Ras—but rather anger. He doesn't flinch from his father's gestures even now, but is always coiled and ready to strike back, harder than he's ever been hit, if Jude would only let him.

"Asshole," she mutters.

He leans back against the headboard, hands behind his head, smirking. "Tell me the rest of the story. About Nikita."

"Do you remember him at all?"

Ras shakes his head.

"I guess you were pretty little," she says. "Sometimes, I forget how young you are."

"Why? What happened?"

"Vance returned from Russia to make his fortune here. He left his family behind for three years. Papa moved in with your mom and the two of them played house until your dad returned." There's a bitter, jealous note to her voice.

Ras raises an eyebrow. "Nadya had an affair?"

Elena snorts with amusement. "It's kind of weird how you call your parents by their first names."

"It's because I don't love them," Ras says.

"I know, baby," she says fondly. "You're like me. You wanna get some food?"

"Can't. I have a date."

They've never been exclusive; neither of them are interested in or capable of monogamy. So Elena just shrugs, swinging her legs over the side of the bed, the long, narrow plane of her back to him.

"Have fun," she says. "I'll text you."

9: Class

I PICK UP the jewelry box sitting on my kitchen table and open it. Inside, a sapphire-and-diamond necklace twinkles at me from the black velvet. The fourth such piece he's acquired in a month.

It's from Reginold's, Ras murmurs, naming a very upscale jewelry boutique. *This must be worth a small fortune.*

"You stole more jewelry?" I ask. "The city is going to run out of diamonds."

She deserves the best. Don't you want to make her happy?

He has a point. Scarlett likes getting jewelry, though I'm pretty sure it's more the fact that they're stolen than the gems themselves. She can't wear the more distinctive pieces in public, but she loves hearing me explain how *I* acquired each one, what venerable estate I broke into, what high-end jewelry store I scammed. I don't like lying to her, and it feels strange taking credit for Ras's work, even though I do it all the time. But her radiant smiles make it worth the deception.

"I do want to make her happy," I say.

Then we agree, he murmurs cheerfully.

"For once," I say. She's the only thing that's ever really brought us together. Ras adores her, of course, and I like her too.

I've started to look forward to the time I get with her, and sometimes when she's not around, I imagine talking to her about whatever I'm doing, thinking of the clever, biting remark she'd come up with to make me laugh, or the intelligent solution she'd have for whatever problem I'm facing.

I'm a little wary, though. Ras wanting to share something so freely, wanting to make me happy, means he's either trying to get something from me, or he's laying a trap.

I want you to take her to dinner tonight. I already made reservations.

"Why? Why do you let me see her at all?"

Because. I want her to know you.

I rub my forehead. "Why? You hate me."

Not true. You hate me. And you're afraid of me.

"Bullshit." I'm certainly not afraid of him, just cautious, like anyone should be when dealing with a wild animal whose behavior they don't completely understand. I don't fear him, and I never have. I don't hate him—he's constantly accusing me of that—but I don't exactly love him either. I never wanted to be a killer, I didn't fucking ask to be a monster, to hurt people so much they beg for mercy. And yet. Even as I fight it with everything I have, a little part of me, no more than an insidious whisper, yearns to be as free and as happy as he is.

And so I date his girlfriend, whose smile makes me feel happy, whose laughter makes me feel free.

Wear one of my shirts. You're taking her to Sonata, not some dive bar like you always take Ash to.

He has a point. Sonata actually has a dress code, though they make an exception for the son of the syndicate boss. I'm not about to wear a coat and tie, but I do want to look nice for her. I pull my shirt over my head and pause, looking at the small bandage on my chest.

"What's this?" I ask, running my fingers over the bandage.

A little cut. Nothing to worry about.

I sigh, shrugging on his button-down shirt. "Elena?"

Yes.

"What about Scarlett? I thought she was the love of your life."

A dark chuckle echoes in my mind. *I don't love anyone. And Scarlett doesn't have to know.*

"That's not fair to her," I say.

Is it fair that you spend half the time telling her how beautiful she is, and then you go moon over Ash?

I shake my head. "It's not the same."

No. Your way is worse.

"How is it worse? That doesn't make any sense."

I'm just cheating with my dick. You're cheating with your heart. What do you think means more to them?

"I'm not cheating," I snap, but I feel a little sick as I button up the shirt. I know there's some truth to what he's saying. I might not want to sleep with Scarlett, but I do love her. And I may never have kissed Ash, but I love him, too, just as madly, just as helplessly.

SCARLETT AND I sit at a cozy table nestled in the corner, a candle flickering between us, white lilies in a tall, slender vase.

She seems uneasy here, watching me coolly and indifferently as though from very far away. I take her hand. I rarely touch her—she's Ras's girlfriend, not mine—but I don't like the distance that's just grown between us. It feels like since we sat down she's started to close in on herself, a flower blooming in reverse, and the loss of our usual carefree connection upsets me more than I would have thought.

Four people have stopped by our table so far to greet her and make small talk. She responds gracefully and easily, laughing her low husky laugh in response to unfunny jokes, promising to call or visit each of them soon. But it's fake. I don't know how I'm sure, but I am.

I take her hand, bring it to my lips, and then hold it between both of mine. Her fingers are slender and cold, her skin impossibly soft.

"I used to come here with my stepfather all the time," she says.

I don't know what her stepfather meant to her, but I can make some guesses from the relieved smile and the sense of satisfaction, of justice served, when she told me about his death.

Two or three years ago, my father and I were looking at a list of city councilors and he put his finger on Chris Bancroft's name and said we should consider blackmail.

"What for?" I asked.

He looked at me for a long time. I was around fifteen, and I could tell he was trying to decide if I was adult enough to have this conversation, a strange thing to wonder about the son he took with him to make deals and collect debts, the son he let torture his enemies and watch him kill.

"There's a lot of ways you can break a person," he said, shaking his head. "Sometimes, I think his way is worse than ours. That poor girl."

I asked for more details, curiosity piqued, but he refused to say more, and, although I kept my ears open, I never came across any rumors. In the end, we didn't blackmail him. My father never explained why, and I thought maybe he'd been wrong, that Chris Bancroft hadn't been guilty of anything of the sort.

But now, in this restaurant where elegance hides so much ugliness, listening to the delicate way she says the word "stepfather" as she drifts away from me like an untethered buoy, I think back to that conversation and wonder what it meant.

"I hate this place, actually," I say, still holding her hand. Still elated to be holding her hand, despite everything. "It's so fucking nice."

"You know I own it, right?" she asks. "Part of the Bancroft empire. My stepfather left almost everything to me."

"I'm sorry," I murmur, and she giggles.

"Don't be. I hate it too. If it didn't make such good money, I'd have it burned to the ground."

"I could arrange that." Several times throughout my childhood, I came back to my body to find a smoldering pile of twigs or scrap wood, or my father yelling at me for almost burning down a shed. Ras liked to set fires, but, fortunately, he's done it less and less as we've gotten older.

She smiles at me, a real, vibrant smile. "Let's get the hell out of here. Take me somewhere that's not nice. Somewhere you like to go."

"WHERE'D YOU COME from, beautiful?" Quinn leans on the bar, grinning at Scarlett. "I could think of a hundred things to do to a girl like you."

"Only a hundred?" Scarlett smiles back, and maybe it's just my imagination but it seems more genuine. In the smoky dark of the bar, she stands out, her posture and her imperious poise setting her apart even before getting close enough to see her diamonds.

"A hundred's better than Jude's got, I'm sure."

Scarlett laughs, and, despite Quinn's teasing, which comes uncomfortably close to the truth, I'm beyond grateful to her for having made my best friend smile.

Now it's my turn to be recognized and pulled into conversations, only my people are hookers, not heiresses; pimps, not philanthropists; thieves and thugs rather than CEOs and lawyers. I keep an eye out for Ash, though I know he rarely ventures this far west, into territory where the gangs still have a presence, despite my best efforts. I don't want him to find out about Scarlett.

It's easy for him to hang a rainbow flag over the bed in his one-room apartment and not give a fuck what anyone thinks of him. He doesn't have a small army of thugs and pimps and drug dealers to keep in line. His father is an orthodontist, and the strain in their relationship is because he's an addict, not because he's gay. He wouldn't understand why I have to play this game with Scarlett, why I lie to her so frequently, why I let her assume I'm someone I could never be. He would just see me hiding. Like a fucking coward.

"Everyone knows you," Scarlett says, sitting across from me in the booth, even more beautiful with the shadows falling over her.

"This is my territory," I say.

"I can see that." She gives me a sly smile. "You know, you promised me a job."

"Right." I wonder why the fuck Ras never told me that little detail. "What kind of job?"

"I want to be the boss." She's not smiling now, and it doesn't feel like a joke. But then she laughs. "Short of that, I'd like to be somewhere where things happen. I don't want to sell crack on the streets. I want to be where the big deals are made."

I have no idea where I could put her. Dad's not going to hire someone for an important position just because I ask him to.

"That might take me a while to arrange," I say. "For now, would you like to work with me?"

She gives me a wide smile, and I feel warm all over, in a way that has absolutely nothing to do with sex.

THE NEXT TIME I see her, I take her to the Warrens with me again, carefully avoiding anywhere Ash might be hanging out. She watches as I talk with the pimps, bribe a stray cop, and collect money from the drug dealers. The people here trust me, and most are willing to talk freely in front of her after I promise she's on our side.

If she has any trace of morality in her heart, any inclination to choose right over wrong, it doesn't show. She can be cold and a little abrasive, but she listens more than she talks. She gives me advice, telling me who she thinks I can trust, when to push and threaten, and when to pull back and be kind, and, for a girl from the city's upper crust, she understands the language we're speaking as well as anyone else.

As we make our way around the slums, two people recognize her, and although the drug dealer clearly knows her from her magazine ads, the other one, a hooker, seems to know her personally. She calls her Rose and asks after her mother, but Scarlett abruptly ends the conversation with a polite "You must be thinking of someone else," and an icy stare. When I ask about it, I get the same cold dismissal, the sense of her folding in on herself, growing distant, and even though I want to know everything about her, I'm so desperate to bring her back that I change the subject immediately.

10: Beauty and the Beast

BESIDE RAS, SCARLETT lies on her back, the curves of her body veiled by candlelight. They've been together for several weeks now, but he still hasn't had enough of her; the seashell curve of her ear, her delighted gasp when he runs his tongue up her thigh, the elegant shape of her neck. Not since Elena has he wanted the same woman more than once or twice, but he's certain he could never tire of Scarlett.

He wants to know everything about her, hear every word she has to say, learn every deep and shameful secret. He wants to own her, body and soul, to possess her like a demon, to lock her in the dark dungeon of his heart for the rest of his life.

She glances at him, a hint of vulnerability in the turn of her lips.

"Can I stay tonight?" she asks. "It's so peaceful here. I sleep really well."

Peaceful? Among the constant noise—the roar of cars on the street below, the neighbors' music and laughter, the sound of their fighting and fucking? Ras is always aware and alert. Some might even say paranoid, and he is still learning to separate noise from threats.

"Of course," he says, getting up to blow out the candles. "I like to have you with me."

Her smile is the last thing he sees before he puts out the final candle and the room is wrapped in darkness.

He drifts in and out of a shallow sleep until the soft squeak of his front door jerks him awake. Heavy footsteps cross the threshold. He gets out of bed and grabs a belt off the dresser, retreating to the dark corner of the room beside the door. Seconds after he's situated, the door is flung open, and a portly silhouette steps through.

"Wake up, punk," Artie says, and Scarlett sits up, startled.

In the dull glow that falls in from the other room, the outline of a shotgun is aimed at her.

She reaches over and flicks on the light. The sheet pools in her lap, her breasts exposed, but she doesn't seem concerned. She crosses her arms, looking up expectantly at the gun barrel trained on her and the man holding it. She must see Ras, silent and still behind Artie, but she never lets her eyes land on him.

"Do you want something?" she asks.

"Where's the kid who lives here?" Artie seems a little off-balance in the face of her cold composure.

She gestures to the right. "In the bathroom. Hiding."

From behind the landlord, Ras grins. Of course Scarlett would know exactly what to do, and be cool and ruthless enough to pull it off. She's luring the landlord away from Ras's hiding spot, ensuring that he'll have his back to Ras, giving the killer an opportunity to strike.

Artie waves at her with the barrel of the shotgun. "Don't you fucking move, missy." He turns, kicking the bathroom door so it swings all the way open. Ras lunges forward, looping the belt around the landlord's neck and pulling just tight enough to make the threat clear.

"Drop the gun," he says.

"Fuck," Artie gasps. "Fuck. Okay." The weapon clatters to the floor, and Scarlett picks it up, studying it with a small, curious smile on her face.

"You could have a lot of fun with a gun like this," she says.

"Please," Artie whimpers. "I'm sorry."

"I don't like guns," Ras says, pulling the noose slightly tighter to remind Artie it's there. "Too loud."

"You're right." She waves her hand imperiously, as though giving an order. "Kill him, then. Make it quick."

Ras knows violence is only for business, never for fun; Jude's will and Vance's commands keep his primal nature in check. He's not supposed to kill, not right here, right now.

And yet Scarlett has the same authoritative demeanor as his father, a strength of will to match Jude's. Her permission, her order, is enough to let him off the leash, to let the darkness in him grow thick and cold and merciless.

He tightens his grip until the struggling, frantic body goes limp, the breath gone, the fight over. He lets the corpse fall to the floor with an ungainly thud.

"What are you going to do with him?" she asks, studying the body with a cool, detached fascination.

"The syndicate has a team of cleaners who take care of this sort of thing," Ras says. "I'll call them."

"Will your dad be upset you killed someone without his permission?"

Ras shrugs carelessly. He hasn't actually considered this. "I'll bribe them so they don't tell him. Just give me a minute to call them."

He gives Scarlett a quick kiss and steps over the body into the other room. But before he can retrieve his phone, the world slips away and darkness overtakes him.

When he returns to consciousness, the clock tells him only a few minutes have gone by. The door to the bedroom is still shut; Scarlett must be getting dressed and putting on her makeup, a time-consuming process that seems almost meditative for her.

On the table before him, their notebook is sitting open to a page covered in Jude's careful, tiny writing.

You irresponsible motherfucker. You were NOT supposed to kill him. Don't even think about calling the cleaners. Dad will find out. Hang the poor guy in his office and start packing. Don't expect me to do it. I'm not cleaning up after another one of your fuckups. And you want to know why I hate you? This is why. Take care of it.

Ras throws the book across the room. He wears an effortless armor of indifference, a complete and flawless arrogance, and few insults even register, let alone injure him. But reminders of how much Jude hates him pierce like arrows. His hurt and anger become a volatile combination; an agitation just beneath the skin, crawling and itching.

He takes Jude's laptop, opens the window, and drops it to the ground ten stories below. Let him pick up the fucking pieces in the morning.

And then he calls the cleaners, a move even he knows will have consequences, he who rarely looks past the satisfaction of the next few hours. A brief conversation, thinly veiled by a simple code, is all it takes to summon them.

"Did you just throw your laptop out the window?" Scarlett asks, as he hangs up the phone.

He glances at the still open window, then back at her. "It was old."

She gives him a skeptical glance, but just shrugs. He'd gladly tell her their secret—he'd gladly tell her all his secrets—but Jude won't let him. There are two rules that govern their life, two places where Jude's will is strong enough to bind him. The first is that he can tell no one about the split in their mind. The second is that he can never harm someone Jude loves. Never. Never.

11: You and Me and the City

SCARLETT BREATHES SOFTLY beside me, the two of us in the center of a bed big enough to get lost in. I stare up at the ceiling and try to concentrate, to let my mind open.

I was in therapy briefly during my freshman year of high school. My mother sent me; my father didn't know about it. When he found out, he put an immediate stop to it.

While I was there, the therapist tried to teach me how to talk to the other parts of my mind. She told me to picture a house and walk through it, looking into all of the rooms to see who lived there. She had the idea that I might discover many hidden fragments of myself, and we'd all live peacefully in the floating dream house in my mind.

But there are no hidden fragments, and no dollhouse. There's just Ras and me, and the city. In the depths of my mind, I conjure up a dark maze of back alleys and garish neon light falling onto wet stone streets. I focus on putting myself there, stepping through a portal into my inner world.

"Come out," I say, standing on the slick cobblestones.

Ras emerges from the shadow cast by a towering stone wall, as though materializing from the plentiful darkness around us.

He grins at me, my own face made unfamiliar by his predatory glee. In his hand, he holds a long knife with a wicked curve. "You want to fight again."

I tried once to kill him, not long after I was first aware of his presence. The first time I returned to my body from an absence to see a mutilated corpse, I was so horrified I dove into my mind and tried to purge him from my consciousness. It almost destroyed us both.

I raise my empty palms. "No. I don't want to fight."

He lowers the knife, a soft shush of rubbed metal as it disappears into a sheath strapped to his thigh. "You want to talk?"

Although a steady rain is falling, droplets catching fragments of light as they tumble downward, the two of us stay dry, facing each other across the length of an alley. Faceless people pass by the mouth of the street, heads down to avoid the rain. The city in miniature, in as much detail as I can render it. There's nowhere else Ras and I would feel at home.

"You have to listen to me," I say. "Dad is going to be furious when he finds out that not only did you kill someone without permission, you bribed the cleaners to keep quiet. They're not going to, and he'll—"

"If he hits me one more time, I'm going to kill him," Ras says, his melodic voice deep with anger. "I mean it, Judy."

"I'll handle it. Just like I handle all your fucking mistakes."

"Why do you hate me?" he asks with a childlike petulance that almost makes me feel sorry for him.

"I don't hate you. I just wish that you'd listen to me."

"You do so hate me. You said so."

Above us, clouds pass over the face of the moon, casting us in deeper darkness, broken only by the artificial lights of the city. Ras glances up for a moment, then back at me, at my hand, and I realize I'm holding a knife, the reassuring weight of a gun on my hip. Weapons summoned into being by my anger.

"A night with no moon," he says, smiling, but with a hand on the hilt of his knife, secure in its sheath. "Like me. All darkness." His smile fades. "You took every good thing for yourself, do you know that?"

I shake my head. "Not true."

Just past him, a streetlight flickers for a second, then dies out entirely. "You lie, Judy." He glares at me. "You lie to me and you lie to yourself. You are cruel to me when all I do is help you."

I step forward, gripping my knife. "You're a monster."

"Then don't ask me to kill."

"I didn't ask you to kill tonight."

He draws his weapon, holding it by his side, watching me warily. From some distant street, I hear Scarlett's voice, though I can't make out the words.

"Go," Ras says, waving at me with the hand that holds the knife. "Talk to her. Be with her."

I watch him suspiciously. "Why? Why do you let me see her at all?"

He smiles, a cold, dark smile. "Because you made her love us. And love is the strongest chain there is. Even I know that."

With that, he steps back into the shadows and disappears. I imagine his grin lingering long after the rest of him has faded, like the Cheshire Cat.

12: A Castle Built on Sand

THE FRONT DOOR to the imposing Victorian mansion is solid oak, creaky as it swings in its wide outward arc. The house, although preserved and maintained, feels like it sags around the opening like a cavernous mouth. I step inside, reminding myself I don't live here anymore and that as soon as I finish talking to Dad, I can go back to my apartment with its wide windows and abundance of light.

I take the temperamental side staircase to the second floor, the dark wood groaning underfoot no matter how lightly I step. Even though my father's not around to hear it, the noise sets me on edge. Ever since I was ten and he first showed us how to walk like foxes, how to place our feet and balance our weight, he's expected Eli and me to always move silently. I do it without thinking now, and rarely slip up, but this aging house is full of creaking floorboards.

I breathe a sigh of relief when I get to the top of the stairs, but the knot of anxiety in my chest doesn't unravel. I can guess why Dad told me to come home, his voice terse and abrupt over the phone when he called.

"This is all your fault," I whisper to Ras, but he doesn't answer.

I knock on the door to my father's study. At his gruff acknowledgment, I step into the dimly lit room, the smell of smoke thick in the air. A cigarette sits in a glass ashtray on his desk, beside a half-full whiskey bottle. I glance at the tumbler in his hand and try to guess how much he's had to drink tonight. He downs the rest of the amber liquid in his glass and slams it on the desk. Not a good sign.

"I just talked to the cleaning team," he says, stepping toward me. "They told me something pretty fucking interesting."

"I can explain, sir," I reply, fighting the instinct to take a step back, as his hands curl into fists.

"I'm disappointed that you killed someone without my permission. I'm fucking pissed because you bribed my own people so they wouldn't tell me. I can't fucking believe it. Do you have any idea how hard it is to find people to do that job? And now I need a whole new crew that doesn't know what a fucking idiot my son is. Jude, what the hell were you thinking?"

A trick question. I sidestep around it. "I'm sorry, sir."

"You're sorry." As he moves closer, I can smell the alcohol on his breath. "You're sorry?"

"Yes, sir."

Dad and I have been sparring partners for years, and, by now, I know all his tells. I see the blow coming long before it lands. I could step aside or block, but that would only make him angrier, and, at any rate, I deserve it. Everything Ras does is my responsibility.

His fist lands on my jaw, a bright, intrusive shock of pain. I've been hit in the face many times in my life, but I've never gotten used to the jarring immediacy of it.

Ras springs into my consciousness with the coiled speed of a jungle cat, woken by the violence. He whispers furiously to me.

Now! You have an opening, Judy, take it! Hit him. HIT him.

I ignore Ras, holding my ground as Dad advances.

"You tried to turn my own people against me," he says, his fist connecting with the side of my head. It hurts, but not as much as it could. He's holding back. He always holds back with me, because he loves me.

Stop him. Stop him! You can do it. I know you can. Now. Hit him now.

I close my eyes for a moment, trying to focus. "It was stupid. It was a stupid thing to do."

He hits me again, this time in the gut, and I double over, struggling to stand upright. He doesn't like to see any show of weakness.

I'll kill him for this. Let me out, Judy. I'll kill him. I'll fucking kill him. Let me OUT.

"No," I whisper, and another punch catches me off guard. I stagger back, resisting the urge to bring my hands to my face and protect myself. I could make this stop. I know what to tell him. I know exactly what to tell him to make him stop. But it involves a lie I never wanted to spin.

"I can't believe this," he says, and the disappointment in his voice is more painful than the blows. "I expect this kind of bullshit from Eli, but not from you. Maybe I promoted you too fast. You've got some growing up to do."

"You don't understand," I say desperately. I can't let him take away the territory I worked so hard to earn. I can't let him be disappointed in me.

"Then make me understand, Jude."

I wipe away the blood running from my lip down my chin. "He threatened my girlfriend, sir." I'm burning with shame as I say it, because she's Ras's girlfriend, not mine. I'm not likely to ever have one; I don't have the energy for that kind of charade, and it wouldn't be fair to whatever girl I caught up in it. I hate deceiving Dad; I hate hiding such a fundamental part of myself from him. But I know how dangerous the truth is.

Dad's fists unclench, his shoulders relaxing, his fighting stance faded away. "Defending your woman? Why didn't you say so?"

"I didn't think it was important."

He slings his arm over my shoulders. "Let's get you some ice."

Downstairs, I wash the blood off my face and he gives me a bag of ice to hold to my eye. The cold feels good on my throbbing skin. He sits across from me with a smile, and I decide he's calm enough I can ask for a favor.

"This whole thing was my fault," I say. "The cleaning crew did exactly what they're supposed to: they came straight to you."

He chuckles, shaking his head. "Your soft fucking heart is going to get you in trouble."

"It'll be really hard to replace the whole crew. And they're not the ones who fucked up."

"You think you know how to run the business, eh?" he asks, but with a fond smile. "Better than your old man?"

Although it hurts to move my lips, I can't hold back a laugh, because I'm so relieved to see him like this. The dad who smiles and gently teases and beneath it, is really proud of me. I know that his moods are like summer thunderstorms, and, no matter how dark the sky or heavy the downpour, the sun comes back soon enough.

"No, sir," I say. "I just don't want someone else to pay for my mistake."

"I'll think about it."

We both turn as footsteps sound in the hallway, my mother's characteristic soft, hesitant tread.

"Nadya." Dad gets up and puts an arm around her waist, giving her a quick kiss. "Get me a drink. We've got big news."

Her gaze lingers on my face for a few moments, lips pressed into a thin line, and then she turns away to open the liquor cabinet. I wish I could tell her I'm fine, that it's really not as big a deal as she thinks it is. That it was my fault anyway. But there's an unspoken, unbreakable rule in this house. Don't talk about it. I would no more go to Mom and tell her Dad hit me than go up to a policeman and admit that I'm a criminal.

"What news?" she asks, setting Dad's drink on the table and sitting in the chair beside him.

"Jude has a girlfriend." Dad sounds almost...vindicated by the revelation. And really proud.

I look away, out into the garden where the acres of rosebushes are starting to bloom. I cut a bouquet a few days ago for my friend to give to his prom date. He gave me a hard time for not going myself, because this is the last time I'll have the chance. But things like school dances and football games don't feel like they fit into my life. I don't feel eighteen and I don't belong among the other rich prep-school kids, not after collecting debts and letting Ras beat up the people who won't pay, not after dealing drugs, not after all the late nights working with my dad.

"You have a girlfriend?" Mom asks, her brow furrowed, studying me like she doesn't quite believe me. It makes me uneasy.

"Yes," I say. "Her name is Scarlett Bancroft."

"The Bancroft girl?" Dad grins. "I'll be damned."

"You know her?" I ask.

"I knew her stepdad. Scum of the fucking earth, that's Chris Bancroft. Glad I got the chance to take him out."

Mom looks away, biting her lip. She hates to hear about the violence we do, but Dad doesn't really try to keep it from her.

"Why?" I ask, leaning forward, eager to unravel a little more of the mystery Scarlett keeps herself shrouded in.

Dad looks at me, considering. "You don't need to know. There's some things that should stay buried."

"I want to know everything about her."

He's silent for a long moment. "Chris did bad things to her. That's all I'm going to say."

I nod. It hurts like an icy blow to the gut, to hear that someone abused her, even though I had already guessed as much. I want to know the details, but at the same time, I'm afraid to. The very thought of it makes me want to cry or throw up or hit something. Or, if Chris Bancroft were still alive, tie him to a chair and let Ras cut him into pieces.

"Is she nice?" Mom asks, and the tension in the air eases somewhat.

"She is. You'd like her, Mom." I'm not sure if that's actually true. If my mother would be able to see past Scarlett's icy exterior to the powerful, graceful person within.

"We want you to be happy, Jude," Mom says. "All that matters."

I nod. Scarlett does make me happy, and, for Ras, she's everything. But my mind always returns to Ash, to the many evenings we spend in dark, anonymous places, laughing and talking, every brush of his fingertips on my arm, every press of his thigh against mine in a small booth, carefully filed away to remember later on the nights I don't see him.

"She's a smart girl," Dad says. "Got nerves of steel. Bring her by Sunday night. We'll have dinner." It's not a request.

"Yes, sir. She'd love that." I recite it mechanically, like a line in a play, this lie I'm supposed to build my life around.

13: Beg, Steal, Borrow, or Barter

I WALK BY a porn store, one of many flourishing in the Warrens, fluorescent insides glowing luridly, and then a liquor store, the brilliant neon signs trapped behind the bars in the windows. Across the street, Bancroft Square is cast in shadow, its once-idyllic pond now a stretch of blackness, harsh lights shining on the graffiti-stained statue at the west corner.

I don't see Ash on the street, so I cross over into the park, slipping quietly from shadow to shadow. I don't usually venture here to find him, where he might be with someone in a dark, secluded alcove.

We've been friends for more than a year now, a friendship that would be as simple as breathing if it weren't for the constant yearning to ask for more. It would be so easy, a handful of pills, a flash of cash, and I could have him. I often wonder how much it would cost, how much money, how many drugs, to make him love me as much as I love him.

But tonight, it doesn't matter. After lying to my mother and father, trying to make myself a chameleon conforming to the pattern they want to see, I'm left furious and ashamed and lonely, all the emotions tangled together in a messy knot in my chest.

An older man, clean-shaven, crisp gray suit, hurries by me without looking up. A few paces past him, I pause outside a curved alcove that leads to a little intimate space beneath a set of stone stairs. When I hear only silence, I turn the corner and step inside.

Ash is leaning against the wall, running his fingers through his tousled hair. He sighs softly, then notices me and smiles.

I don't speak, and, for once, I don't think, striding toward him and pushing him back against the wall.

I tilt my head upward to meet his lips, pressing my hand to the cool stone wall behind him. At the brush of his tongue against my lips, I open my mouth, and the rest of the world fades into a gray background, washed out and meaningless, and only we are in color, a vivid red-orange like flame where our lips touch, and spreading from there all through me.

The bite of winter air on my face, the sweet, wet taste of him, sweep away thoughts of everything but this, now, here. I have enough presence of mind to press some cash into his hand before I get on my knees on the cold concrete.

"Baby, you don't have to—"

His words are cut off with a soft, strangled sound when I take his cock in my mouth. He makes moans as sweet as the crooning of a slow love song, his fingers tangled in my hair, pulling hard on the strands when he comes.

Getting up off the concrete, I kiss him and kiss him, guiding his hand below my waist. "I want to see your face," I whisper, and he laughs softly against my lips.

"You're such a romantic," he says, but meets my gaze, the both of us raw and exposed and fiercely intimate, until I can't keep my eyes open anymore, burying my face in his neck and calling his name.

After a few moments, I pull away, looking uncertainly up at him, but he gives me a warm smile.

"What was that for?" he asks.

"I saw my father today," I murmur. "I told him I had a girlfriend. I lied. I lie to him every time I see him. I just... Tonight, I wanted to do something that felt true. Something that felt right."

"Did it?" Ash asks, studying me intently. "Feel right?"

With an unsteady fingertip, I trace the curve of his ear, then over the line of his jaw to the center of his chin, and down his throat to press my index finger gently into the hollow beneath it. Following the lines of his body like a map, like a road that might lead me home.

I can't tell him that I love him. And I can't possibly expect him to fall in love with me. I can't tell him how precious he is to me, when I know that to him, I might be a friend, but just as importantly, I'm someone who has drugs and doesn't always make him pay for them. Someone who will loan him money and never expect it to be paid back. And now, probably, someone he can fuck and then ask for anything he wants.

"Come home with me tonight," I say.

I MAKE PANCAKES, even though it's almost midnight, and Ash eats ravenously, like usual. Afterward, we do the dishes, and as I'm standing with my hands in the soapy water, he hugs me from behind, putting his head on my shoulder. All the air leaves my chest at the gentle press of his warm body, at the shock of his affection. I've wanted it so desperately and for so long that, now, it doesn't quite seem real that I might actually have it.

"Why are you so good to me?" he asks.

"I'm not that good to you, Ash." Or he wouldn't be sleeping in his car in the chilly spring weather and skipping dinner to save money.

"Let's play a game." He sounds almost melancholy. "Just for tonight."

I dry my hands and turn to him. "What kind of game?"

"Let's pretend you're my boyfriend. Like, maybe we were in a coffee shop and you looked at me across the room and just had to come talk to me. Maybe you took me to dinner and I took you to the library and we kissed and you didn't think you had to pay for it. Let's pretend we're a normal couple. Just for tonight."

He sounds like he's mourning the loss of that possibility, the chance for something innocent and fresh, untouched by our seedy reality. But even here, in Ghost Town, where a person can buy anything if they have the cash, in a shitty apartment where the blue light from a garish billboard illuminates each night, where sirens wail past and addicts shoot up in the alley behind the building, that kind of miracle can happen.

"Ash," I say. "I still remember exactly what I sold you the day we met. You painted your nails rainbow colors and you were carrying a copy of *Jekyll and Hyde* with a torn black cover. You talked to me about the book and I sold you the drugs at half price because I knew I had to see you again."

I want to touch him, but I'm not sure how or if it would be welcome. The simple fact of his presence is overwhelming in a way it's never been before, his heady, earthy scent, the dark hair on his bare forearms. His golden skin, his long, slender fingers with their chipped black nail polish. I feel all of it—all of him—acutely and at once.

"I fell in love with you," I say.

His eyes widen, but he says nothing. I thought he already knew.

"And if you want me to take you to dinner, I will. I'd like to. We can go to the library; we can go anywhere you want. I just want to be with you."

"You mean that?" he murmurs.

"Tomorrow night. I'll take you on a date. Somewhere fancy. The Sonata." After a second, I look away, realizing what a bad idea that would be. "No. Somewhere else downtown, maybe."

He crosses his arms. "Yeah. I get it. I'm not really the type of guy you take to a place like that."

"That's not it. They know my father there."

"Oh," Ash says softly. He understands how bad it would be if Dad found out about us. "That's okay, baby. I could go anywhere with you."

I turn those words over in my head. *I could go anywhere with you.* Does that mean he cares about me? Does it mean I'm special? Or would he say it to anyone?

"Somewhere nice," I say. "I promise."

He gives me a smile like the sunrise and I ache with the desire to kiss him. I still don't know what this is or what we are, but right now, it doesn't really matter. It doesn't matter if he's here for money or drugs or me or maybe all those things at once. What matters is that he's here.

"Can I...?" I ask, sliding my fingers just under the hem of his shirt.

His smile doesn't waver as he puts his arms around my neck. "Anything you want."

ASH LIES ON his back, staring up at the ceiling. Wondering what the hell he's gotten himself into. Beside him, Jude is on his side, an arm slung over Ash's chest, head nestled against his shoulder.

He didn't know it would be like this, that Jude would be so eager and so sweet, like a puppy, wanting only to please. That the second time it would be slow and would feel like making love. The tenderness, the murmured endearments, the lingering kisses unnerved him. He worries that Jude will want something he's not capable of. He worries more that he himself will want it.

Although there's a fluidity to hustling, arrangements and favors offered in an unspoken agreement, men he calls friends (but of a certain kind), in his scholar's mind he keeps a ledger, black ink for each transaction. A blowjob: a handful of pills. Sex in someone's bed: a place to sleep. Every means of survival, every quick, dark intimacy, must be paid for. His keenest desire is to be given something unearned. His sharpest fear: to accept it.

A cynical survivor, he wonders what favors Jude—drug dealer and apparent sentimentalist—might do for someone he loves. Beneath it, his heart beats a heady rhythm. He loves me. He loves me. He loves me. Undeserving as Ash might consider himself to be, there could be no question of Jude's sincerity.

He feels Jude's gaze on him and turns his head. "What?" He feigns annoyance he doesn't really feel in the hopes that it will put some distance between them.

"Do you like roses?" Jude asks shyly, and Ash feels something inside himself crumble; a castle wall, a fortification. "I mean, if I were to give you some. Would that be okay? Or is that not something you bring for a man?"

Ash laughs softly, turning on his side to face Jude. "You're so fucking cute. I'd love it if you brought me flowers."

"My mother grows them in her garden. An acre of them, all different colors."

Ash glances at the clock—closer to morning than to night—and feels the old drag and scrape of craving start to pull at him. He puts a hand on Jude's hip and doesn't quite meet his eyes, feeling oddly reticent despite the intimacy they just shared. Or maybe because of it, because the Ash who cons and charms and plays Jude like a puppet on strings is not the same Ash who fervently, desperately made love to him.

"Jude, baby," he says, his words dissonant to his own ears, out of tune with the night's music. "I left all my stuff at home."

Jude is quiet for a moment, and Ash's chest constricts with anxiety. Maybe Jude will say no, and then how will he get high tonight? Maybe Jude will say yes, like always, and would that really be any better?

"Do you need it right now?" Jude asks.

Ash wants to say no, but the word that leaves his mouth is yes.

Jude gets up and walks into the other room, his wiry body all lean muscle and pale skin, a fading bruise along the rib cage. A body that speaks of precision and discipline, that earned the karate trophies on the dresser. Ash has seen Jude punch someone only once—a tall, barrel-chested man who called them a "couple of fags"—but that one hit was enough to knock the guy out cold. It was done with such accuracy and force and calm intent that Ash knew those hands were capable of killing, even if Jude himself was not.

"Here." Jude sets one Oxy tablet and one Valium on the nightstand with a glass of water. And how is it they've become so intertwined he knows what Ash takes every night?

"Thanks," Ash says, and swallows the pills.

Jude sits beside him and presses a kiss to his temple. "Will you stay?" he murmurs into Ash's hair.

"'Course I will." Ash lies back on the pillow, his body relaxed and languid now that he's gotten his pills. It's not about getting high—his tolerance is such that he hasn't felt "high" in a long time—but about staving off the inevitable withdrawal.

"Stay here as long as you want," Jude murmurs, nestling against his shoulder again. "Forever, if you want."

Ash blinks at the ceiling, a little stunned, but puts an arm around Jude and pulls him closer. The bodily intimacy he's grown used to as a hustler is always fleeting, half over before it's begun. He can't begin to conceive of an embrace that could possibly last so long.

The Second Fracture

IN THE SEVENTH grade, Jude had liked a boy. This was not unusual, as he always had a crush on some sweet dark-haired boy or fiery, vibrant girl. This boy was called Trevor, and Jude had written the name in his notebook, and then drawn over it with his pen until he had made a solid rectangle of black ink to hide it.

Whenever he smiled at Trevor, Trevor smiled back, thin lips pulling upward, pale blue eyes sparkling. Trevor was the smartest in the class, and Jude would watch dreamy-eyed as he gave book reports on heavy tomes much more advanced than anything they were assigned.

Jude knew being gay was a bad thing, knew it from the things the other boys had said on the playground, insults thrown in the cafeteria, and the words his father used. But he didn't think of himself as gay. He liked girls, their pretty laughs and flowing hair, curves just starting to develop. And he liked boys, wiry bodies all knees and elbows, awkward with the task of growing. Liking boys seemed such a natural, fundamental thing, and so harmless, that he didn't quite connect it with the words people said and the hatred with which they were hurled.

That day, he sat under the big oak tree on the edge of the school campus, and Trevor sat with him, talking about nothings, school and music and movies, as a cool spring breeze made the leaves overhead sway as if in a slow dance.

He had never been so happy. And when he reached out and took Trevor's hand, their fingers lacing together, warm skin against his palm, his heart felt as though it might burst and light would come out, bright as the sun peeking through the green canopy above them.

"It's true," said a shocked but gleeful voice approaching them. The biggest kid in their class—and, as if by default, the class bully—grinned down at them. "Jude is a fag after all."

Jude reluctantly released Trevor's hand and stood. "Fuck off."

The bully snorted. "You just wait until after school."

At this, Trevor winced. He had been on the receiving end of this kind of violence before. But Jude told him not to worry, that as long as they stayed together, they would be okay.

And they were. At the edge of the parking lot, the no-man's-land out of sight of any of the buildings, the bully and a few friends were waiting for them. After that fight, they no longer called Jude fag, but rather psycho, with an uneasy respect. And although Trevor became something of a pariah among most of the boys, for which he'd always blame Jude, no one beat him up until they went to separate high schools.

After the fight there was a parent conference, which Dad attended, which Mom did not. Driving there, Dad was amused by Jude's account of the fight, proud that his son could hold his own. But at the conference, where all the parties involved were present, the reason for the confrontation came out. And all the way home, Dad was tight-lipped, thrumming with fury like a heavy bell rung so hard the vibrations continue for what seemed like hours.

When the front door shut behind them, Dad started hitting him in the foyer, unable to wait until they got all the way into the house. Jude remembers the sheer terror, the father he knew replaced by something else, a frothy-mouthed beast with bloodshot eyes, and the pain, the slam of his shoulder against a wall, the impact of Dad's fist to his jaw, a kick in the ribs. And then nothing.

"HE'S GOING TO be okay, Mrs. de Haven," said a hushed woman's voice. He opened his eyes to the sterility of the room, the woman's white lab coat and the thin black snake of a stethoscope around her neck. Her name was Dr. Amelia, and he'd seen her many times before, because she was the syndicate doctor and worked for his dad.

"The CAT scan didn't turn up anything abnormal," she continued. "You can take him home soon. Just watch that he doesn't fall out of any more trees. Tell the boss to...be more careful."

"Thank you," Mom said, her voice halting and hesitant.

Jude closed his eyes again. When he opened them, the room seemed empty, but then he saw his father in a chair beside the window. Dad laughed, relieved, and hurried over to the bedside.

"Jude," he said gently. "How do you feel?"

"Why am I here?" Jude was muddled, hazy. He felt cold and betrayed, but his father's affectionate smile, the hand carefully rustling his hair, warmed him.

"You got hurt. A bump on the head. We wanted to make sure it was nothing serious. And it isn't. You're going to be fine."

Jude nodded.

"Which is good," Dad said with a fond smile. "You're going to need all your smarts if you're going to be my consul someday."

He attempted a smile, but moving his face made his head hurt worse.

"I'm so proud of the way you took on those boys," Dad said. "I could tell they were afraid of you. You did good."

Dad squeezed his hand, then got up to call the nurse.

I love you. He watched his father walk away. *I hate you.* And his mind broke a little further.

14: Dynasty

ALTHOUGH HE ASKED her to call him Ras, in her head, Scarlett sometimes thinks of him as Jude. The name seems to fit better in times like these, when he's in one of his moods, more intense and less exuberant, carrying an unrelenting tension rather than moving with his usual easy grace. He even talks a little differently, his voice huskier, lower. The differences are so subtle she thought at first that she imagined them, but after the reckless and constant intimacy of the last few months, she's realized that he changes from day to day, a boy of stark contrasts, shifting from one affect to another like an unpredictable pendulum.

"Call me Jude when we're here," he says, pulling up to a stately mansion that looks authentically Victorian, dark wood pillars and curtains drawn across the many windows. "My parents don't know that I call myself Ras."

"Sure." She wonders if he tries to hide that aspect of himself from his parents, along with the name. Or if he keeps it from his father because Ras does so many things in the Warrens that aren't strictly sanctioned by the syndicate and hasn't kept a low profile about it.

"Thank you." He sits in the car for a moment before turning off the engine and opening the door. She feels like she should be reassuring him, even though this is his family.

The entryway is imposing, dark paneling and a vaulted ceiling. A crystal chandelier offers insufficient light and shadows linger in the corners.

A butler appears to take their coats, giving Scarlett a sympathetic smile, though she's not sure yet what the sympathy is for. Jude leads her down a long hallway to the kitchen, where a woman sits in the sunlight shining in from the only open windows Scarlett has seen so far. Her long black hair hangs to her waist, and, when she gets up and greets them, the resemblance to both her sons is striking. Jude introduces her as Nadya, his mother.

She smiles at Scarlett, but the corners of her eyes don't crinkle, and Scarlett wonders what she's done to already earn this woman's dislike. A possessive mother, maybe. Or maybe Vance has told her about Scarlett's past, about the things she did for Chris and the kind of woman he made her into. In the past year, she's tried to put that shame behind her, but it follows like a wet woolen cloak, clinging to her shoulders, dragging on the ground, pulling her backward into memory.

"Your father won't be back until after dinner," Nadya is saying when Scarlett returns to the present moment, restless memories tucked away. "He said to eat without him, and he'll meet Scarlett after."

"I'll cook, then," Jude says, and Nadya smiles at him. Scarlett feels an unfair pang of jealousy at the affectionate gaze, the kind of fondness her mother would never show.

He moves around the kitchen, some of the tension in his shoulders eased away. He likes to cook, and he's good at it, always showing up with a cake for her or fresh bread or cookies—things a model can't really eat, though she appreciates the gesture. But he only cooks when he's in these moods, when he's Jude, not when he's the sinister man she first met on the yacht, the one she has sex with, the one she calls Ras.

"How did you meet?" Nadya asks.

"At...a party," Jude says, without turning around, his hesitance making it clear he's lying. Nadya must see it, too, frowning at him.

"It wasn't just any party," Scarlett says with a warm smile. Unlike Jude, she is an accomplished liar. "It was the Bancroft Foundation's yearly gala. I organized it. Jude showed up without a tux and swept me off my feet."

Jude keeps his head down, intent on whatever is sizzling on the stove. Nadya doesn't seem pleased, her brow furrowed as she looks out at the garden.

"You do charity work?" Nadya asks.

"Yeah," she says. "And I'm a student at Vintir." The exclusive private college rolled out the red carpet for the heir to the Bancroft fortune, but Scarlett was glad to find the professors still demand rigorous perfection, no matter the student's last name.

Nadya's lips turn up just a bit, and Scarlett feels a surprising rush of relief at her approval, however slight it might be. "You go to college," Nadya says. "What do you study?"

"Political science. I'd like to be a politician someday."

"You want to make world into better place?"

"Something like that," Scarlett answers, though in truth it's nothing at all like that. For all her life, until she pulled the trigger and put a bullet in Chris's brain, she has been powerless. Things happen to her, not because of her. But that will change. Ambition burns in her, hot as the sun, bright enough to blind, this desire to be something, to claim something. She sometimes wishes she lived in the age of the great conquerors: Genghis Khan, Napoleon, Alexander the Great. A time when the world was ripe for the taking for those with a strong enough will and a hard enough resolve. Politics is a poor, pale substitute, but still a direction, a path to power of some sort.

"Hey." Eli stands in the doorway, smiling his charming smile at Scarlett. When they met at the gala, she was surprised that Jude—whose looks could at best be described as "interesting"—had such a handsome brother. "Good to see you again."

Scarlett greets him with a warm smile, and, instead of shaking her hand, he lifts it to his lips and presses a featherlight kiss to the back. Jude is absorbed in whatever he's cooking and doesn't seem to notice.

"Hey, Eli," he murmurs, looking up with a hopeful smile. "I'm making *piroshki*. Your favorite, right?"

"It's okay," Eli says. "Dad won't like it, though."

Hurt flashes in Jude's green eyes for a moment before he looks down, studying the food on the stove.

"Your father won't be here," Nadya says. "Jude can cook what he wants."

Eli shrugs. "Scarlett's probably bored to death sitting here while you cook, though."

"I'm not bored," Scarlett says.

"How about I give you a tour?" Eli asks. "I'll show you all the secret passageways."

"Go ahead," Jude says. "This might take a little while."

"Okay." She is curious about this dark, foreboding Victorian mansion.

Eli leads her through a lot of stiffly formal, shadowy rooms, the silence oppressive, dust motes almost still in the stuffy air. He stops on a narrow stairway, running his finger down a long gouge in the wall.

"When Jude and I were kids," he says, "we thought it would be fun to fight with real knives. We got some from the kitchen and chased each other around the house. He almost got me here, and then I stabbed him in the thigh. And the whole time, he was laughing, even when I stabbed him, even when he was sitting here with blood running down his leg."

She's not surprised at the brutality of the "game." Jude has many similar stories, though few that ended quite as violently. Still—unfairly—she thinks he had it easier in this dark house than she did in Chris's gilded cage. At least he was allowed to fight back.

"How long have you two been going out?" Eli asks.

"Four months."

He nods, brushing his palm along the banister. "Have you noticed anything strange about him?"

"Like what?"

"Like...I don't know. I never figured it out. He can be like two people sometimes. He'll speak Russian just fine one day and not know a word the next. He got really upset because he hit a squirrel with his car. But the next day, he went to work and cut some guy up and didn't flinch. I think he's bipolar or something."

She doubts it. It's not his mood that shifts, but his personality.

"Look," Eli continues, "I don't want to be a jerk, but what I'm trying to tell you is he's not who you think he is. The guy who cooks for you and is so fucking sweet and sensitive? That's just half of him. The other half is dark and fucked up, and...you should be careful, is all I'm saying."

She lets a cold silent moment linger before answering, annoyed that yet another man has decided she can't handle the harsh reality of the world. Another man who thinks she will break like porcelain, when really she is hard as diamonds.

"I know who he is," she replies. "I've seen what he can do. I'm not a child. I can handle it."

"I didn't mean it that way." Eli remains calm, unruffled by her anger. "He freaks me out sometimes too."

"He does what's necessary."

Eli shrugs. "That's all I wanted to say. I'd rather talk about you. Let me show you the gardens and you can tell me about yourself."

They walk through the cool spring evening, among rosebushes and azaleas, and through a wide green lawn with a fountain in the center. Eli sits on the edge of the fountain, and she perches beside him.

He's a good listener, patient and thoughtful, and she finds herself talking much more than she should. Revealing her plans for the future, not just the desire to go to law school but the schemes that will take her far beyond it.

"It's a long ladder to climb," she says, "but my aunt already wants me to follow in her footsteps as the next DA. After that...I think I'd like to be the mayor."

He nods, letting a thoughtful silence linger for just a moment. She likes this about him, that he takes the conversation slowly and seriously, like he's really thinking about what she's telling him.

"So that's what you really want," he says. "To run the city."

"When you put it like that...yeah. It's exactly what I want." She turns toward him, aware that she's been doing most of the talking. "What do you want? Out of everything you could have in the world?"

"Isn't it obvious? I want to be here with you, right now."

She raises her eyebrows. To want something so simple, so sincerely, is inconceivable to her.

"I like to think of the past and the future falling away like sand," he says. "So all I stand on is a moment."

The sentiment strikes her as achingly beautiful. To let the past fall away like sand; if only she could.

"That's how I live with myself, I guess," he murmurs, looking away.

Without thinking, she puts her hand over his, wanting to soothe, an impulse largely foreign to her.

He looks back at her, and this time when he raises her hand to his lips, the attraction between them doesn't crackle, but rather flows like a deep river.

"We should get back," she says.

AFTER AN AWKWARD dinner of long silences, Nadya studying her like a specimen under glass, Vance arrives.

Scarlett holds her breath, wondering what he'll say to her, what he's said to Jude about her. He knew how thoroughly defiled Chris left her. He saw how broken she was when she fired that gun, when she collapsed to her knees after Chris crumpled lifelessly to the ground.

How could he possibly want someone like her dating his favorite son?

He strides into the living room where the four of them are sitting on overstuffed formal couches, severe Victorian decor to match the severe Victorian house. With a gun at his hip and his cocky swagger, he looks like an action hero. Like he belongs in a movie where, after a long series of explosions and car chases, good defeats evil.

He grins at her, and when she gets up to greet him, he pulls her into a hug. She lets out the breath she'd been holding in a long sigh.

"It's good to see you, sweetheart," he says, letting her go. "If I knew you'd go for Jude, I'd have introduced you two a long time ago."

She laughs softly, breathless with relief. "It's good to see you too."

After some small talk, she, Jude, Eli, and Vance retire to the game room for a round of poker. Vance doesn't ask

Nadya to join them, and she doesn't seem interested, making an excuse and disappearing down a narrow hallway.

Chris used to host a regular poker night with some of the most powerful people in the city, Vance among them. They'd bribe and bluff as they made deals that affected thousands of people. Corruption ran deep in the city's government, but a number of politicians cleaned up their acts and started to fight crime. Most got killed for their trouble, including Chris.

During those poker games, Scarlett would tend bar, wearing a short dress and stiletto heels. Wandering hands squeezing her curves or sliding up her thigh as she served drinks. She feels a small thrill now, sitting down at the table instead of hovering around it with cocktails, a player in the game, not a decoration, with one of the few men who never touched her, who always looked at her with something like pity. Now, she thinks, maybe that pity could turn into respect.

Sometime between the poker game and dinner, her lover slipped away and came back with his usual fluid grace and a wide, gleeful grin, his strange affect evaporated into the ether. Like a shapeshifter, he walked away as Jude and returned as the man she thinks of as Ras.

"Call," he says, laying down a pair of fours. She stifles a laugh. He's terrible at the game, fidgety and bored, unable to focus long enough to read his opponent. He leans back in his chair during the next round, folding early and then playing with the little switchblade he keeps in his pocket. As the blade flicks out and folds in, his other hand settles on her thigh, and although it's a touch she loves, a touch she craves, in this setting, it stirs her ever-restless memories. She tries to focus on the cards, but the symbols swim and dance in front of her eyes.

The knife flies through the air, over Vance's head, to land in the center of a dartboard at the far end of the room. The crime boss doesn't even look up from his cards.

"Can't you sit still for five fucking minutes?" Eli asks.

"Jealous, Eli?" Ras smirks, gesturing to the dartboard. "You can't even hit the target."

"I'm not the one who's stupid enough to bring a knife to a gun fight."

Ras narrows his eyes, leaning forward. "It was because I didn't need a fucking gun. You—"

"That's it," Vance says firmly, though he sounds more amused than angry. "You two go downstairs to the gym and work this out. Come back when you can act like civilized people." He turns to Scarlett. "I apologize for my sons. They'll calm down once they've thrown a few punches."

"It's about time I kicked your ass," Eli growls at Ras.

"It has been a while, hasn't it," Ras replies as the two walk out. Though their bickering is amusing on the surface, Scarlett senses a deeply hidden current of hatred beneath it that makes her uneasy.

Vance picks up his cards again. "What do you think, sweetheart? You gonna call?"

She wins the last hand, and he pours them each a whiskey, which makes her feel as though pleasantly warm embers are kindled to life in her belly. She's been drinking all night, and now she finds herself speaking the words that have been weighing on her, unable to stop.

"You're not angry with me," she says softly. Furious at herself the moment the helpless words leave her.

He gives her a puzzled look. "Now why would I be angry at you?"

"You know what Chris did to me," she says. "You know what kind of person he made me. Do you really want me to date your son?"

Vance is silent for a moment, and she fights the urge to step back, to run.

"I saw you kill a man," he says slowly. "There's nothing that shows your true self like the way you are when you kill someone. You were strong enough to pull the trigger and smart enough to do it right. That's the woman I want dating my son."

She nods, bowing her head to hide the tears gathering in her eyes.

"You're a good kid," he continues. "And Jude is crazy about you. As far as I'm concerned, you're a part of the family."

"You mean that," she says, looking up at him. Heart catching in her throat.

"I do. That's how I know I can trust you, even though you're working with the DA." He sips his whiskey. "Your aunt is a fucking piece of work, isn't she?"

"You don't know the half of it. But I bet you'd like to. I'll see if I can find something for you in her office."

"That's my girl," Vance says, and she feels a warmth that has nothing to do with the whiskey.

15: The Evil Twin

WHEN I WAKE up, I'm curled around Scarlett like a shell, her soft body nestled against my chest, her breathing deep and even.

If it's possible to love your best friend, in a way that has nothing to do with romance, then I really do love her. But her feelings are for Ras, not me. She adores him because he's strong, dangerous, and reckless—all the things I'm not. And if she knew how weak we are at the core, how broken our mind is, she'd leave us.

I start to disentangle our limbs and she pulls away, turning to give me a sleepy smile. "Morning," she murmurs.

"Morning." I kiss her on the forehead. I've come up with a number of affectionate gestures that feel platonic to me, but might seem romantic to her. It's one of the many, many ways I constantly lie to her.

"I had fun last night," she says.

I nod, keeping my expression neutral. I have no idea what she and Ras did after dinner at my parents'.

"We went out drinking," she says.

"I know," I mutter, sitting up. "I was there."

She gives me a suspicious glance. "Were you?"

I scoot away, getting quickly out of bed. What the hell is that supposed to mean? "I'm going to take a shower." I back away from her and dart into the bathroom, breathing a sigh of relief when I shut the door solidly behind me. I strip, grateful Ras is too paranoid about nocturnal attacks to sleep naked very often, and step under the stream of warm water.

The bathroom is the most run-down part of this apartment, with peeling paint walls and brown linoleum that curls up in the corners, but there's always hot water. I let it run over me, my mind foggy from the hangover Ras left me with.

Fingertips brush my skin and I startle, spinning to face my attacker. I grab her wrists and pin them to the wet wall behind her.

"Shit," I murmur as the adrenaline wears away and I realize it's just Scarlett, grinning at me. "Don't sneak up on me."

She playfully bites her lip and raises an eyebrow. "Aren't you going to punish me?"

"I..." I let her go and step back, wishing that Ras would come and take things over, but he's dormant, and I can't sense him in my mind at all.

I knew this would happen eventually, and I'm not ready for it.

She watches me expectantly. Droplets of water cling to her skin, beautiful even in the sallow light from the bare overhead bulb. Her body, the valley of her waist, the swell of her hips, seems as untouchable and fraught with meaning as a work of art on a museum wall. A beauty as deliberate and cultivated as the red roses in my mother's garden.

"Next time," I say, backing away until I bump against the frosted-glass door to the shower.

She looks me over, her smile gone. "You don't want me."

"I'm allowed to have an off-day." I twist the shower knob to stop the flow of water and reach for a towel. This is dangerous, and I need to get the fuck away from her before she figures us out.

"You never want me," she says.

"What are you talking about? We have sex all the time."

"Not you." It sounds like an accusation. "I have sex with him. You never want me."

"I don't know what the hell you mean."

"I've been waiting for you to tell me," she says. "Are you just going to lie to me forever?"

I shake my head wildly, pulling clothes on over my wet skin. "Tell you what, Scarlett?" I ask harshly. "You don't know anything about me."

"You weren't with me last night," she says, stepping toward me, wet and naked and as imperious as if she were wearing ermine and diamonds. "It was someone else. Wasn't it?"

"You think I'm crazy," I yell, so loudly the neighbors must have heard it. "I'm not fucking crazy and I don't have to listen to this."

I dart out of the bathroom and slam the door behind me.

"Jude," she calls after me. "Don't you dare run away from me." But I ignore her, running through the apartment and out the front door, pausing only to grab a jacket to pull over my bare chest. I don't realize I've forgotten shoes until I'm halfway down the sidewalk and a sharp pain in my left foot tells me I've stepped on some of the broken glass that litters the streets of Ghost Town. I limp over to a nearby stoop and pull out the bloody shard. I stick my foot into the crust of snow on the dead grass beside me and wait. For what, I don't know. For her to be done with me, I guess. Beneath my foot, a red stain spreads through the snow.

"Hey." Scarlett waves at me from down the street, then runs toward me. She's carrying my shoes. "Did you cut your foot?"

I nod, and she kneels in front of me and wipes away the blood with a handkerchief she retrieves from her purse. I lean forward and put my hands on either side of her face. She looks up at me.

"I love you," I say. "What we have right now is so good. Can't that be enough?"

"If you love me, then trust me. Just tell me your name."

I shake my head. I can feel the words inside me, eager to spill out, but I force them down.

"It's Jude, isn't it?" she asks, gently enough to break me. "You're Jude, and he's Ras."

I take a deep breath and lean my forehead against hers. "Yes."

"Wow," she murmurs, as we pull apart from an embrace as intimate as a kiss. "I was pretty sure, but it's still just—"

"Crazy. I know."

"It's not crazy." She brushes her hand down my arm. "If this is how you've survived all these years, maybe it's a strength, not a weakness."

I wonder if she knows I've waited my whole life to hear that.

I HOBBLE BACK to our apartment, and she cleans and bandages the cut for me. She asks me how it works, Ras and me. Her curiosity doesn't feel hostile or judgmental, just friendly. I tell her how we can talk to each other, and, when we can't, we leave each other notes.

She asks to see our notebook and flips through it, frowning. "You guys don't seem to like each other very much."

"He's a monster." I snatch the notebook from her. "What's there to like?"

"Let's get one thing straight," she says. "I'm never going to take sides. I care about you both."

I nod, glad we're not going to have to fight each other for her affection. We have enough to fight about anyway.

"What happens when you switch?" she asks.

I set the notebook on the coffee table and turn so I'm facing her on the couch. "I can show you, if you want."

I close my eyes, and, in the warm darkness of my mind, I drift deliberately backward, detaching myself from the reality of the world around me. For a moment, as I float, there's an emptiness, a void where a personality should be. And then Ras springs forward eagerly, filling the space with his exuberant presence.

He pushes Scarlett back onto the sofa, pinning her arms above her head and grinning at his prize.

She stares back at him, mouth open. "That's... Your face just went completely blank. Like there was nothing there at all. Did you just switch?"

"Yes." He gives her a kiss, keeping her securely pinned. "I'm Ras. Your favorite one."

"I don't have a favorite," she says.

"Hmm. We'll have to work on that," he says, leaning down to kiss along the line of her throat, nipping at the soft skin. He likes to leave a mark, so everyone will know she's taken, she belongs to him.

She leans her head back with a sigh. "Figures you'd come out to have sex and leave the rest to Jude."

Ras releases his iron grip on her wrists and pulls away. "I do no such thing."

"Then what is this?"

He sits up, watching her curiously. Powerfully aware of his own clumsiness, he who is always so deft with a knife, in the darkness, on the streets.

"What do you want from me?" he asks. Not accusingly— he really does want to know. "This is what I know how to do."

"So learn," she says.

He raises an eyebrow. "Learn what?"

"To love me."

He shakes his head. She might as well ask a cat to bark. "I can pretend," he says, with no trace of shame. "But you would probably see through it, and anyway, I don't want to play games with you. Jude loves you. Isn't that good enough?"

Still on her back, long hair spread over the couch cushions, she looks up at him. "No. It's not good enough. I love you as much as I love him. I want you to love me back."

He studies her, eyebrows raised, as though she is a strange new specimen, grown a pair of wings or a mermaid's glossy tail.

"You love me?" He sounds startled. "No one has ever loved me before. Jude is the one people love." He says it without a trace of anguish or bitterness. It has always been this way, and he assumed it would always be this way, and has never given it much thought. It was just one more way they divided their life. Love was clearly Jude's responsibility, just as violence was his. Jude would step forward when their parents were affectionate, just as he would appear when there was bloody work to be done.

"You're my monster," she says with more fondness than Ras thought anyone would ever show him.

He leans over her again, kissing her gently on the forehead and on the throat. "Sex is how I show you that I love you."

She rolls her eyes. As expected, she can see right through him but returns his kisses anyway, her fingers tangling in his hair.

But there is something to it, something about the physicality of the act. When the pleasure rises and rises until her embrace—the wet heat of her, the long legs locked around his waist—renders him powerless, he feels something utterly foreign. Like sugar crystals are dissolving throughout his body, like finding the answer to a question he forgot to ask. A yearning so deep it overwhelms him, so potent he can't look her in the eye because this feeling he's never felt before might drown him.

It comes to him as clearly as a word below an illustration in a children's picture book, a concept he's never understood.

Love. Sweeter than heroin, and so, so much more intoxicating, bleeding into Ras's dead heart like ink through thin paper. For a single breath-held second, his two halves merge. Jude's tenderness and his violence coming together as one person made whole, to worship his queen and defile her, to hold her with a single set of arms, to fuck her with a single cock, to love her and love her and love her, together, as one.

But as he pulls away, the strange feeling recedes, until it no longer makes sense, no longer matters to him, an old love letter so faded and worn the words are gone, and all that remains is the vague sentiment. He and his gentler half separate as oil on water.

And yet, what he feels afterward, lying beside her in bed—respect for her strength, her ruthlessness; admiration for her devious nature; a lust for her body that borders on worshipfulness—isn't nothing. He has never wanted anything like he wants her, to possess her, to own her. To be owned by her, as he was in that moment when she gave him her imperious glance and told him to kill. He would drown this city in blood if she only gave the order.

He wants to show her these feelings, the depth of them, the unfamiliar way they tug at him. He wants to be closer to her, to share a boundless intimacy. He thinks for a moment on how to do this, then turns on his side, running his fingers through a long lock of her hair.

"I have a hit to do," he says, "tomorrow night."

She turns to him with the intent curiosity she always has when he mentions his work. "Who's the target?"

"He's a businessman. He cheated on his wife so she took out the hit." He tugs gently on her hair. "He has a thing for brunettes, you know. And I need to get him alone. I could use some help."

Her full lips turn up in a wide smile. "You want me to help you kill someone?"

"Yes. Will you?" A strange anxiousness fills him as he waits for her to answer, he who is never anxious about anything.

"I thought you'd never ask," she says.

The Third Fracture

JUDE HELD UP his new shiny knife, turning it and admiring the way it gleamed silver as it caught the light.

"Don't play with that," Dad said, but his tone was fond, indulgent. Tonight, Jude was dressed in black, black everything, even his socks, because he was going with Dad to work for the first time. Eli had been working with Dad for years, but finally, at twelve years old, it was Jude's turn to tag along. To start to learn.

He sheathed the knife and stared out into the darkness as Dad drove them across the city. He wanted to ask a hundred questions about where they were going and what they would be doing and who would be there, but, in an attempt to appear more mature, he said nothing.

The car pulled up beside an abandoned building, and they got out. Dad picked the lock on the back door and let them into a shadowy room with ominous sheet-covered shapes in the corners, a counter where a cash register might once have sat at one edge. Light from a streetlamp outside peeked in between the boards on the front door.

Dad gestured to the top of a flight of stairs in the corner. "Hide. No matter what, you have to be perfectly quiet, or I can't take you anywhere. Got it?"

Jude stood up straight. "Yes, sir." He dashed up the stairs and huddled on the landing. When he was hiding, he liked to imagine pulling the shadows around himself like a cloak. Like fabric, different shadows had different textures and thicknesses, and he knew the ones he was wearing now were like heavy velvet and would conceal him entirely.

The back door opened, and two men walked in. Like Dad had taught him, he scanned them for weapons and saw that each was carrying a gun in a hip holster. The tall one moved with a boisterous confidence, his heavy frame almost bouncing with each assertive step. The skinny one beside him seemed tense, rocking back and forth on his heels, muttering something.

Dad and the men started talking, a conversation that quickly became animated, the boisterous man throwing his hands up in the air and shouting. Jude didn't follow everything they said, only that they were talking about drugs. Dad was very strict on the subject of drugs; when Eli tried cocaine, he was hit so hard he lost a tooth. Dad said drugs were okay for some people to do but that Jude and Eli should be better than that. He said you could never trust someone who did drugs and that he needed to be able to trust his sons, if they ever wanted to work for him.

A bang broke through Jude's thoughts, so loud his ears rang in protest. His head jerked back toward the skinny man, who was now slumping to the floor.

Jude felt himself disconnect from his body, watching the corpse and the violence that followed, Dad hitting the man with the pistol, then shooting him in the knee, asking for something—but Jude couldn't follow the words anymore. There was a part of him that was shaking with terror, with fear, with empathy for the guy begging for his life. But that part grew more and more distant as he floated away from himself.

He also left behind the part of himself that watched Dad intently, fascinated by the raw power in his ready stance.

How his fists and his feet and his gun were tools he used to win, and how, right now, he could make that man do anything. This was something he wanted to learn, something he wanted to be, even as he grieved for the man bleeding on the floor, who had once been a human being and was one no more.

16: The Godfather

AS RAS SLIDES his switchblade along the edge of the sharpener, light from his apartment's tall windows falling over him, the world narrows to the long slow strokes, the familiar coarse hiss of metal on the water stone. A meditative ritual to settle into the calm alertness he'll need to take down his prey. Reckless as he is, even he sees the need to prepare before each job. And he enjoys it. Like a sadistic magpie, he likes sharp, shiny things.

He dries the knife and turns it edge up. No reflection along the blade's edge, no shine, no imperfections to catch twinkles of light. A straight, perfect line.

He sets it aside and picks up a longer knife, sinking into the cold, clear focus that slows the world, sharpens the colors, amplifies the sounds. Controlled adrenaline, Vance always called it, and taught it by pitting his young sons against the criminals he intended later to kill. Fighting someone who wanted to kill you, even under Vance's watchful eye, was excellent practice. Ras learned to fight like water, adaptive, graceful. Merciless as a riptide, relentless as a river.

In much the same way, Eli became stone; unmovable, unbreakable. His fists like boulders, a hit to throw you back against the mats, a blow to break ribs, if he chose to do so. Together, they're unstoppable.

Ras has great respect for Eli, the way he can take a punch to the face without flinching, the power in his ready stance. He's also fond of his bigger brother, perhaps because of the many indiscretions Eli never told their parents about. Or it might be that Eli represents a challenge; someone he can't manipulate, someone he can't intimidate. Someone worthy of being called a friend.

A knock sounds on the door and he lets out an exasperated sigh, putting down the knife. Eli stands outside with a large duffel bag slung over his shoulder.

"You live here?" he asks, glancing around Ras's apartment dubiously before tossing his duffel bag on the couch. "Seriously? This place is a shit hole."

Ras rolls his eyes, unbothered by the scrutiny. Eli's disdain is mostly jealousy. Ras has a shitty apartment in Ghost Town because Vance expects his favorite son to be self-sufficient and earn his own way. Eli lives in a luxury condo downtown because Vance throws money at him as a means of shutting him up.

"How many guns did you bring?" Ras asks, eyeing the bag on the couch.

"Enough. And the sniper rifle." Eli looks through the bag while Ras returns to the table and picks up his knife again.

Eli sits beside him, setting a pistol, gun oil, and rags on the blue tablecloth. "*Knives*?" he says. Speaking in Russian to see which half of Jude he's with. He doesn't know Ras's name or the extent of the split in Jude's mind, and Ras is forbidden to tell him. But he knows the break is there.

"*I like them,*" Ras replies.

"You are one sick fuck," Eli says. His tone more teasing than condemning. He seems to like Ras better than Jude.

"Says the man with the brass knuckles."

Eli's smile fades. "That was one time. Dad asked me to. How am I supposed to tell him I can't? You know what he'll say."

"He'll insult you, questioning both your gender and sexuality, beat you up, and then get drunk. Why don't you fight back?"

Eli crosses his arms. "Because he's my dad and I love him. Why don't you fight back?"

Because of Jude's fucking pain-in-the-ass rules. He can never hurt someone Jude loves. No matter how much he might want to. But he can't tell his brother that.

He imitates Eli's expression and inflection. "He's my dad and I love him."

"I never know when to believe you." Eli expertly dismantles the gun, carefully spreading the pieces on a towel. "Are you ready for this?"

"Yes. I probably won't even need you."

Eli rolls his eyes. "Well, I'll be there just in case. I hate you, but I don't want you to die."

Ras grins. "I hate you, too, big brother."

They both laugh, an easy camaraderie that would make Jude furiously jealous. The banter, as they ready their weapons, is as relaxing a ritual as the sharpening and cleaning and checking of guns and knives.

At the sound of the doorknob, they turn toward the bedroom door. Jude's boyfriend walks through it, big black eyes sleepy and half-lidded, shirtless, the top button of his jeans undone. Ras has never met Ash, only seen him through Jude's eyes, mostly indifferently. But now he imagines running his tongue up the long line of Ash's throat, tangling his fingers in Ash's dark curls, a little surprised at the direction of his own mind. He's never wanted to fuck a man before. But something about Ash draws him, a spark, a sweetness. A brush of Jude's passion against his own dead heart.

"Ash, this is Eli," he says. "My brother."

"Oh." Ash takes a step back from Eli, whose eyebrows are raised, mouth slightly open. "Hey. Hi. Are you guys..." He trails off, looking over the table of weapons. "I guess you're busy. I'm gonna go take a shower and then I'll get out of your hair."

"Hey." Ras grabs him by the waist and gives him a kiss, letting it last longer than he probably should, just to see if he likes it.

Is Jude the jealous type? Maybe not. Although it's tiresome to pretend to be him, it might be worth it to get this lovely creature into bed.

"Stay," Ras says. "When I get back, I'll get you high."

"Yeah?" Ash smiles. He's not that pretty, certainly not the beauty Jude thinks he is, Jude who sees inner beauty as clearly as outer. But there's something to his lanky body, the awkward glances directed at Eli, an uncertainty of being that Ras, who is never uncertain, finds endearing.

"Here." He pulls forty dollars out of his wallet and tucks the cash into Ash's pocket. "Go buy something. Maybe a book. Is that enough for one?"

Ash laughs his low, husky laugh. "Do you really not know how much a book costs?"

"Jude doesn't read," Eli says, turning in his chair.

Ash shifts his weight nervously, attempting a smile. "I guess not."

"Buy something nice." Ras pulls Ash close again and kisses him on the lips and once on the jaw, grabbing his ass. "Okay, baby?"

Ash nods, something in him subdued. "Yeah. Thanks."

FROM THE NARROW snarl of streets in the Warrens, Ras merges onto the freeway that flows through Ghost Town, suspended above the slums on huge concrete pillars. It curves between high-rise tenements and garish billboards glowing in the dim gray light beneath unrelenting clouds. He pulls off when they reach the Stacks, stopping about a mile from their destination. Better to walk, or the car waiting outside the meeting spot will give their presence away.

As they continue on foot, the hard-packed dirt silent beneath their steps, Eli glances over at his brother.

"You know, I accept you," Eli says awkwardly. "It's okay that you're gay. Doesn't bother me."

The corners of Ras's mouth twitch upward at the absurdity. A creature of pure arrogance, it's never occurred to him to worry what anyone thinks about anything he's ever done. He knows that some people (his father among them) consider homosexuality to be abhorrent, but it makes no more impression on him than it would to meet someone who has different taste in music or food. Declarations of morality—people who tell him killing is wrong or that stealing is a sin—are met with the same indifference.

"That's such a fucking relief," he says. "I lay awake at night worrying, *what will Eli think of me?*"

Eli glares at him. "Fuck you, man. I was just trying to be supportive."

"Why?" Ras asks, with genuine curiosity. "Why would I need that?"

"Sometimes you care a lot what I think."

Ras tilts his head, considering this, and finds it to be true. Jude would care a lot, so easily wounded by world's sharp edges. When cruelty comes their way, Jude gets hurt, but Ras gets even. And then some.

"Maybe sometimes I will care about what you said, then," Ras tells him. "But not right now."

"You're so weird," Eli mutters.

"Am I?" Ras wonders if this could be true. He'd always thought of himself as completely normal, the template from which all others should be judged. "Do you really never hear a voice in your head?"

"No." Eli frowns at him. "Most people don't. Are you hearing that voice again?" Shortly after Ras was created, Jude confided in Eli, panicking about the new presence in his mind, which he didn't yet fully understand.

Ras smirks, amused by Eli's concern over something that is, as far as he can tell, perfectly harmless. "Yes. The voice is telling me to punch you in the face and take that sniper rifle for myself."

"Seriously." Eli stands in his path, facing him. Studying him. "Do you still hear voices? Are you hearing them right now?"

"Eli." Ras draws the name out like a whining child. There is work to be done and he doesn't want to wait. "I don't want to talk about it. Come on. We have people to kill."

"Yeah. People who want to kill us. I need to make sure you're not going to freak out on me."

"I haven't freaked out on you since I was fifteen," Ras says. *And that wasn't even me*, he thinks sullenly.

Eli lets out a long sigh. "Fine."

They climb onto the roof of a two-story warehouse, and Ras watches over the building across the street as Eli sets up his sniper rifle, an old but reliable relic of Vance's time in the armed forces. A theft pinned on the Russian mafia, like so many other valuable things he took with him when he left Moscow.

"Nikita is gonna hear this even across the street," Eli says. "So get him restrained right away. Don't play with him like a fucking cat."

Ras rolls his eyes. "Fine."

"Get him talking fast," Eli says. "If you hear a second shot, that means he's got backup. If that's the case, you kill him and get out of there, got it?"

Ras, who has no intention of following any of these orders if they don't suit his mood, puts on a solemn face. "Of course."

Eli lets out a long sigh. "Get to it."

CAPTURING NIKITA PROVES disappointingly easy. It was simple enough for Ras to skulk through the abandoned machinery, moving from one hiding spot to the next among the decrepit conveyer belts and forklifts. Simple enough to work his way closer, even with the sunlight falling through the high narrow windows, illuminating the room and casting stark bands of light on the floor. Simple enough to connect the butt of his pistol with the back of Nikita's head and knock him out cold.

The old Russian must have gone soft, Ras thinks, tying the unconscious man to a chair. He prefers rope to handcuffs, likes the texture of it between his fingers, the tactile pleasure of tying solid knots.

He sits on a slab of concrete facing his prisoner, cross-legged, and waits, playing with his switchblade, several other knives of various sizes set out before him.

Elena will be angry, Ras knows, but she's nothing if not pragmatic. She will understand why this is necessary. And she'll eventually forgive him. He's been spending less and less time with her anyway, growing apart as Scarlett occupies more of his mind and his heart. He no longer needs Elena's guidance—she's taught him everything she knows.

Nikita leans his head back, groaning, then blinks a few times and studies Ras. "Eli?" he says, eyes wide. "No. Jude."

Memories rush toward him like floodwaters, hazy recollections from when Jude was young, years and years before the split that called Ras into being.

The sound of Russian words, spoken freely and without fear, spoken through laughter and with smiles. Strong hands lifting Jude onto a swing and pushing him to fly higher and higher. The current of memories tugs at him, then sweeps him away, backward into the dark mindscape he inhabits when he's not out. He fights to stay in place, because this is his turn, his kill, and Jude will only fuck it up. But the swell of emotion that accompanies the memories is too much for him, and after the blank-nothing moment of the actual switch, I step forward into our body.

"Jude." A familiar voice is frantically saying my name. "Jude."

I open my eyes. Nikita sits before me, looking almost the same as he did the day I left Russia, a solid frame and a sturdy jaw, but the lips I remember as always curving in an easy, open smile are frowning now. He's tied to a chair, but the concern in his eyes is for me. He's saying something I can't understand, repeating it urgently, the syllables familiar but nonsensical.

"I don't speak Russian," I say. "I'm sorry."

"Are you okay?" he asks, through a thick accent. "Your face, it was..."

"I'm fine. Nikita. What are you doing here? What's going on? Why are you...?" Slowly I realize that I have a switchblade in my right hand, and that the rope binding

Nikita to the chair is the thin nylon cord Ras likes to use. The late-afternoon sunlight glints off of the collection of knives lying in wait beside me.

"You're our target," I whisper.

He shakes his head slowly. Not a denial, but a surrender.

"Someone's framing you," I say, putting the knife away as quickly as I can. I'm clumsy with my right hand, though it's Ras's dominant hand. "Someone's been stealing from the syndicate and Dad thinks it's you."

"No one is framing me. I'm trying to draw your father out of his hiding holes."

"I don't understand. You and Dad were friends."

He sighs heavily. "Yes. A long time ago."

"What happened?"

He shifts in his bindings, not in the manner of a man trying to escape, but as though he's settling in to tell a long and heavy story.

"I was police in Russia," he says. "Your father was spy from this country, but he came in good faith. Together we worked to stop many criminals in Moscow. He became great friend to me."

I nod. I know this part of the story, that Dad was in the military and then became a spy and that he went to Russia to take down the Russian mafia. But he never talks about why he came back to the city.

"But then he betrayed me," Nikita continues. "He betrayed police and mafia too. He took stolen moneys and ran."

"Why would he do that?"

Nikita shakes his head sadly. "Who can understand such man? He even left his family behind."

"He came back for us," I snap, though I'm not sure if I'm angry at Nikita for his words about my father, or if deep down part of me is still furious that my father left us, that, for years, I didn't have a dad.

He did what he had to do, I remind myself. He built a life for us here.

"I cared for you," he says evenly. "For years, I cared for you and Eli and your mother. Then your father returned, and he took you from me."

I vaguely remember my mother's tearful goodbye, Nikita's strong arms hugging me close, his voice speaking Russian to me—*Be good for your mother. Be strong. I love you.*—just before we walked away.

"Why did you come back?" I say, my voice thick with the emotion I'm trying to hide. "Why are you doing this?"

"Your father is criminal," Nikita says. "I will bring him to justice. Or I die trying."

"You have to give this up," I say frantically. "If you promise to forget it and go back to Russia, I'll let you walk away."

"And if I don't do as you say?"

My turn, Ras whispers gleefully, waking again at the possibility of violence.

"You used to pick up insects off sidewalk so no one stepped on them," Nikita says. "You used to be good person, with most gentle of hearts. Has your father really made you into such monster?"

"Please," I whisper. "Just stop this. You can stop this."

"Your father must answer for his crimes, Jude."

I shake my head wildly, turning away from him. He has to die. It's what Dad would want. It's what's best for the syndicate. I know what I have to do. And yet...

Let me out, Ras whines petulantly as a little kid stamping his feet and clenching his fists. *It's my turn.*

"No," I say softly, and Nikita looks up at me. "Wait."

What the fuck?

I step a few feet away from the prisoner and turn my back to him, as though that could keep him from hearing me.

Let me out, Judy. Let me the fuck out. We have our orders. Don't get fucking soft on me now.

"Since when do you give a fuck about orders?" I hiss.

Since you became such a huge fucking pussy.

"He's our godfather." I rub my forehead, a headache threatening as Ras strains to be let out, to be set free so he can cut Nikita's throat. "You fucking monster."

I'm your monster, Judy. You made me. You need me. And everything I do, I do because you secretly want me to.

Nikita murmurs something, but I barely hear it, his voice a distant background. I run a hand through my hair, taking a few agitated steps. Ras is right, and I know it. All of the blood on his hands is on mine, because I let him attack, because I let him kill. But tonight, I'm trembling, fists clenched, with the effort of holding him back.

Judy. His whisper fills my mind, insidious and almost tender. *You want to.*

I look down at my fingers, curled thoughtlessly around the hilt of his knife. I flick the blade out and study it curiously. What would it look like, adorned with blood?

You want to.

His cold shadow falls over me, and in the darkness that bleeds from his wicked soul to mine, I smile, hefting the knife.

You want to.

I close my eyes and fight it back, the seductive darkness, wrapped around me like black satin. I want to and I don't. My fingers tighten around the hilt of the weapon, to cast it away or to bury it in Nikita's chest. Around me, nothing makes a sound, save for the beating of my heart. Our heart.

You want to.

"I can't. Stop saying—"

A gunshot cracks through the still air, and I turn quickly. Nikita slumps forward in his chair, his dark hair slick with blood.

"You really should see a shrink," Eli says, holstering his pistol.

I stagger back, still reeling from the battle with Ras and its abrupt end. "I don't—"

"Relax. I'm not going to tell anyone."

"He took care of us," I say, studying Nikita's slumped form. "For years. He was good to us."

"It doesn't matter now," Eli says bitterly. He grabs Nikita's hair and tugs upward so he can study the dead man's face, blood running down his forehead and into his eyes.

That blood could have been on my hands. Not Eli's. Not Ras's. Fear and horror spread through my chest, but beneath them, something dark, something eager, thrilled at the sight of blood, the proximity of death.

Next time.

A headache starts spreading, so intense it feels like my head is being crushed, from the effort of forcing Ras back, of maintaining the walls that keep us neatly separated.

"You're a monster, Eli," I say through gritted teeth, and walk outside.

"I'm the monster?" he says, his voice sounding from somewhere distant. "I'm the fucking monster, Jude? Really?"

I lean back against the warehouse wall, sliding down until I'm sitting in the dust. Closing my eyes doesn't help with the colossal headache, but I do it anyway, so I won't have to look at my brother, who knows exactly what kind of monster I am.

Everything Ras does is my responsibility. But I thought that we were separate. Because he likes to kill, and because I can't. But back there, for just a fragment of a moment, I wanted to. I did.

"You look like shit," Eli says. "Are you okay?"

"Leave me alone," I mumble.

"Fuck that. Wait here. I'll get the car and take you home."

IT'S HARD TO hate Jude with his eager smile and his bright eyes, but Eli tries, because he has to hate someone. Sometimes, he succeeds, achieving the brusque distance he wants to keep between them, and other times, like right now, Jude slung over his shoulder, murmuring incoherently, he fails completely.

Jude is a person sharply divided, and is it really so strange that Eli's feelings about him would be so starkly split as well? Sometimes, Jude is a cold, sly bastard, and Eli gets on with him okay because that guy's not the real Jude, the heart or the soul. That persona is just a weapon, like a fist, an extension of Jude, but not his true self.

He can't recall ever liking Jude all that much, but he does feel responsible for him, in the way he might feel responsible for a scruffy, helpless kitten left on his doorstep. Any residual fondness from their childhood days has been carefully quashed. Eli has built a cold wall of hatred between himself and his brother, who has succeeded in everything Eli has failed at.

He carries Jude through his parents' darkened mansion, setting him on his bed so their mother can hover anxiously over him, pressing a hand to his forehead even though they both know this isn't a fever, but a sickness of another kind.

Eli leaves Jude in their mother's hands—this isn't the first time he's passed out like this, and he always wakes up just fine.

Downstairs, their father is in his study. He looks up from the papers on his desk when Eli walks in.

"Nikita...Nikita's dead," Eli says, standing at attention in front of the desk. "Jude freaked out at the end, so I killed Nikita myself. I don't think he would have done it, Dad."

He knows this won't be enough to erase the five years Vance has spent making his disappointment in Eli clear. But maybe it will shift the balance between Jude and Eli a little bit. Eli's sin was showing mercy, and now Jude has done the same thing.

Vance looks up, mouth pressed into a grim line. "Jude would never rat you out like this. You know that, right?"

"I know," Eli says, and the absurd thing is, Vance is right. Jude would never say a word against Eli—but then again, he never has to. He's the favorite, the golden boy, and he has the luxury of loyalty.

Vance nods and looks down at his paperwork again. "Quit telling lies about your brother."

Dimly, Eli wonders why he's so surprised. Of course their dad would take Jude's side. He gave up on Eli years ago, when Eli let Nikita escape a similar trap, a betrayal Vance has never forgiven him for. And he's not the type of man to change his mind.

"There's something wrong with him. There's something wrong with Jude. You have to have noticed it."

"Get out," Vance says without looking up from his desk. And when Eli hesitates, he growls again. "Get out."

For a moment, Eli is seized by the wild urge to draw his gun and fire a few bullets into the desk or the walls or the windows, just to make Vance fucking look at him for a few moments.

But instead, he turns tail and walks away. Like always.

Jude is waiting in the hallway outside, and the sympathy in his eyes makes Eli want to deck him.

"I'm sorry I called you a monster," Jude says gently. "And I...I know that Nikita meant a lot to you. If you want to talk—"

Eli punches him, because he can't bear to hear one more fucking word, one more pitying syllable.

Jude staggers back, his head tilted down, black hair falling in his face. For a few moments, he's perfectly still, features shadowed in the dark hall. And then he looks up at Eli with that half-mad glint in his eye and grins.

"Go ahead," he says. "Hit me again. I dare you."

"There is something so wrong with you," Eli says, before he can stop himself.

Jude lunges at him, all flying elbows and fists and knees, the dirty street-fighting techniques they were raised on. They're pretty evenly matched—strength versus speed—and so familiar with each other's fighting styles that they can spar the way some people hold conversations.

But not today. Today, they are both furious, scrabbling and cursing, barely holding back. Blood is running from Eli's nose, his jaw tender from a blow he failed to dodge, when he hears Vance shouting for them to stop. They pull apart, both breathing raggedly with rage and exertion.

"Jesus Christ," Vance says, standing in the door to his office, regarding them furiously. "What the hell is going on?"

"Just practice." Jude leans against the wall, his posture deceptively relaxed, his expression taut with anger. Blood trickles from his lip down the side of his chin.

"Yeah," Eli echoes. "Practice."

Vance lingers in the doorway for a moment, as though debating whether or not to believe them, but then he just shrugs. "Keep it down," he says, before walking back into his office and shutting the door behind him.

Not a surprising outcome. He's always preferred his sons work out their issues independent of his guidance.

"You always fuck with me." Jude grins, a white cut of teeth in the darkness. "I should cut your fucking throat in your sleep, Eli."

Eli shrugs. The threat and the expression on Jude's face and the shiny switchblade in his hand might be enough to make a normal person tremble with fear, but not Eli. Jude says shit like this every time he gets angry, and Eli has gotten used to it.

"Go to hell, Jude," he says mildly. He walks away, keenly aware that Jude's green eyes—the eyes everyone says look just like his own—are fixed on his back.

The Fourth Fracture

JUDE WAS THIRTEEN, and for a year, he had been immersed in violence. He'd heard people beg for their lives and saw their prayers ignored or answered. He'd learned to hide his horror and his sorrow, to distance himself from his own heart, beating in time to the hearts of those suffering around him.

He avoided acknowledging or thinking about his malevolent part, his shadow, his darkness. He pretended that the evil belonged to someone else, that it was someone else who wanted to grow up to be just like Vance as he was in those moments: powerful, dangerous, unstoppable.

But there came a day when Vance called him out of his hiding place and put a knife in his hand, nodding his head at an unfortunate debtor tied to a chair.

"Go ahead," Vance said. "Just a little. Just enough to teach him a lesson."

He needed no further instruction; he knew what to do. He looked at the knife, and his dark half was disappointed the blade was matte, a dull gray, not shiny to gleam in the harsh industrial lights.

He tried to raise the knife but couldn't. At the terror in the victim's eyes, his heart beat a similar anguished rhythm. You are the same, you and he, it said. To break him would be to break yourself.

He felt cold, his knees weak, unable to disappear from his body as he normally would, to float away into the thin air of the atmosphere and watch as a distant, emotionless observer.

"Go ahead, Jude," Dad said, impatience shortening his tone. "Let's get this over with."

Jude stared at the man, at his eyes peeled wide with fear, the irises blue as day. "I can't," he whispered.

Dad's hand gripped his shoulder. "You can. And you will. Now, Jude."

Jude shook his head so hard the room blurred around him.

Dad heaved a heavy sigh and gave the knife to Eli instead, who did what he was told without any expression at all.

"This was your mother's doing," Dad muttered on the way home, hands clenching the steering wheel, knuckles white. "She makes you too fucking soft."

And from then on, Jude wasn't allowed to cook with his mother or spend time with her in the garden, tending her rosebushes. But it didn't help. Night after night, he was unable to follow his father's orders; unable to bring himself to harm another living being. Beatings and lectures and his father's sullen disappointment weren't enough to change him. It wasn't that he wanted to be disobedient; in fact, he wanted desperately to make his father happy. It was that he simply could not do it. It was like running into a wall.

But always there was that insidious whisper, that murmur beneath his thoughts that was not a voice, not yet, telling him it could be done, that all he had to do was close his eyes and surrender to it. The presence scared him, the malignant darkness within his own mind, and so he pretended it belonged to another person, a separate entity. At night, he would lie awake in bed and think of every good part of his day—a hug from his mother, a cute boy or girl at school, a smile from his father—and hold them close to his chest. Then he would take the bad things—a night working with Dad, a bruise on his mother's face—and give them to his dark half, as though putting them in a vault. Only then, when the day's violence was put securely away, could he sleep.

17: Possession

AT THE EDGE of Bancroft Square, a boy of maybe twelve or thirteen years huddles in the doorway to an abandoned store, arms wrapped around himself, looking around with wide eyes. Clearly out of place. A runaway, Ras thinks as he passes by on his way through the square and southward to a bar he frequents when he wants to get into a fight. It's been weeks since Nikita's death, and the fight with Eli, but he still feels strange about it, uncharacteristically restless.

"Hey, kid." A low, guttural voice comes from behind Ras. "You wanna make fifty bucks?"

"What do I have to do?" the kid asks, his voice high-pitched and trembling.

Ras turns. A skinny middle-aged man is standing too close to the child, looking him over with shrewd, sunken eyes.

"It's easy. Just take you five minutes. Fifty bucks," the man says.

Ras eagerly makes his way toward the two. He likes to catch child molesters because not even Jude cares what he does to them.

"I don't think so," he says, stepping between them and grinning at the man, his smile full of teeth. With a little click, the blade of his knife flicks out, shining under the streetlamp. "Get the hell out of here, or I will cut you open, you fucking pervert."

"I didn't do nothin'." The man backs away slowly. "You can't prove nothin."

Fortunately, Ras has never felt that explicit proof is all that necessary. His gut feeling and the circumstances at hand are enough. He memorizes the plates on the man's car as it squeals out of the parking spot and quickly down the road. Thanks to an information broker who owes Jude a number of favors, that should be enough for the two of them to stay in touch.

"What was he going to do to me?" the kid whispers.

"Nothing good." Ras looks the child over curiously. He's dressed in a sweater vest and khakis, still clean, if somewhat wrinkled. This is probably his first night on the streets.

"Please." The kid blinks away tears. "I'm looking for someone. Can you help me? His name is Ash."

Ras raises an eyebrow. "What do you want with Ash?"

The kid makes a soft huffing sound that could be a stifled sob. "My mom kicked me out. I can't go home anymore. I don't know what to do. I tried to sleep at the train station, but the lady there said I couldn't. She said to come here and find Ash, and that he would help me."

"Well, let's go find him," Ras says, wondering why someone would send a terrified homeless kid Ash's way. "What's your name?"

"Theo."

"I'm Jude." Ras would like to give his own name—Jude's name chafes like a too-tight, itchy sweater—but he has to keep up appearances. Although they've met, once, Ash doesn't know Ras exists as an entity separate from Jude. All he knows of Ras are the rumors that spread like viruses on the streets. Ever the narcissist, Ras delights in these stories, the way they make him seem like a boogeyman, exaggerating his skills and sadism.

Ras leads the kid down the sidewalk, through puddles of light cast by streetlamps and the darkness between. "Do you read comic books?" he asks.

The kid glances over at Ras, a hint of a smile crossing his face. "Yeah."

"My favorite is Batman," Ras says, grinning back. He loves superheroes and sometimes wishes there was a force for good in the dark city, just to make things interesting. He reads them with the delight and wonder of a child, while Jude, ever the responsible adult, calls them a waste of time.

It turns out Theo is a fan of Spiderman, above all others, and he and Ras discuss recent storylines until they come upon Ash, sitting on his usual bench, a heavy book in his hand.

He greets them with a smile, not at all surprised to see a shell-shocked runaway out in the middle of the night looking for him. Theo spills the story again.

"Why did your mom kick you out?" Ras asks.

Theo gets very quiet, kicking at a pebble on the sidewalk. "I kissed a boy," he mumbles, almost too softly for them to hear.

"Hey." Ash takes Ras's hand and smiles at the kid. "It's okay. You can trust us."

Theo's eyes get wide, looking at their interlaced fingers, then back at Ash. He raises his chin defiantly. "I'm not sorry. I'm not sorry I kissed him."

"You have nothing to be sorry for," Ash says. "Now, have you eaten today?"

Theo shakes his head. "We were supposed to have breakfast after church but..."

"It's almost midnight." Ash hides his dismay behind a cheerful smile, but Ras can see it all the same, the way Ash's heart is breaking for this child. "You must be starving. Jude, baby, will you buy your two hungry street urchins some dinner?"

"Of course," Ras says. This is so intriguing it's almost better than getting into a fight.

AT THE DINER, Ash cheerfully hands over all the money in his wallet (there isn't much) and gives the kid advice about staying alive on the streets. Ras finds this kindness both inexplicable and compelling.

Under the table, he puts a possessive hand on Ash's thigh. Lit with sparks of Jude's love, perhaps, or just the need to claim this strange man for himself. A desire to own this true heart, the likes of which is unheard of in his dark underworld, the way he might covet an exotic and priceless piece of jewelry. Something beautiful to make his own.

"But I don't think it will come to that," Ash is saying. "There's a shelter set up just for queer kids like us. I spent a lot of nights there when I was younger. It's not a bad place."

"Did your mom kick you out?" Theo asks.

"Nah." Ash gives him a sad smile. "I ran away. I had a lot of problems. But you? You're on the straight and narrow. No drugs. No fighting. You're gonna make it out okay."

Theo nods, staring down at his half-eaten pancakes.

"Eat up," Ash says. "They feed you at the shelter, but it's not the greatest food."

"Where are you going tonight?" Ras asks the kid.

"I don't know," Theo says, his lower lip starting to wobble.

"Well, the shelter won't take someone this late," Ash replies. "So I was hoping..." He gives Ras the sweet, wide-eyed smile that always convinces Jude to hand over more cash.

Ras sighs. He is not overly fond of children, particularly in his living space. But Jude would undoubtedly say yes.

"Fine," he says. "Just for tonight."

RAS AND JUDE have recently upgraded their living arrangement to a new place in Ghost Town with a second bedroom and a little communal garden just outside their windows that Jude has planted roses and tomatoes in. Theo takes the spare bedroom, mumbling a grateful good night.

In the kitchen, Ras catches Ash by the waist, taking the bottle of wine out of his hand. "I saw you taking a few Xanax at dinner," he murmurs in Ash's ear, surprised by how much the proximity of Ash's body affects him. "No booze."

Ash sighs, sagging against him. "Maybe I wanna black out for a few hours."

Ras pulls away, surprised. "Why?"

"I don't know, Jude." Ash sits heavily on the couch. "That kid looked at me like I was someone he could respect. Someone he could look up to. But I'm not. It just gets to me sometimes, what a fucking mess I've made of my life."

Ras sits beside Ash, watching him curiously. Why would someone feel this way? He can't think of anything Ash has done that's particularly bad.

"And now I have to ask you for money again," Ash says, "because I can't send that poor kid away with just the forty bucks I gave him, and I don't have anything else."

"Is that where all your money goes?" Ras asks. Jude gives Ash a lot, and Ash seems to have no problem spending it, but never has better clothes or nicer things. He doesn't spend it on drugs, because he relies completely on Jude for those. And right now, watching Ash glow like a beacon, alight with the kind of goodness he's never seen before, Ras is glad. The drugs are like a leash, they make sure this enchanting man never gets too far away.

Ash shrugs. "Some of it, yeah. A lot of people know me. They know I look out for kids if I can. I don't do much."

"Why? Why would you do that? They're never going to pay you back."

"I dunno. I just want to."

"Why would you want to?"

Ash hunches his shoulders, turning away. "Just makes me feel a little less worthless, I guess."

"Worthless?" Ras is thoroughly confused. How could a person believe himself worthless? Particularly when Jude's love for him is so fervent it borders on worship?

"Yeah. You know what I mean." Ash speaks with heavy conviction, as though the answer is obvious. Ras isn't sure what to do to shake his certainty. Jude is the one who is good at emotional situations, not him.

"You are a nice person," Ras says. "I find this very strange. But I like it about you."

Ash bites back a laugh. "You find it strange? You're nice too."

"I am no such thing." Ras climbs into Ash's lap, straddling him, pressing rough kisses to his neck. "Take it back."

Ash makes a contented humming noise, running a hand into Ras's hair. "What if I don't?"

"Then I won't be gentle," Ras whispers in his ear, then nips at his earlobe.

"I didn't think you had any other setting," Ash says, laughing, head leaned back.

"I'm full of surprises." Ras gets up and lifts Ash off the couch, throwing him over his shoulder and carrying him to bed. Jude might be mad; Scarlett almost certainly will be, but in this moment, he doesn't care, too entranced by the light shining in Ash's heart. And, he figures, they don't really have to find out.

Ras opens the drawer on the nightstand and fishes out a length of silky rope. He runs it through his fingers and raises an eyebrow.

Ash laughs, lying on his back in the bed. "I didn't know you were into that. Sure. Looks like fun."

Ras gives him a predatory grin. "It is."

"I've never seen this side of you," Ash says, as Ras ties each wrist securely to the bedposts. "You even sound a little different, you know?"

Ras makes a contented humming noise, looking over his ensnared prey. The opportunity to play with someone so pure, so sweet...

"Is that a...riding crop?" Ash asks, as Ras pulls something else from his nightstand drawer. He isn't smiling now, and he looks a little nervous, but also intrigued.

"Yes." Ras runs the crop along Ash's inner thigh, the dark leather against his lover's golden skin, then lands one hit on the sensitive flesh. Hard enough to sting, hard enough to give Ash some idea what he's getting into.

Ash gasps softly at the impact, but then his smile returns. "Is that the best you can do?"

Ras slaps him. He knows how to hit a person, the way to hold his hand, the angle, the force, to cause pain or to avoid damage. He can break a jaw in a single blow or simply leave a stinging red mark that will quickly fade but was enough to render Ash speechless for a moment, mouth open in shock.

"Jude," he whispers, a small bright spot of blood on his lip. "All this time, I thought you couldn't even hurt a fly."

"You only see the best in me," Ras says, tracing the contours of Ash's bare chest with the crop. "Not the darkness."

"Okay." Ash's tongue darts out to lick away the blood on his wounded lip and Ras watches, captivated. "Show me, then."

Ras grins, wide and wicked like the Big Bad Wolf. "Tell me if you want me to stop."

But Ash doesn't say no, never asks Ras to stop, his cock hard despite the pain and humiliation (or maybe because of it). Until Ras is caught as surely as Ash is; the twisted ways they begin to twine around each other, the light inside Ash that so fascinates this creature of darkness.

IN THE STILL, silent moments afterward, Ash tied down on the bed like a fly in a web, Ras runs his hand over his lover's chest, tangling his fingers in the coarse, sparse hair.

"You're mine now," he says. "So you had better stop hustling because if you fuck anyone else I will kill him."

Ash laughs, and then his smile fades. "You're serious."

"Yes."

"I'll think about it."

"No. No thinking about it. Just say yes."

"Why do you care?" Ash asks, shifting his weight uneasily, spread out on the bed. "You know it's different with you."

Ras sits back, running a possessive hand down Ash's thigh. "I'm not going to untie you until you say you'll quit."

Ash frowns, uncertainty flashing in his dark eyes. "What's with you tonight, Jude? You're acting so weird. Like a different person."

"Stop hustling." Ras runs gentle fingertips over Ash's body, tracing idle lines and circles, calm as the surface of a river but with a deadly current beneath.

Ash tugs at his restraints. "What's wrong with you?"

"You're mine, Ash." As Ras thinks of the many people Ash has been with, jealousy rises in him like a hot, whipping wind. "I don't. Fucking. Share."

"You're scaring me. Let me go. Please."

Ash's eyes are wide and shimmering, mingled fear and shame, and Ras is taken aback as powerfully as if he'd been punched in the chest. *I did that*, he thinks. *I hurt him.*

And for a fleeting moment, he feels a strange, heavy weight tugging down at his heart. Regret. Remorse. Guilt. He's never felt it before, and it is so acutely painful, so draining, that he can only bear it for a few seconds before retreating into the depths of his mind, detaching himself from a world with thorns he didn't know existed, leaving only a void for Jude to fill.

ASH SLEEPS BESIDE me, curled up into a little ball while I stare up at the ceiling and let it fade away, tunneling inward to meet Ras on the pale stone streets of our city beneath a dark sky. He remains half in shadow, leaning against a wall just at the edge of the puddle of light cast by a streetlamp.

"What did you say to Ash?" I ask, my hands clenched into fists so tight they ache. "You made him cry."

"I didn't mean to," Ras says, looking oddly vulnerable, eyes wide and bright. "Did you fix it?"

When I came back to my body, I cut Ash free from where Ras had tied him up. Then I held him in my arms, and he told me some of the horrible things he believes about himself—that he's worthless, that he's a failure, that he's ruined his life. I don't know what Ras said to bring all that up, but I tried to convince Ash that none of it was true. I tried to show him how perfect and precious he is, but I don't think he believed me.

"It's not something you can just fix, just like that," I say. "It takes time and patience and love. I'm doing the best I can, but—"

"I want to do it too." Ras steps forward eagerly. "I want to love Ash. I want to love Scarlett. Show me how."

"You can't," I say.

Something flickers across his face, sorrow, maybe. "I want to."

"You can't."

"How do you know?"

"I can't kill. You can't love. That's just how we were made."

Fog starts to roll in, wisps of gray that cast soft halos around the streetlights. In the distance, the indistinct murmur of people walking the streets floats toward us. Even so, we're alone in this city, the people as much a mirage as the stone walls and the thickening mist.

Ras stands straight, shoulders back, with a menacing grace like a cat stalking easy prey. "You took every good thing for yourself. And you left me with nothing but darkness. And even then, I don't hate you. You are the one who hates me."

"That's not true," I say, my left hand on the butt of my gun. His right hand clenches the hilt of his knife. One more insurmountable difference between us.

He bares his teeth. "If it weren't true, you would let me love them. You would let me have it too."

"It's not up to me." I take a step back, my fingers tightening around the gun. "You are who you are. I didn't ask for you to be a monster. It just happened that way."

He draws his knife, and in a smooth, flawless motion, throws it at me, the blade glinting as it passes beneath the streetlamp, piercing the fog, to bury itself in the wall just beside my head. I raise my gun with an unsteady hand and keep it trained on his heart.

"If you want to fight, let's fucking fight," he says.

I shake my head. "I don't want to fight."

He approaches me slowly. "You're the monster," he says, reaching past me and jerking his knife free of the wall. "You made me what I am."

"I didn't mean to make you at all," I whisper, as he turns abruptly and stalks off into the shadows, holding the knife at his side. Around me, the city fades into black, as though night has fallen utterly and completely.

The Fifth Fracture

JUDE WAS TWELVE, light-footed as a cat, creeping downstairs to the kitchen for a late-night snack. He paused at the edge of the parlor, the formal one the family never used. Among its stuffy sea-green furniture threaded with accents the color of tarnished gold, his mother and father stood facing each other.

"How can you do this?" his mother said. "He is your son and you treat him like dog."

And Jude understood that they were talking about Eli, because they couldn't be talking about him. His father loved him, and everything done to him was done for his own good. But something inside him—not a voice, not yet—rebelled all the same. Sometimes, he would shake with the effort of keeping that dark thing inside his heart from bursting free and into the world, where it would leave a trail of devastation in its wake.

"Be careful, Nadya," Dad said, and his voice was very low. In the darkness, Jude tensed because he knew that tone and what it foreshadowed.

"Please, Vance," she said. "For our children."

A familiar thud sounded, and he peered into the room as his mother staggered backward, a hand pressed to her face. His father stood tall and straight, fists clenched and furious.

Jude's focus, guided by his evil half, landed on the heavy poker by the fireplace. He felt himself tugged, as if someone had grabbed his hair and jerked toward it, and he started to tremble with the effort of holding that darkness inside. It would be so easy to grab the heavy iron implement and charge at Dad and set things to right.

He stepped into the room, hands still shaking, but didn't move toward the fireplace. "Dad," he said. "Dad, please don't hit her."

"Go to bed, Jude." Dad barely looked at him.

"Jude," Mom whispered. "Go to bed, honey."

He felt himself being pulled, being stretched like taffy, stretched and stretched and pulled and pulled until the center thinned and started to fracture.

I could kill him. It would be so easy. And then no one would ever hit me again.

"No," he shouted aloud to banish the thoughts that hadn't quite become distinct voices but had gotten louder ever since he'd started to work with his father, late nights watching Vance break noses and knees, collecting his debts, establishing his authority.

"No," he said, and looked up at his father with wet eyes, the kind, cruel face he loved and hated. "Please don't hit her. Promise you won't hit her."

"Jude." His dad spoke gently. "You know I always have a reason for what I do. Sometimes, your mother needs to be taught a lesson too."

Someone should teach Dad a lesson, whispered his shadow, and he shivered.

"Go to bed," Dad said reasonably. "It's late."

"I don't..." He glanced from one parent to the other. It was clear enough what would happen the minute he was out of earshot. He took four steps forward, four big, assertive steps, until he was standing between his mother and his father.

"Please don't hurt her," he said.

Dad's mouth contorted with fury, fists balled, but he didn't hit Mom, not on that night, not on the many nights to follow. He would beat Jude instead, Jude who was becoming such a disappointment to him with his soft fucking heart, Jude who was a fucking sissy, Jude who would never be able to follow in his footsteps.

18: Broken Walls

SCARLETT LIES BESIDE Ras in her big bed and listens to his deep, even breathing. She's helped him with a few different kills now, but tonight's wasn't sanctioned by the syndicate. Tonight's kill was her decision, after weeks of gathering information in the Warrens, careful conversations with hookers and pimps that led them to the ringleader of a human-trafficking operation. Maybe Vance would have agreed if he'd known the circumstances, but Ras doesn't need his father's permission anymore. Vance no longer holds the monster's leash—Scarlett does. She gives the orders, and Ras kills for her. It's a heady, breathless rush each time.

But now the excitement has faded, and she lies awake, staring up at her chandelier of falling stars. She often feels as though she's been patched together by glue and tape, rattling with broken pieces put in the wrong place but cohesive enough on the exterior to fool anyone, even Ras. Even Jude, who is closer to her heart than she thought anyone would ever be.

Memory intrudes less often when they fill her mind, but it still makes itself known, demands its due now and then.

She wriggles out of his grasp and tiptoes across her room, feet softly scuffing the thick carpet. Her closet is large enough it could be a room in its own right, clothes on hangers ringing the edges, while in the center a plush couch and monstrous chest of drawers sits in shadow.

Pursued by the memory—hands on her thighs, a rough-bearded kiss—she steps inside, pausing to grab a tall bottle of vodka from the set of drawers, and makes her way to the darkest corner. There she sits, secreted away behind the long evening gowns hanging sequined and dazzling.

Of course he comes looking for her after a little while; she wonders if deep down she wanted him to. He must spy the bare feet poking out from her corner, because he parts the dresses, frowning, but asks no questions. Instead, he sits beside her and puts an arm around her, pressing a kiss to the side of her head.

"If you're not feeling well," Jude begins, and she almost laughs aloud at the understatement, "you should wake me up."

"You don't get enough sleep." An excuse, and a poor one.

"You're more important." He puts an arm under her legs and pulls her so that she's seated in his lap, cradled in his arms. "Is this about your stepfather?"

She tenses, back straight, wondering what Vance has told him. Enough to ask, at least.

"You don't have to say anything," he continues. "But if you want to, you can."

"No," she says, her voice stilted and stiff. "I don't want to."

"I have to ask one thing, though, and you have to be honest with me. Promise you will."

She nods, her head moving against his shoulder, but she doesn't mean it.

"Do you like having sex with Ras?"

She's silent for a long moment, trying to put it into words. To explain that sometimes it's a welcome escape or a way to show affection for someone she loves. And yet, other times, it's an unwanted intrusion, one she doesn't know how to say no to. For years, saying no was the worst offense, and it came with the harshest punishment. Now, she can feel the word catch in her throat like brambles, stuck there.

"We'll love you, no matter what," Jude says. "We just want to make you happy."

She lets out a long breath. "Sometimes. I like it sometimes."

Jude brushes away the tears she didn't realize were on her cheeks. "Thank you for telling me."

She leans against his chest and, after a long silence, begins to explain why she can't say no, why the word is forbidden, stolen from her. The words fall from her like dead things, toneless, expressionless, and Jude holds her, murmuring soft words of love in her hair when she can't continue.

After her story is finished, he lets a long silence linger. Then Ras says, "If I could kill him all over again, I would."

She leans her head against his chest, breathing him in, that rainwater scent. It always takes her a moment to adjust to his switches.

"I would do it slowly," he says.

"I know," she replies. "I wish I had taken my time when I killed him."

"You killed him?"

"I had help. Your father did the cover-up, made it look like a mugging gone wrong. But I shot him."

"Of course you did," he says.

She smiles at the clear note of pride in his voice.

He lets her go and pulls away so he can see her face, brushing back a stray lock of hair. "I never want to be like him. I never want to hurt you. I can't love you—I don't know how—but I will protect you. Protecting is my job."

The set of his jaw makes his face look more angular than Jude's, shadows falling over high cheekbones and a pronounced nose. Even sitting still, he has a languid, easy grace, lacking the constant tension Jude carries. Now that she knows what to look for, what to listen for, it's not difficult to tell them apart.

"You protect Jude?" she asks.

"Yes. That's why I was made."

"How did it happen?"

"Don't distract me," he says. "We need to talk about you."

They talk until daylight replaces the moonlight falling in a wedge through the closet door. Ras wants to know what she likes in bed, what she doesn't, what scares her, what brings back memories. How she can tell him no.

It doesn't fix everything; some nights, she still sleeps on her closet floor or drinks until she can't remember anything at all, not Jude, not Ras, not her life before. But it gives her a sense of safety, makes it easier for her to be around him. It's one more disguise she's able to lift away, one more layer of armor she can shed. One step closer to the two of them and the heart that, deep down, she knows they share.

RAS ANSWERS THE phone when Elena calls, even though he knows he should just let it ring. Scarlett doesn't stir as he sneaks into the next room, deeply asleep despite the sunlight falling over her bed. He's glad to see she can finally get some rest. She has too many tortured, sleepless nights, and if he could hunt down and kill the demons that torment her in the hours between sunset and dawn, he would gladly do so.

"I have a riddle for you, Ras." Elena's voice is thick with fury on the other end of the line. "Two brothers walk into a warehouse to kill my father, but only one of them fires a shot. Which of you was it?"

"I didn't think you'd be so upset," Ras says. "I didn't think you even liked him."

"I barely knew him. But he was my father. This isn't about love. It's about honor. If it were love, I'd shoot both of you like dogs. But honor only demands that I kill the person who fired the gun. Who was it, Jude?"

Ras hesitates. It would be so easy to simply tell the truth and let Elena send her dogs after Eli. And why shouldn't he? Eli was the one to kill Nikita, after all. And Eli hates him and hates Jude. There have been times over the years when Ras wished he could kill Eli, when their older brother made Jude cry or fold in on himself with sadness. Eli deserves nothing but indifference.

"If you don't tell me who it was, I'm going to have to kill you both," Elena says.

Ras thinks of Eli on the afternoon of the kill, walking the hard-packed dirt alongside him. Saying, *I accept you.* Saying, *I'm just trying to be supportive.* He thinks of sparring with Eli, the exchange of pulled punches and grappling throws, fluid and easy and almost friendly. He would not be so skilled a fighter without Eli to constantly test himself against.

A strange feeling wells up inside Ras when he imagines Elena's thugs coming for Eli. Both brothers are strong and fast and cunning, and Vance will protect them as well. But no protection is infallible, and Elena is a dangerous foe.

"Give me a fucking name," Elena growls. "And don't lie to me."

Ras has always acted on instinct rather than following rational lines of thought. He rarely makes more than the most rudimentary of plans, preferring to let circumstances lead him where they will. And so he doesn't think, just gives an automatic answer.

"It was me," he says. "I shot Nikita."

On the other end of the line, Elena sighs softly. "Get ready for a fight."

After the call has ended, Ras stares down at the phone, wondering how he could possibly be so stupid. And yet, buried deep beneath the cold pragmatism is a hidden satisfaction.

Maybe Jude was wrong. Maybe Ras isn't as broken as he says.

19: A Heart of Gold

LATE-MORNING SUNLIGHT filters in through the window beside us, bright on Ash's golden skin and the vibrant red roses on the nightstand. I lie on my side, propped up on an elbow, studying him. He's on his back, his whole body exposed, and I brush my fingers over a birthmark on his abdomen, through the coarse hair on his chest, and down the long, thick scars that run along the inside of his forearms.

"You want to know what happened," he says.

"I want to know everything about you. But only if you're willing to tell me."

"I was in high school. I wasn't exactly out, but people just knew I was gay. I got bullied a lot. This one kid...he left a note on my locker every day telling me to kill myself. Eventually, I took his advice."

I force myself to breathe evenly, to stay still, even as my chest constricts so tightly it's hard to breathe at the thought of Ash so hurt, at the thought of someone treating the man I love with such cruelty.

"We only had one bathroom at my house," Ash says. "I don't know how I thought I could get away with it. I didn't even remember to lock the door. My sister barged in before I even finished the other arm."

He lifts his left arm and turns it so I can see what remains of the unfinished cut. I take his hand and pull it toward me so I can kiss the inside of his wrist, where the scars start. Bowing my head as though in a benediction of gratitude that the scars don't continue any farther, that the wounds weren't deep enough to kill.

"I'm sorry," I say.

He shrugs, speaking with a calm detachment, as though it's just a story about someone he doesn't particularly like. "They made me see a doctor who put me on some meds. I liked the way the Valium made it all go away, so I found someone to sell me extra at school, and told the doctor I needed a higher dose." He sighs, leaning back. "I had Ritalin for when I had to study, my benzos for sleep, Oxy for everything in-between. It got me through high school and the first year of college, but then my parents found out what a druggie I was. They cut me off, so I dropped out. I started hustling and pretty much made a fucking mess of my life."

"You could go back to college," I say.

"What are you, a fucking guidance counselor?" he snaps.

"Wouldn't it make you happy?"

He turns on his side, facing away from me. "I've had this conversation with everyone in my life. I'm not having it with you."

I run my hand down his back, over the ridges of his spine I can feel beneath his smooth skin. "I'll pay for it."

He turns back toward me, tangling his fingers in my hair and pressing his lips to my neck. "I don't want to talk right now," he murmurs. "Let's do something more fun."

I know he's using sex to distract me, like he so often does. But my blood heats anyway, and I meet his eager kisses, running my hands down his bare back, pulling his hips hard against mine.

"I love you," I say, moaning the endearment into his neck when I climax, and his fingers dig harder into my shoulders. He's never said it back, but he doesn't have to. Whatever he's willing to give is enough.

"You're cuddly," he murmurs as we lie together in bed, my head on his chest so I can feel the rise and fall of his breath, the steadiness of his heartbeat.

I pull away and raise an eyebrow at him. "You are too."

"Yeah, but I'm not the one who walks around the worst parts of the city with a gun and knife doing whatever it is you do out there."

"The weapons are for show," I say. "If someone gets out of line, I let Ras take care of it."

"So you tell me." He studies me with dark, shrewd eyes. "And I've heard enough about Ras to know he's a really bad guy. He probably doesn't mind doing the dirty work. But you've never broken someone's knee when they couldn't pay their debts?"

"What would you think if I had?" I ask, watching him carefully.

He presses his lips together, silent for a long moment. "I just didn't think you were capable of something like that. I guess it would mean I don't know you as well as I thought."

I lean forward and kiss his nose. "Of course I've never broken a knee. Or anything else."

"I knew it," he says with a triumphant grin. "I knew you had a soft, squishy heart. Big enough to be an easy target."

I press my hand to my chest. "You got me right through it."

He laughs, the sound as golden and sweet as the morning sunlight. I snuggle against him, wondering what he would think if he knew that Ras and I are the same person and that I bear the responsibility for every knee Ras has broken, every kill he's done, every life he's destroyed. I can't lie to Ash forever, but I don't know what else to do.

I COAT MY hands with flour and start sprinkling it over the counter, the dough sitting in a bowl beside me, ready to be kneaded.

"Baby, you didn't have to do all this," Ash says, standing beside me and looking over at the freshly baked cake. "She's just my sister. Nothing special."

"I want to make a good impression."

"You will. No matter what. Now sit down and relax." He playfully swipes the bowl of dough.

"Hey. I need that."

He laughs, holding it above his head, his long arms suspending it out of my reach. "Come and get it, baby."

"Mmm." I look him over, his long, slender form, his lips turned up in a sly smile. "I have a better idea." I put my hands on his ass and pull him against me, tilting my head upward for a kiss. He sets the dough aside as his mouth moves with mine, but I find it hard to care about bread right now.

"Isabella is gonna be here soon," he says, as my hand moves to his groin.

"You started it," I murmur against his neck.

"Jude," he says solemnly. "You're going to make the best impression."

I pull away. "How can you be sure?"

"Because I've never been happier in my life."

A knock sounds at the door and I let him go. "That must be her. I'll let her in. Start some coffee brewing."

I open the door and Dad is standing there with a warm smile for me and a bottle of whiskey in his hand.

"A little housewarming gift," he says. "Heard you'd moved. Thought I'd..."

He trails off, staring past me at Ash, at the floured handprints on the back of his dark jeans, and, when he turns, on his crotch and chest.

"Jude," Dad says softly, staring at the flour on my hands. Then louder: "Jude. Who the hell is this?"

I let him into the apartment and close the door behind him. He doesn't seem to notice as I take the bottle of whiskey from him, moving mechanically as though caught in the slow, surreal motion of a nightmare.

I glance at Ash, who doesn't seem afraid at all. In fact, he seems angry, his shoulders back and his slim chest puffed slightly out, the way he got when he saw the bruises on my face from the last time Dad beat me up.

"Dad, meet Ash." I breathe deeply and try to stay calm. This is my dad. He's going to be angry, and he's going to hit me, and then he's going to forgive me, because he loves me. He always loves me. "He's my boyfriend."

Dad's jaw tightens and he clenches his fists as Ash takes my hand. I squeeze his fingers and tug him to my side.

"This isn't funny, Jude," Dad says.

I hold his gaze. "It's not a joke."

"I want you to tell this boy to leave." Dad speaks very slowly and deliberately, giving instructions to defuse a bomb. "I want you to tell him you're never going to see him again."

I shake my head.

"We all make mistakes," Dad says, in that same cautious tone. "Now's the time to own up to it and make it right."

Ash is watching me intently, fearfully, like he thinks I'm going to obey.

"I would never leave him," I say.

"Jude," Dad says, his hand dropping to his hip, "this is for your own good."

For a moment, I'm fourteen years old again, watching his draw, trying to copy his technique, emulate his dizzying speed. And all the times since that I've seen him shoot, the cold glint in his eyes when he intends to take a life. It flashes past me so quickly that by the time his hand is on the butt of the gun I'm moving, darting sideways, standing in front of Ash as the barrel raises and the sound of the shot cracks the still air around us.

The impact feels like it was made by something much bigger than a bullet, a hammer to the left side of my chest. I stumble backward into Ash but stay on my feet.

"Ash," I say, gritting my teeth, adrenaline coursing through me so intensely I don't even feel the bullet, "on the count of three, I want you to run for the door."

"I'm not leaving you," he says.

"One," I say, standing straight, staring at the gun my father is still holding steady. "Two."

"I'm not leaving."

"Three." I rush Dad as he raises the pistol again. My heart races as though I've just run a mile, my muscles trembling and weak, but I grab the barrel of the gun and keep it aimed at my chest.

"Jude..."

"Ash," I yell. "Get the hell out!"

I struggle with Dad, every bit of attention focused on keeping the gun pointed directly at me, so that Ash is little more than a blur running past us and out the door.

"Jude." Dad wrenches the gun free, and the momentum sends me crashing against the wall.

"I won't see him again," I say, sliding down the wall. I pull my knees to my chest, my heart beating a rapid, erratic tempo. "If you leave him alone, I won't ever see him again."

It's an easy promise to make because I know, sitting here with blood slicking the front of my shirt, hands shaking, breath coming in ragged gasps, that I'm going to die. Dad shot me, and now I'm going to die.

After talking on the phone for a few minutes, Dad kneels beside me, pushing my knees down so he can press a dishtowel to my chest. "An ambulance is on the way," he says.

"It doesn't matter," I say. "I'm going to die."

"Jude." He puts a hand on the side of my face, speaking with the kind of tenderness he's never shown me before, not even when I was a little kid. "I never meant to hurt you. I only ever wanted what was best for you."

"I did everything you wanted," I murmur, leaning my head against his palm. "He was the only thing I wanted."

Tears run down my cheek and over his hand, but, for once, he isn't angry at me for crying.

"You're going to be just fine, Judy," he says, and I feel a pang of longing for the days when he used to call me that, when I was a little kid who just arrived in a city that seemed so bright and bursting with promise.

I close my eyes and I see Ras, standing on the other side of an empty street, and he reaches for me, but, behind him, night falls fast, shadows rolling in like the tide, and he is swallowed up, and then I am.

The Final Fracture

JUDE, DRESSED ALL in black, met his father and Eli at the door to the garage. That night, they were going to meet with a few gun runners and maybe make a deal. But Dad shook his head, looking Jude over.

"Give me your gun," he said.

Jude frowned, a little confused, but handed it over.

"And your knife," Dad said.

Reluctantly, he pulled the weapon from its sheath on his thigh, and, after studying it for a moment, gave it over too.

"You won't need these anymore." The disappointment in Dad's face made Jude's stomach sink and unbidden tears gather behind his eyes. "You're done, Jude. You stay home."

Around Jude, the world crumbled. The tower he'd climbed as a child, the city stretched beyond it, reduced to rubble, the love of the father who held him up to see the vista stolen away, leaving only a cold emptiness behind. Even his dark half was subdued, equally devastated.

"One more chance," he said. "Please, sir. I can do it. Give me one more chance."

"You've had enough chances," Dad said. Eli watched the exchange, expressionless, even though this meant he had won the vicious competition that had dominated the last two years. He would be Dad's consul, and Jude, so long the favorite, would be nothing.

"Please," Jude said as Dad turned away. "Please. I know I can do it. I know I can." Though he himself was not so sure. He'd tried so hard to obey Dad, to hurt the people Dad wanted him to hurt, but he'd never been able to, not once.

"Jude." The word was a low warning, but Jude ignored it.

"Just one more time," he said. "Please, Dad."

Behind him, a soft meow from Pounce, whose suppertime was rapidly approaching. Dad spun on his heel, scowling, and glanced from Jude to the cat he despised. The cat that liked to run with Jude through the yard like a dog or spend an hour curled up on his lap as he read or watched TV.

"Kill that fucking cat," Dad said. "If you can do that, you can do anything."

As the door slammed shut after Eli and Dad, Jude looked over at the fluffy black ball of fur.

"I can't," he whispered, and his dark half whispered back, *I can.*

He baked a salmon fillet and let the cat eat his fill, then sat on the couch with the animal in his lap. He held the warm body in his hands.

"No," he said, fingers sunk into the cat's thick fur. "No. No."

Inside him, night fell like a velvet curtain. Jude retreated into the labyrinth of his mind, and, in that cold empty space, Ras was born. Fearless. Heartless. And he whispered back.

Yes.

Part II

20: Solitary Confinement

RAS LIES IN the hospital bed, resting listlessly against the firm white-sheeted mattress, inclined so he can sit half upright. A tube extends from his chest to a little machine, which whirs happily as it sucks blood from him.

Vance and a doctor in a white lab coat stand to the side of the bed.

"It's a one in a million shot," the doctor says. He glances over at Ras. "You're an incredibly lucky kid."

"They said the bullet struck his heart." Vance is pale, mouth set, grim as death as he puts a heavy hand on Ras's shoulder. Ras tries to squirm away, but the doctor stops him.

"Ah-ah," he says, giving Ras a kindly smile. Beneath his lab coat he wears an impeccable blue sweater vest, his face narrow and accentuated by thick glasses. "Hold still. You don't want to dislodge that chest tube, trust me."

Ras scowls up at the ceiling like a petulant child as Vance tightens his grip.

"The bullet must have glanced off a rib," the doctor says. "So when it hit your heart, it landed in the muscle and stuck there. It's safer to leave it there than to take it out. Scar tissue will form over it eventually."

Ras snorts, looking up at Vance. "You shot me in the fucking heart and you couldn't even kill me."

The doctor looks up from Ras's chart, eyebrows raised. "I'll give you a moment, boss." He quickly leaves the room.

"Watch what you say," Vance tells Ras.

"Why? Everyone in this fucking city is lining up to kiss your ass." Ras jerks his shoulder away from his father's grip. "Don't touch me."

"Jude." Vance sits on the edge of the bed, studying his son with a worried frown. "This isn't like you."

"I'm not Jude."

"I know who you are. You're my son and I love you. And we're going to get through this together."

Ras looks away. He wants to feel anger, to breathe life into that old, cold hatred, but he is empty. As though his soul has leaked away with all the blood pooled on the floor of the home he shared with the only person he could ever love.

Jude is dead. Each heartbeat reminds him. Jude is dead. And for the first time, he is alone.

"How do you feel?" Vance asks gently. "Are you in pain? Talk to me, Jude."

The silence inside his head is maddening, the silence inside his heart—worse. He feels a brittle hollowness, as though he has been only a shell and Jude the true center.

Jude is dead. The beat of their heart, now his alone. Jude is dead.

"You're goddamn quick," Vance murmurs, a haunted expression crossing his face. "I never meant to hurt you."

"For someone who never means to hurt me, you're pretty fucking good at it."

"Let's not do this now," Vance says, in a low, soothing voice. "You're angry at me. I understand. I tried to take away something you thought you wanted. Jude, I—"

"I'm not Jude!"

"You're tired." Vance stands up. "And you're in pain. You don't know what you're saying. I'll get the nurse to give you a little more morphine."

Vance walks out and, a few minutes later, returns with a nurse, who puts something in the IV that not only makes the pain fuzzy and distant, but the room and the people in it. They stand, quietly conferring as blackness overtakes him.

WHEN HE NEXT wakes, he's alone in the white-walled room. He needs Scarlett, needs her desperately, and, as soon as he's awake enough to function, he's fumbling with the ancient-looking phone beside the hospital bed, his own vanished god knows where. But as he dials the number, he remembers the last time he saw her. The way she'd laughed, kissing him on the tip of the nose, the words she'd said: I love you. Now, those words seem to rattle mockingly in his ears, stripped of the meaning they once had. The sweet stirring she created in him vanished like mist on a hot morning, replaced by the arid air of a desert, nothing living for miles and miles.

What will he have to give her? Without Jude, she'll no longer feel loved. And what will she do once she realizes that the love is absent?

He hangs up the phone. Better this way.

BY THE TIME they discharge him, Ras is fidgety and irritable, desperate to be anywhere else, anywhere but in this fucking hospital bed. No one has come to visit besides Vance, who probably hasn't even told Nadya or Eli about this yet.

Today, Vance walks into the hospital room as Ras is sitting on the side of the bed, dressed and ready to leave.

"Dad." He puts enough cold mockery into the word to chill the room. "What do you want?"

"I want you to come home. Let your mother look after you for a little while, until you get better." Vance looks weary and disheveled, as though he hasn't slept or changed clothes in days. As though he's barely left the hospital since they arrived. Maybe he hasn't.

Ras barks a bitter laugh. "You're fucking kidding me."

"I'm not." Vance sits on the bed, and Ras scoots away. "I worry about you."

Jude might have fallen for this conciliatory bullshit, but Ras won't. "Go to hell."

"You're angry. I understand. Come home and we can talk this out."

"What is there to talk about?"

"What happened..." Vance hesitates. "You know I was only looking out for you. That boy poisoned your mind."

Fury swells in Ras, but he hides it behind a cold smirk, standing and facing his father. He wants his words to hurt, to wound, to destroy.

"You know, he wasn't the only one. He wasn't the only one who fucked me. I slept with every man I could get my hands on."

"Jude...don't do this." Vance closes his eyes, sighing. "Not now. Not here."

"I'm not Jude."

"You don't know what you're saying."

"I'm saying I'm not him. I'm not your fucking son."

"You need to come home. You need to recover." Vance puts a hand on his arm, and the touch burns like fire.

Ras jerks away.

"Jude, I—"

"I'm not Jude!" He springs forward with the fury of a wildcat, fighting madly, desperately. His jab lands on Vance's chin, a knee dug into Vance's gut, but he's weakened from the gunshot and the hospital stay, and his father subdues him easily, pinning him to the ground with his wrists above his head.

"Hey," Vance says in the soothing tone he always adopted when a much-younger Jude would wake in the middle of the night from terrifying dreams. He and Ras are both breathing hard from anger and exertion. "It's going to be okay. We'll figure this out. Just...come home."

"Do you want to know what it's like?" Ras asks, his upper lip curling into a snarl. "To be with a man?"

"Don't," Vance says, and now his voice is very low, an eerie calm settling over his face, the one that always precedes a violent storm. But Ras feels no fear, only fury, only a desperate need to dig in his claws and rip Vance to shreds.

"It's good," he says. "It's so good. The men that fucked me, they—"

Vance slaps him, hard enough that he can taste blood, hard enough that his ear rings for a moment.

He spits, the red-tinged saliva hitting his father's cheek, and starts laughing. "Look at you. Vance de Haven, syndicate boss, so fucking tough. Beating up your kid since he was six years old."

The crime boss wipes away the saliva with a slow, deliberate flick of his hand. "You'll leave the city. You won't see that boy again if you want him to live. You're dead to me, and you're dead to everyone you've ever known. You're not my son, and I never want to see you again."

Ras grins at him, wide and feral. "Try not to miss me too much." He leans his head back and laughs as Vance walks to the door. Vance is right. Ras is not his son. His son is dead.

21: A Dying Wish

SETTLED IN A posh spot between downtown and the river to the west, Green Street is lined with distinguished stone buildings, most of which are hundreds of years old. They stand like gray rain-streaked sentinels, reminders of a time when the city was young. A better time, some say, but Ras knows that these streets have run with blood before, and they might again, if someone were strong enough to challenge Vance.

He may have come up with slick new names and a shiny modern image for his criminal empire, but the syndicate is as old as the city itself, a long dark shadow constantly by its side.

The syndicate's time-honored traditions were discarded after Vance's coup, a move that made many people uneasy. Perhaps he thought that fear alone would be enough to inspire loyalty, that they no longer needed the vows or rituals to bind each person to the whole.

Jude liked the rituals and researched them in secret, memorizing the words a consul was meant to say to the boss, a promise of obedience and sacrifice. He wanted so much to stand beside his father and rule their empire together.

And Ras? He wonders now what it was he truly wanted. Not to stand above the city and know that he owned it, but to be on the streets in the dark and feel power at its most raw and visceral. To bring Scarlett the heads of their enemies and lay them at her feet. But now—now he can't bear to see her. To hear her voice and feel so acutely everything he's lost.

He walks into one of the office buildings, his footsteps silent on the polished marble floor in the hushed entryway. The security guard nods at him as he passes by. He's been here many times before.

Gideon looks up from his desk as Ras walks into his distinguished, opulent office. His blond hair is perfectly groomed and styled, and his neat, manicured fingers tap on the lacquered black desk as Ras takes the chair on the other side.

"Jude," he says, eyes wide. "Shit. I'm so sorry, man."

Ras raises an eyebrow.

"Your dad told me," Gideon says, his usual levity disappeared.

"Told you what?"

Gideon shifts his weight uneasily. "That you're dying."

Ras leans back his head and laughs. "You're fucking kidding me," he says when he regains his composure.

"No. That's what he said. Are you dying?"

Ras grins. "Worse."

Gideon leans forward, elbows on his desk. "Worse?"

"I'm gay." It's not true, not anymore, but, for this task— the last one he must complete before leaving this city for good—it's a necessary lie. "When Vance said I was dead to him, apparently he meant it literally."

"Holy shit," Gideon says. "I knew he was a ruthless fucking asshole, but I always thought he cared about you."

"I need a favor." Ras leans back in his chair and puts his feet up on the desk. Gideon eyes them, frowning, but says nothing. "Think of it as my dying wish."

"You're not dying."

Ras looks out the narrow window to the street three stories below, people with black umbrellas hurrying about in the rain.

"As far as this city is concerned, I am."

RAS SITS ON the fire escape outside Ash's window, hidden in the thick darkness cast by the streetlight he knocked out before climbing up here. Even he knows better than to contact Ash directly after Vance's solemn threat. And in truth, he isn't sure he wants to. The shine within Ash, the beacon of goodness he once was drawn to, now seems dull and tarnished. Ras no longer has any capacity for goodness, and, like Scarlett, Ash is only another reminder of what he's lost.

Leaving is the only way to escape.

Inside, Ash is handing Gideon a cup of coffee. In his thousand-dollar suit and designer silk tie, Gideon looks out of place in Ash's studio apartment, sitting on a chair Ash rescued from a nearby dumpster, holding a cracked white mug.

If Gideon seems cool and composed, Ash is a wreck, his hair messy and unwashed, dark circles beneath his eyes.

"I think you should sit down," Gideon says gently.

"Is he dead?" Ash's voice breaks on the last word.

"I'm sorry," Gideon murmurs, and Ash sinks onto the couch and draws his knees to his chest.

Ras feels nothing at all. A cold, vast silence where there once was something as beautiful as a song. He's not here because he loves Ash. He's here because, although Jude never made a dying wish, he knows what his other half would have wanted him to do. Jude's heart was too big, too soft, too open, and, when it was broken, he died. This gesture is the best way Ras can think of to honor him.

"Thanks for telling me," Ash says when he finally looks up.

"That's not the only reason I'm here." Gideon sets a folder on the table. "Jude left a modest amount of money behind."

"I don't want it," Ash blurts out. "That's not why I was with him."

"Look, Ash." Gideon leans back on the sofa, feathers unruffled. "If you don't take this money, it goes back to his dad. Jude really wanted you to have it."

With detached fascination, Ras wonders at the tears sparkling on Ash's cheeks, the clear signs of his suffering. What would it be like to love someone so intensely that losing them seemed like losing the entire world? Jude was never sure if Ash's affections meant love, but Ras knew that they did.

"Okay," Ash says. "Okay."

"There are directions for how this should be spent. But the long and short of it is that it will cover a year's worth of college tuition at Vintir and your living expenses for that year."

Ash draws in a shaky breath. "What did he say about me? When you talked to him about this. What did he say?"

"He said he loved you very much," Gideon says smoothly. And Ras is grateful to the accountant for the lie. There's no reason Ash needs to know that to Ras, this was just one more matter to settle before he can get the hell out of this haunted city.

"Why don't I love you?" he whispers at the hunched figure in the warmly lit room, his words fogging the window. "Why can't I?"

Of course neither of them hear him.

RAS STANDS ON the deck of a boat in the harbor, a duffel bag slung over his shoulder. The bruises on his face mostly healed, the tooth Vance knocked loose taken care of.

As the boat makes its slow way into the bay, the sun sets behind the city. From the water, it's cast in silhouette, the skyscrapers that form its distinctive, uneven skyline towering in the distance, the flat planes of Bayside apartments and strip malls lying before them. To the west, the smokestacks of the industrial district stand sentry, and, in the east, the river flows into the rapidly darkening waters of the bay.

Ras feels a strange longing as the city slowly shrinks, the brilliant orb of the sun dipping behind it. If he ever loved anything at all, it was the dark city, the narrow, twisting stone streets of the Warrens, the haphazard Ghost Town tenements, the slick glass storefronts that made up the downtown. The smell of rain on concrete, the way the shadows fell so deeply he could almost feel their ghostly caresses.

But it was Jude's city as much as it was his own, and to walk those streets is to be reminded how hollow his own heart has become. Who would have thought that emptiness could ache so keenly?

In a new place, he can start again, he can be himself, untethered by Jude's rules and his strange feelings. In a new world, he can forget Jude, and he can forget what it used to be like when he could almost feel Jude's reckless love.

22: To Drown in Black Water

SCARLETT KNOCKS ON Eli's door with some trepidation, but also some excitement she has tried to ignore. Something about him draws her, a stillness, a deliberate grace.

When he lets her in, he's on the phone, and he gives her an apologetic nod before turning away, speaking Russian in his low, rumbling voice into the receiver.

The apartment resembles a cool but luxurious cave—bare, smooth concrete for one wall, rugged brown rugs over a wood floor. Eli hangs up the phone and, instead of turning to her, stares into the fireplace, palm pressed to the dark stone hearth.

"What's going on?" she asks after the silence lingers long enough to be uncomfortable.

"I, uh..." He clears his throat. "I guess no one's told you. I kind of figured."

She steps closer. "Told me what?"

Eli turns his head away. "Jude's dead."

She feels nothing. No, not nothing. A blank white, like shock. A hollowness beneath her skin. A distinct sense of unreality in the air around her, thick enough to touch.

"What happened?" Her voice drifts from far away. She grips the straps of her purse so tightly her fingers ache, but her face remains serene.

"He got shot." Eli pulls away from the fireplace and turns to face her. "I'm sorry, Scarlett. If you want to talk or anything..."

"No." The word is curt, almost cold, and it echoes in the cavern that is her heart. "I should go. Thanks for telling me."

"Yeah. If you need anything, just call me."

She graces him with a nod and polite goodbye, then walks out the door.

In the black asphalt heat of the parking lot, she takes out her phone and dials Ras's number, then Jude's. The phone rings and rings and rings.

She sinks to her knees beside her car, the ground rough and hot beneath her bare knees, her palms. Staring numbly at pavement.

Warm arms wrap around her, pulling her back into the embrace of a broad, solid body. Eli sits on the dirty ground of the parking lot, holding her as she shakes, as the world fragments beneath her. As her heart falls and falls, he holds her close, murmuring soft Russian words into her hair.

When the storm is spent, he lifts her easily as a child and carries her back inside. She's soothed by the rocking of his steady steps, her cheek against his chest, breathing his scent, musky with a hint of spice, like Earl Grey tea.

On his couch, wrapped in a blanket, she tries to comprehend the magnitude of her loss. Eli sits beside her, waiting patiently.

"What happened?" she murmurs.

"He got shot. Doing a hit for Dad."

She shakes her head. "That doesn't make any sense. If he had a hit to do, why wouldn't he tell me about it?"

"I don't know," Eli says. "Maybe it came up at the last minute. Dad won't talk about it."

She wraps her arms around herself, thinking of Ras and Jude dying somewhere cold and distant, a place she'll never see. She wonders which of them was the last to leave this world, or if, in the end, they departed together. She always knew they could become one person, given enough time. But their time has been cut short.

SHE ARRIVES AT the funeral late and in the red dress that has always been Ras's favorite, lipstick to match. Six-inch heels sinking slightly into the grass. The air muggy and warm on her arms, her legs bare to the mid-thigh.

The other mourners glance her way, disapproving frowns, the occasional whisper. She ignores them, arrogant chin set. Not one of them knew them like she did. Loved them like she did.

A priest begins to speak, but the words brush senselessly by her. She does not cry or listen, studying instead the lines of the black coffin.

When he is done, she throws a single red rose into the grave. She waits as the grave is filled, each person casting their handful of dirt, murmuring soft goodbyes. Their faces blurring into one mask of mourning. She is indifferent to them. Their sorrow means nothing to her, consumed by the selfishness of her own despair.

She waits still, as the last of them leave, and the gravedigger comes to fill in the gaping hole. He gives her a nod that is polite but nothing more.

Standing sentry, she tries to conjure them. The subtle electrical thrill of Ras's proximity, the tenderness of Jude's touch. The ease of their smile. She pictures a shade, a cold presence drifting just behind her shoulder. One that will never leave her. One she cannot lose.

She moves closer to the mound of dirt, to examine the inscription on his tombstone. An angel, wings spread, eyes cast heavenward.

"Did you know?" Vance's voice comes from behind her, cold and harsh. When she turns to face him, his expression is dark as a shuttered window.

She gives him a puzzled frown. "Did I know what?"

"Were you really his girlfriend?" Vance asks, stepping closer. A flask gleams in his left hand and his breath stinks of whiskey. "Or was that another lie?"

She holds her head high. "I loved Jude," she says, heart breaking to hear herself use the past tense. "Maybe you think that I'm a gold-digging whore, but Jude knew that I loved him, and that's all that matters." She refuses to look away, refuses to let him see her cry.

"I don't think that," he says quietly and hands her the flask. "What I meant was that Jude had some secrets from me. But it sounds like he didn't share them with you."

The whiskey burns her throat, kindling a fire in her chest. "What secrets?"

Vance slowly shakes his head, staring down at the grave. She hands him the flask and he takes a long drink.

"You come have dinner with us sometime," he says. "Don't be a stranger."

JUDE HAS BEEN dead for forty-seven days when Scarlett next steps into the de Havens' Victorian mansion, the foreboding house dark and silent as a tomb. Her high heels click on the wood floor in the shadowy entryway.

The housekeeper shows her to an imposing oak door, steady and solid under her knock.

"This better be pretty fucking good," Vance calls from within. The housekeeper shrinks back, then hurries off down the hall, leaving Scarlett to open the door and step in alone.

Amber light falls in through a high-set stained-glass window, casting the room in a warm glow as though from a hearth. Vance looks every bit the crime boss, with a tumbler of whiskey and smoke drifting whimsically upward from a cigar in an ashtray on his massive wooden desk.

He looks up and raises his heavy eyebrows, mouth turning up in a grim semblance of a smile. "Scarlett. What can I do for you?"

She stands before his desk and opens her mouth, shuts it again. Unable to speak, to ask for what she wants, what she needs from him. Just seeing him is enough to bring her best friend and her lover back strongly enough to steal her voice away, to shake her unshakable resolve. How did she ever give them so much power over her?

"Do you want to stay for dinner, sweetheart?" Vance asks, and she nods gratefully.

In the dining room, Nadya is already sitting at the long, narrow table, large enough to seat a dozen, places set for four. She looks up at Scarlett, her skin as white as bleached bone, the sheen of a prescription daze in her eyes.

"Hello, child," she murmurs, getting up. She doesn't seem surprised at Scarlett's presence, but then, she seems so sedated she probably wouldn't be surprised at anything short of Jude walking through the archway leading to the shadowy hall behind her.

Instead of Jude, Eli appears, moving with the same silent grace. He looks so like his brother that it seems he wears a ghostly mask for just a moment. But then he smiles. Calm, steady. The rock that the rest of them, adrift on an ocean of grief, could grasp for.

Dinner is a quiet affair. Nadya barely speaks, her hands trembling, knife and fork clacking against the plate until Scarlett leans over and cuts her meat and potatoes for her.

When she sits back, Eli is watching her with an expression she can't place.

"Jude and I had an idea," Scarlett says, glancing across the table at Vance, who sits at the head. The idea was really hers—Jude's input was minimal and Ras had nothing to contribute once she made it clear no violence was necessary. But she thinks Vance will be more likely to take her seriously if she reminds him they were involved.

"An idea?" Vance asks.

"Jude used to...we used to talk a lot. About what he was doing for the syndicate. I helped him sometimes."

"Did you, now?" Vance studies her face. She can't tell if he's encouraging or skeptical, and her heart skips anxiously under his scrutiny. Vaguely, she wonders if this is what it would be like to have a father—this overwhelming desire to earn an approving smile and a kind word.

"I was the one who figured out which detective was helping Nikita, and it was my idea to give him a fake lead," she says. "I've helped Jude with some of his contract kills—drawing out his targets. And we worked together in the Warrens sometimes."

Vance raises his eyebrows, a hint of a wry smile on his face. "I'll be damned."

She outlines briefly her plan for a very lucrative scam. A charity gala, the kind she attends on a regular basis, with the proceeds flowing through a fictitious charity organization right back to the syndicate. Vance listens without interrupting, nodding thoughtfully now and then.

"Jude was luckier than he knew to have you," Vance says when she finishes her explanation. "That's a goddamn brilliant idea."

She blushes, a pleased heat creeping over her neck and cheeks. "Thank you."

"Make it happen," he says with the ease of a man accustomed to giving orders that are obeyed without question. "Eli will make sure you've got everything you need."

She blinks at him. She hadn't expected her idea to be accepted so quickly, so easily. "It's not without risks. And it's not cheap. I—"

"Scarlett," Vance says, gently holding her gaze. "I wouldn't be where I am if I couldn't take the measure of a person. You'll get it done, and you'll make it work."

"Yes, sir," she says. "I'll get it done."

His smile is fond as he gets up and pats her shoulder on his way out of the room. "Welcome to the family, sweetheart."

She bows her head, biting the inside of her cheek to keep from grinning. Such exuberant emotion seems almost obscene in the face of the grief that hangs thick as smoke in this house. But she can't keep her heart from racing with the exhilarated certainty that her life is about to start.

23: Grace

IT HAS BEEN a hundred and seventeen days since Jude's death, and Scarlett and Eli are walking the mansion's darkened hallways. Eli's hand brushes hers as they make their way to Vance's office, and she feels that same flow of affection and attraction, a desire so steady it seems like it's always existed, even before they met.

It's past midnight, but Vance will be awake, waiting for news of their success or failure.

Tonight, it's success, a hit on a wealthy business owner who knew a little too much. Like usual, Scarlett was the one to fire the gun, not because Eli is incapable, but because he doesn't like to kill. It eats away at him in quiet moments, but he forces his conscience aside to be the man his father needs him to be—Jude's replacement.

With a gun in her hand, Scarlett feels no fear and no remorse, just a simple split-second calculation: her target lives or her target dies, and, from there, she extrapolates the results and makes a clean, decisive choice. She has yet to feel any semblance of remorse.

"Nicely done," Vance says with a fond smile, and she feels her chest puff up with pride.

"Thank you," she says.

Eli is standing, as he so often does, just to her right and a little behind her, like a shadow. If it bothers him that she has taken Jude's place in their father's regard—a place that really should be his—he hasn't given any sign.

"I don't know what I'd do without you, sweetheart," Vance says. "Now go get some rest. We're going shooting bright and early tomorrow."

She smiles, inclining her head. "Yes, sir."

There's a bedroom on the east side of the mansion she has made her own for late nights like this. When she can't sleep, she slips through the maze of hallways to Jude's room and climbs into his empty bed.

But tonight, she hesitates on the landing between the brothers' doors. Eli's is slightly ajar. An invitation he could not voice. It silently swings inward and she steps into the room. Eli sleeps without a sheet to cover him, shirtless, broad shoulders and a muscular torso.

She steps closer, with only the shuffle-scuff of a foot on the carpet to announce her arrival. Eli stirs but doesn't wake.

The bed sags slightly as she sits on the side, and, in a lightning-strike instant, she's on her back, pinned by her wrists, the controlled weight of a knee on her chest.

"I got you," Eli mumbles, eyes glazed with sleep. "I fucking got you."

"I'm not Jude," she says.

He blinks a few times, then looks at her with clear eyes. He lets a long, potent silence linger, holding her wrists firmly to the mattress, then leans down to press his lips to the curve where her neck meets her shoulder. Gentle kisses trace the line of her collarbone.

"Try to forget him," he says, his tongue dipping into the hollow at the base of her throat. "Just for a little while. Just for tonight."

She closes her eyes, and Eli's lips press to her eyelids soft as the sweep of a paintbrush. "The past and the future falling away like sand," she says.

"And all we have is this moment."

She opens her eyes. In this moment, there is nothing else, not the cruel stretch of her past, not her shroud of grief. In this moment, the past and future fall away and there is only Eli, kissing this and that of her, the curve of her jaw, her breastbone, her cheek.

When she rides him, hands on his hard chest to steady herself, he groans endearments in Russian, tender words that need no translation. She tries not to think of another pair of green eyes, not here. But there is a second where the ghost slips into her mind again. A second of longing for his dark and his light, his boundless tenderness and the violence at her command.

Afterward, they lie beside each other, not touching. She wonders if this is a betrayal, and, if so, which brother she's betraying.

Tonight is the first time since Ras and Jude's death that she's felt alive, if only for a few fleeting moments. Is it because of Eli's passion, which burns like a torch in this darkened house? Or just that he looks so, so much like his brother?

"Please don't go," Eli says.

The hands that just caressed her with such fervor lie helplessly on the sheets at his sides, as he stares at the ceiling. She takes one of them and laces their fingers together.

They talk of trifles, of nothings, the tight knot of sorrow in her chest unraveling at the sound of his voice, until light begins to stream in through the French doors leading out onto his balcony.

"Why are Jude's doors boarded up?" she asks. "Does he have a balcony like yours?"

"Yeah." Eli sighs, putting his hands behind his head. "It was a long time ago. I think he was in middle school or maybe just starting high school. Dad told him to kill his pet cat. I didn't think he would. I didn't think he could. But when Dad and I got home from work, Jude was sitting at Dad's desk, the dead cat by his feet."

Could that be the moment, Scarlett wonders. *Could that be the moment when his mind split, when Jude's dark half became its own entity, became Ras?*

"I've seen a lot of bad people. But Jude scared me that night. He was like a completely different person, sitting at Dad's desk, waiting for us to come home. He smirked at Dad and said, 'You owe me a new cat.' Dad just laughed. But..."

Eli gets up and walks to the balcony. Scarlett joins him, looking out over the garden. She shivers and he puts a blanket around her shoulders.

"That night, he jumped through his glass doors. I heard the crash and ran over there. I found him on the balcony, kneeling on the shards of broken glass with his hands over his face. He kept saying 'what did you do?' over and over."

"Oh," she says softly, surprised at how it can still hit her like a punch to the gut, the realization that he's gone. She imagines him on the other side of the boarded-up doors, trapped and scared, in a place she can never reach him.

24: Mercenary

THE LONDON NIGHTCLUB pulses with heat and bass, the press of bodies, beautiful people yelling to be heard above the music. Ras makes his graceful way through the throng, stalking like a jaguar among a jungle of sequined dresses and bare shoulders. The bouncer by the door in the back gives him a curt nod and steps aside.

"Ah, there you are." KL stands in the center of the room, wearing an expensive blue pinstripe suit more appropriate for a stockholders' meeting than a nightclub. His black hair is silver at the temples, and he has the distinguished air of a well-traveled gentleman.

"I've been waiting for you. The man of the hour." He raises his glass of champagne and glances around the room; all of his sycophants—beautiful women in short dresses, two solidly built and serious men openly carrying guns—do the same.

"They said you were good," KL continues after a theatrical swig. "But I had my doubts. Frank was a careful man. Paranoid, one might say. And he knew you were coming."

"Yes." Ras grins, pulling a signet ring from his pocket. KL likes to have trophies, irresponsible as such a practice is. "It was fun. He put up a fight. You'd be surprised how rare that is."

"Well. Good." KL clenches his fist around the signet ring. "Glad he's dead. Dangerous fellow. I suppose you are, too, at that."

He picks up a bulky briefcase sitting beside him and hands it to Ras. "Here's ten grand. The rest is in your bank account. But you should stay. Have a drink with us."

The girls beside KL echo his sentiment, smiling more at the briefcase full of cash than at Ras. He sits beside a pretty one with long brown hair and a full pouty mouth.

"You look like someone I used to know," he tells her as KL is relating a long boring story with great gusto to one of his bodyguards, two of the other girls leaning in to giggle at appropriate moments.

"Someone you loved," the girl says. Her voice is reedy and thin but has a pleasant dreamlike quality to it. "Am I right?"

He laughs then, unable to keep the bitterness out of it, the hollowness rattling like a dead leaf in the wind.

"Everyone falls in love," she says, in her wispy way. "Even monsters."

"Could you love a monster?"

Her eyes dart to KL, and he can't tell if it's a calculating gaze or a truly enamored one. "There's good in every person," she says. "You just have to find it. I'm sure there's good in you."

He pictures Ash, dark curls spread on a pillow, a crooked smile. A true heart.

"There was," he says, "but I left it behind when I left home."

"I don't believe that. You can't just leave a part of yourself behind."

He doesn't want to think about it, to think about Ash, who once fit against him as neatly as a puzzle piece clicking into place. The goodness he was lacking, glowing in one man. A man he could possess, a man he could have made his own, if only they'd had more time. His precious gem, his stolen heart of gold.

He refuses to remember, leaning toward her and murmuring in her ear, "If you want to know me better, let's dance."

She glances skeptically at him.

"You can learn a lot about someone by how they dance," he says.

She lets him lead her to the dance floor. Ras likes to dance, to feel the vibration of the music move through his body, and he's good at it. Unlike Jude, whose self-consciousness made him clumsy.

Ras lets the noise of the club wash over him, the heat of bodies, the press of the crowd. These are the good moments, the moments when thought and memory are chased away by the immediacy of the body. When he fights, when he fucks, when he gets high. The chains that once bound him, the bare minimum of morality, the love, the cautiousness, are gone. He can do anything; the world is his for the taking, ripened and ready to be plucked. And yet, the things he wants most of all—the ice queen, the true heart, the city that should be his—are beyond his reach. Jude's ghost lingers on those stone streets, haunting the shadows that once were a sanctuary.

He buys the pretty girl a drink—her name already forgotten—and sits by her at a little table in the corner. Like everything else in the nightclub, it gleams a chrome and purple, the light pulsing over them in time with the bass.

KL slides into the table beside them, sitting close to the girl, clearly enthralled—she must be his choice for the evening. Maybe more than an evening; she is beautiful, soft features like Scarlett, whose full lips and large brown-sugar eyes hid a will of iron.

"How did you do it?" KL asks, leaning in.

"A good assassin never gives away his secrets." And Ras is the best in the world. He'd put it on business cards if he had them. If he was in a profession suited to such niceties.

KL shrugs. "I just want to know if you made him suffer."

"Yes."

Beside KL, the girl shivers but quickly composes herself.

"You lived up to your reputation," KL says. "How did you get so good?"

"Practice." Ras isn't about to share his secrets. Vance de Haven is well-known in international crime circles and does business with a number of KL's associates.

"Baby—" KL squeezes the girl's thigh. "—go get us a few more drinks."

She glances at their half-full cups but simply shrugs and walks away, unperturbed at the clear dismissal.

"It's funny," KL says. "I met someone who looks quite a bit like you."

Ras raises an eyebrow, tensing slightly.

"Eli de Haven," KL continues. "Vance's kid. He mentioned he had a younger brother."

The handle of Ras's switchblade is smooth and reassuring beneath his fingers. "Jude de Haven is dead."

"I think someone went to a lot of trouble to make it look that way. I don't know why you ran away, but it doesn't really matter."

"I didn't run away," Ras growls, although in many ways that's exactly what he did.

"Have it your way," KL says, with a good-natured smile. "What matters is I know who you are now. And I know how much your life is worth to the right people. I don't know what you did to piss off the Russian mafia, but all it would take is a single phone call to bring Elena Nikitichna and her people down on your head."

Ras takes a deep, calming breath, releasing his grip on his switchblade and placing both hands on the table. A submissive gesture to show he is not a threat, not now, not here. He's certain he could protect himself if Elena were to come after him, but it's better to be cautious if he can afford it.

"I know that you are not a loyal man," KL says. "Until now. I'll keep your secret, Jude, as long as you're useful to me."

Ras scowls, meeting KL's gunmetal-gray eyes furiously. He thought he would never have to endure being called Jude again. It's enough to make him want to start stabbing.

"My name is Ras," he says. "You have to call me Ras."

"Of course," KL says. "Of course. I'm glad we could come to an agreement."

Ras bows his head, a gesture of agreement and also surrender. For now.

THE DOOR TO KL's apartment is unlocked, the alarm system and cameras disabled by a tech-savvy friend. From inside, it resembles a glass box, walls all segmented windows, the furniture sleek and modern. Ras rather likes the aesthetic, the luxurious austerity.

He doesn't flick on the lights; the moon shines bright as a spotlight, casting its pale glow over thick white rugs and a dark wood floor, silent beneath his feet. Knife strapped to his thigh, gun at his hip, switchblade in his right pocket, garrote in his left. He's not about to let a man like KL own him.

He takes a marker and draws his smiley face, two sharp slashes for the eyes, a wicked curve of a smile, on a floor-to-ceiling window, the mouth stretching as wide as he can spread his arms, grinning out over the Thames.

In the bedroom, KL sleeps on his back, one arm nestled beneath his head, mouth slightly open. Beside him, the pretty girl who talked to Ras about love lies on her side, bare shoulders above the blanket. Her hair messy like Scarlett's would be when she slept over, a slight flaw in her usually perfect appearance. How he once adored those imperfections of hers, reminders that beneath all the grooming and poise, there was a woman, vulnerable and beautiful, visible only to him.

Now, those memories have taken on an emptiness, a bitterness to replace the sweet. He pushes them away, drawing a knife. (He hates to use guns—too loud, too impersonal.) It's a simple thing, to stand by the edge of the bed and cut KL's throat, blood spurting from the artery and pulsing onto white sheets, black in the moonlight, until KL's body goes limp in death. Messy, but satisfyingly so. Better than the abrupt, deafening blast of a gunshot.

The girl stirs, then jerks awake. He puts a hand over her mouth.

"Shh," he whispers. "Don't move."

Her eyes are wide and wet, tears running down her cheeks and onto his fingers, still clamped firmly over her mouth. She is afraid; she is so afraid.

Scarlett would never be afraid.

He cuts her throat and watches her die. When she lies still, brown eyes open wide and sightless, for a moment he sees Scarlett's face, steady resolve absent, frozen in death. He steps back as the unnerving vision—imagination, nothing more—fades from his mind, bringing his phone to his ear, so automatically and thoughtlessly he's almost surprised when she answers.

"Hello?" Her voice is low and husky on the other end of the line. And he feels nothing, hearing it. Just a bitter, empty space where that infatuation once lived.

A long silence lingers between them as the corpses bleed into the white bedsheets.

"Hello?" she says again, and a small spark, a single star in a black sky, flickers briefly inside him, and then all is dark.

He hangs up the phone, looks over the two dead bodies, and walks out of the room.

THAT NIGHT, HE dreams of the city and wakes with a longing like a rope tied around his chest and pulled tight.

He gets high. He doesn't do drugs often, because he's almost always on some job or another, but, tonight, he goes through the ritual: the spoon, the brown liquid, the syringe. He likes heroin because of the sweetness, the expansiveness that feels almost—almost—like the fleeting warmth of love.

He thinks of calling Scarlett, of showing up on her balcony and taking her in his arms, or kissing Ash in a back alley, their bodies pressed flush together. But he doesn't want to hear their voices and feel the emptiness where there once was something he didn't understand but craved. Jude took every good thing for himself. Until now, Ras has never borne any resentment for it. But as the chemical euphoria fades, he finds himself bitter and angry.

"You took Scarlett," he says to the empty apartment, to the man no longer living in his mind. "You took Ash. And everything else."

As always, there is no answer.

25: You Can't Fix a Rose

NARROW AND TINY even for a six-year-old, Jude always moved recklessly, skipping, running, yelling, unaware of how fragile he looked to Eli, who, at twelve, felt he was nearly an adult, old enough to accompany his father as he worked, old enough to pick up the family trade.

Eli perched on the edge of the fountain as Jude walked along the rows of their mother's rosebushes, blushing red blossoms not fully opened. He stopped at a low-hanging flower, level with his face.

Jude studied the rosebud, bending forward to sniff it, hands folded behind his back as though leaning into a chaste, delicate kiss. Straightening, he reached for it, then jerked his hand away as though stung, the prickly stem bouncing slightly.

He reached again, fingers closing around the stem, and leaned in slightly to smell it.

"You fucking whore." Their father's shout and the clash-clang of a thrown pan spread through the open kitchen door and across the garden.

Jude stood, startled and stiff as a fawn. Slowly, he pulled his hand away, the red flower on his palm. He turned to Eli with wide, watery green eyes, and held it out like an offering.

"I broke it," he said.

"It's okay," Eli said. "It's just a flower."

"No." His little lips trembled, water starting to spill in shining rivulets. "I broke it."

"Shh," Eli whispered nervously, glancing at the kitchen door as Jude's shoulders shook, whimpers forming on his lips. "Be quiet. It's okay."

Jude sat heavily in the dirt, flower still in his open palm, and sobbed. "I broke it. I broke it."

Eli held back a heavy sigh, but beneath the exasperation was a melancholy he couldn't then articulate, a sorrow for Jude, crying because he had broken a rose when, in a few years, he would be taught, as Eli had been, to break so much more.

He knelt in the dirt and put a hand on Jude's arm. "I'll fix it. Okay? Just wait here and be quiet."

Miraculously, Jude's sobs stopped. His pitiful green eyes fixed on Eli. "Okay," he murmured.

Eli darted across the yard, bare feet clapping over gray stones, a path worn smooth. He wrenched open the sticky screen door and walked inside, his mad dash slowed to hesitant steps. Fear caught in his throat. He wasn't supposed to be anywhere near when Mom and Dad were fighting. And Dad's anger, which was now focused on Mom, could switch targets at a dizzying speed.

His mother stood back against the counters, chin tilted down, face hidden behind a curtain of black hair.

"Nadya." Dad gripped her chin between thick fingers, tilting her face up toward him. "Look at me when I fucking talk to you."

"I'm sorry," she whispered.

He raised his hand. Eli's soft whimper was lost in the heavy smack of Dad's palm against her face. Mom didn't cry. She never cried, just looked back at her husband with dark, dead eyes.

Eli moved foot by cautious foot across the floor behind Dad, listening to the Russian words, bad words, words he was never, ever supposed to say. He crossed the kitchen without a sound, slid open a drawer, reached in. After a moment of frantic rummaging, he closed his fingers around the cylindrical mass of black electrical tape.

Prize clenched firmly in his left hand, he darted across the floor, shoved the screen door open, and dashed outside. No one came after him.

By the rosebushes, Jude hadn't moved, the blood-red blossom still centered in his palm. Eli took it from him and helped him to his feet.

"Okay," he said. "I'm going to fix it. Close your eyes."

Jude squeezed them shut tight and waited as Eli put so much tape on the stem it was as though a second ugly black flower had bloomed behind the red one. But when he pulled his hand away, it stayed.

"You can look," he said.

Jude stared at the rose, then at Eli, grinning, wide-eyed like his brother had worked a miracle. He gave him a tight hug around the middle, then walked his cheerful, bouncing walk away over the uneven stones.

Years later, when Jude killed his cat, when he changed so profoundly and in a way Eli didn't quite understand, Eli would remember that day in the garden, the little boy who was devastated because he'd broken something beautiful. When he saw Jude kill someone for the first time, the gleeful confidence with which he held the knife, Eli remembered those green eyes filled with tears over a flower.

Now he looks out over the garden from his balcony, Scarlett sleeping in the bed just behind the open glass doors, and wonders if she loves him or if, in Jude's absence, she's settled for the next best thing, as his father has. He puts his hands on the railing, sturdy fingers, thick knuckles. Enforcer's hands, for breaking jaws, for collecting debts. They seem so clumsy, caressing her delicate body, a fragility he knows is deceptive and yet is deceived by daily.

Their father was always harder on Jude, pushing him to be better, while Eli had only his own ingrained discipline to thank for his skill and achievements. He was as quiet as Jude, stronger, but not as fast. He could shoot more accurately; Jude had a quicker draw. He had a head for numbers, Jude a knack for leading people. They were meant to complement, not to compete, but there was only one prize, and Jude had won it.

He hated Jude for it, up until the day his brother died, and even his grief couldn't wash away the years of bitterness he carried inside him like stagnant water. He used to wish that Jude would disappear, be gone from his life forever, so that for once someone might see him. Someone might love him. And now it's happened, a victory so hollow it can hardly be called a victory at all.

Soft footsteps sound on the carpet and Scarlett wraps her arms around him from behind, pressing her forehead into his back. He tells her the story of the broken rose, speaking evenly and calmly, without pausing to let her respond, and she stands at the railing and listens.

"But after Jude walked away, I turned back," he says, "and the rose had fallen off again." It lay there, red as a wound on the dust, and Eli had felt something twist in his chest, a sorrow, a betrayal.

She puts her delicate hand over his. "You can't fix a rose."

In the moonlight, white silk flowing over her curves, she shines like a goddess. He has never loved like this before and often wonders what it was in him that chose her. It wasn't her beauty but her grace that first drew him, not her sensuality but her strength. The core of her, hard and cold as steel, and for all the times he's cut himself on her sharp edges, he wouldn't dull them. She is a warrior, she is a queen, and, as always, he is in awe.

"Marry me," he says, words escaping before he can stop them, words that have been on his lips for months now, words that, if he were truly honest, have been in his thoughts since the first time she came to his bed.

Her eyes meet his, and the corner of her mouth turns up in a sad smile. "Eli, I..." She looks out at the night sky, "I'm like a star. A tiny point of light, very far away. And even if you crossed that cold distance, you'd find I'm already dead."

"I know," he says, brushing the cool skin of her cheek with his fingertips. "But I love you enough for the both of us."

Her eyes shimmer in the moonlight, and she bows her head. "I love you. I really do."

"Then marry me."

When she looks up at him, she smiles. "Okay. Yes."

SCARLETT SETS ANOTHER tumbler of whiskey before Vance. He doesn't object. He never objects to booze.

"How's Eli treating you?" he asks. Vance and Nadya accepted the news of her too-soon, too-sudden engagement with subdued happiness, Ras and Jude's absence as tangible as their presence ever was. She and Eli have only been together for eight months, but she is desperate for something to hold on to, someone to belong to.

It's not just Eli she's marrying, but his family. Nadya, with her quiet warmth and gentle touch. Vance, who treats her like a daughter, who lets her step into Jude's place at his side. She never met her own father and didn't realize there was such a void inside her where a father's affection might lie. She doesn't mind that the love she receives is nothing more than the love he harbors for his dead son, displaced onto the nearest acceptable substitute.

"Eli is good to me," she says. "You don't have to worry."

"He'd better be," Vance replies gruffly. Eli receives no more of his father's attention than he ever did, but he doesn't seem to resent Scarlett for it.

The photo Vance usually keeps hidden away in a drawer is sitting in the center of his desk. Jude grins at them from the frame, several years younger than when she first met him.

She finds it hard to look at.

"I miss him too," she says, standing beside Vance's chair. His hair is now more gray than blond, his face, though largely unchanged in terrain, has lost the youthful vigor it had only a year ago. In running the syndicate, his ruthlessness has turned to indifferent cruelty, a clumsy heavy-handedness that she finds painful to watch. *I could do better*, she thinks at every misstep. Imagining, in her heart of hearts where no reality intrudes, that she might someday take his place, stand in that office above the city and, wielding both money and violence, rule it.

Vance drains his glass of whiskey in one tip of the tumbler, like a rough-mannered soldier, then stares morosely at the photo. She reaches out and picks it up, studying the haunted boy in a middle-school uniform, his face still childish and round. She wonders if it was taken before his mind split.

"It's my fault. I regret it every day, Scarlett." Vance's voice is rough with barely restrained feeling. "If I could, I'd tell him to come back. I'd welcome him with open arms."

He presses a hand to his face. "I love him. I love my son. You have to believe me."

She moves closer, placing a gentle hand on his shoulder. "I believe you." Vance is a monster, true, but he loved his son. She is the one who does not love, who cannot love, who feels for Eli only a fraction of what she should. Her heart a brilliant red berry that bloomed in the hostility of winter and is now encased in ice.

Vance makes a soft sound that might be a sob. "I was wrong. If I could find him, I'd tell him. I'd bring him home. But he's disappeared. He's hiding from me."

Scarlett squeezes his shoulder. Once, when she stayed the night with Eli, she found Vance sitting in the kitchen in the dark with a gun on the table, staring intently into the dull metal. His moods have become erratic, even more mercurial than usual. But speaking as though Jude is alive is strange, even for him.

"Jude's dead," she murmurs. "We can visit his grave if you want."

He looks up at her with wet eyes. The king laid low by love. A lesson, if there ever was one.

"He's not dead. I sent him away." Vance chokes back a sob. She tenses as he grabs for her, but he just rests his head against her breasts, clutching her close. "It was a mistake. I was wrong."

"You sent him away?" Her hands tremble, perched on Vance's shoulders. "What do you mean?"

He lets the story spill forth, face buried in her bosom. Sketches it in rough, heavy strokes, the bare outline but enough for her to understand.

"I shot him. I shot my son. He was in the hospital with tubes coming from his chest, pumping out the blood, and, even then, I couldn't forgive him. I told him to get out of my city and he did."

"He's alive," she whispers, but Vance doesn't seem to hear.

"Forgive me. I didn't know what I was doing. Please, forgive me."

He's speaking to Jude, but Scarlett runs a hand over his graying hair and answers anyway. "I forgive you."

As she speaks the comforting words, her eyes rest on the drawer where he keeps a loaded pistol. But a quick, painless death is too good for him, for this man who treated her like a beloved daughter while stealing away the one person she loved most. Nothing has ever hurt as much as the news of Jude's death and the quagmire of grief she had yet to escape. And now she has someone to blame for that suffering. Someone who almost broke her and then, when she was lost and lonely, pretended to love her so skillfully she fell for it, quickly and completely.

Killing him is not enough. First, she will take everything he holds dear. First, she will ruin him.

26: The Ambush

RAS WALKS DOWN the slushy Moscow street in the heavy boots he hates to wear because they make his footsteps so loud. The night sky twinkles with stars, the moon absent. He carries enough weapons to fight his way out of an ambush—two guns, a boot knife and a switchblade, a smoke bomb, and a garrote—because he is very likely walking into one right now. A client, unknown to his handler or anyone in their secretive network, asked that he meet in person and in private. He should have said no, but when he found the client was from his city, he was too intrigued to walk away.

Lately, restlessness has been blowing through him like a hot, dry wind, and nothing, not drugs, not sex, not the highly lucrative contract kills, can alleviate it. He'd been hoping for something dangerous and exciting to enter his life, and this invitation could not have come at a better time.

He steps into a ritzy hotel, plush red carpet and gold trim, mirrors on the lobby walls to reflect the well-dressed people milling about. After a short second to memorize the layout should he need to make a quick escape, he takes the stairs in case someone is waiting for him just outside the elevator. The fourth floor was a clever choice, he thinks, as he walks down the hallway. Keep him from escaping out a window if things get dicey.

He knocks on the door, and, immediately, she answers it.

She's existed solely in his mind for more than a year, a phantom he sees when he closes his eyes in the late nights. But his memory is of a younger, softer woman. Had her eyes always been so cold and cruel, her cheeks so gaunt beneath those elegant cheekbones? Had she always been so slender, her collarbones prominent above the low neckline of her white shirt?

Had she always been so beautiful?

"You son of a bitch," she says, standing in the doorway.

It isn't the greeting he would have hoped for, but he understands. He left her. He left Ash. He left his city.

"How could you do that to me?" she whispers. "Vance told me you were dead. I mourned you. I missed you so much I thought I'd die."

"He's not wrong. Jude is dead." Ras brushes past her into the room and walks to the window, restless, agitated. He has become a ghost, he realizes. Heartless. Soulless. He imagines walking right through her and, even then, feeling nothing.

"Jude can't die," she says. "He's a part of you. As long as you're alive, he's alive."

"He's gone. If he were there, I would know."

"He's not gone." She sounds so certain, and he desperately wants to believe her. But this time, for the first time, she is wrong.

"You don't know." He stares out into the rapidly darkening sky. "You don't know how quiet it is now."

"Jude." Gentle arms circle him, the press of her soft body against his back, her low, husky voice in his ear. "Jude. I know you're there. Come back to me. I love you."

Ras spins, pushing her against the wall, agitated at her intolerable tenderness. "You know nothing. Do you think that I loved you? Jude was the one who loved you. And now it's gone."

She takes his hand and puts it over her throat, tilting her head back in a startlingly erotic gesture. "Hurt me, then. If you don't love me, show me."

She stands there, vulnerable and helpless and fearless, maybe because she trusts him so implicitly or maybe because she simply doesn't care about the outcome.

She should be afraid. Without Jude to restrain him, Ras has killed out of anger when his agitation and frustration simply become too much to contain. And why not? Who gives a fuck? All the people on the streets, all the people that he knows, are meaningless and transient as shadows before the sun is high.

"I don't love you," he says, his hand very still on her neck. "I don't give a fuck about you."

Her pulse beats a regular rhythm beneath his fingertips as she waits, cold and distant as a dead star.

"Don't fuck with me," he says, applying gentle pressure, enough to pin her back against the wall, not enough to bruise, not yet. "You think you know who I am? You don't know a fucking thing."

"Then do it."

It is her calm that infuriates him most, the cold distance between them.

"You don't love me," he growls. "I know this now. If you loved me—"

"If I loved you, I would what? Come to Russia and track you down just so I could see you again?"

You would fix me. If you really loved me, you would bring Jude back from the dead.

He tightens his grip, for just a second, but no fear flashes in her eyes. He jerks his hand away, turning from her. Furious at his inability to feel anything for her—a desire to harm her, a desire to hold her.

"Go back home," he says, pushing her away as she attempts to embrace him. His anger is for Jude, but it overflows his meager capacity for emotion, boiling over like a teakettle left unattended and scalding everything nearby.

He stalks away from her, desperate to put distance between them, to avoid the tenderness that should stir him but doesn't. If only he had never shared the world with Jude. This emptiness wouldn't hurt so much if he didn't know what was missing. If he had never seen her through Jude's eyes, she would be just another beautiful woman, one he would fuck, and then forget.

"I don't love you. I don't want you. I didn't ask you to come here. Go the fuck home, Scarlett."

She opens her mouth to speak, then closes it, pressing her lips together in a thin line. She holds out her left hand, where a magnificent diamond sparkles on her ring finger.

"Who?" he growls, his eyes on the shine of the gems.

"Someone who loves me much more than you do."

Jealousy, yes, he can still feel that. Anger, hot and thick as tar, he can feel that too. He grabs her wrist, digging into her skin with hard fingers, and jerks her closer.

"You were dead," she says. Coldly, distantly. "Did you expect me to mourn you forever?"

If she wasn't in danger before, she is now. And oddly enough, even as he tightens his grip on her wrist, his other hand clenched into a fist, a part of him fights back. He wants to hurt her and he doesn't, the impulses warring within him.

"He's good to me," she says. "Better than you ever were. I'm everything to him."

He shoves her backward and she falls onto the bed, brown hair fanning out behind her head as she lies there.

"Don't," Ras says, looking down at her. "I don't love you. I don't want you. I don't want to see you again."

Something like hurt flickers in her eyes, quickly disguised. He turns quickly before he can change his mind and walks out of the room, letting the door drift shut behind him.

HE WANDERS MOSCOW, and, although it is so unlike his city—so gray, so utilitarian—he has found that all cities share a certain social geography; the distance between people narrowing in the press of crowds. The easy exchange of goods, everything from a haircut to a prostitute can be found somewhere.

Ras walks with a restlessness borne of boredom, of his inner emptiness. His long strides devour sidewalks, silent steps leading nowhere. He steps into an alley, a shortcut back to his home, absorbed in his frustration, in his thoughts of Scarlett. He doesn't hear the footsteps behind him until it's too late. He's reaching for his gun when something heavy hits the back of his head with a dull thud of pain, and the world goes dark.

RAS WAKES IN a cell, three solid walls and a line of bars with a padlocked door. The room is frigid, and his coat and scarf have been taken away, along with his phone, gun, and switchblade.

He slowly gets to his feet, wincing at the sharp stab of pain in his temple, and makes his careful, silent way to the door. But the lock is a combination lock, not a key lock, and he scowls in frustration, the lockpick he keeps in his sleeve rendered useless.

He examines the cell. A thin blanket sits atop a frayed mattress about an inch thick. A toilet juts from the wall and a high, narrow window lets in a tiny rectangle of gray light. An old Soviet jail perhaps, one that's fallen into disuse, if the layer of dust covering everything in the room is any indication.

The wall is perfectly smooth, impossible to climb even if the window weren't barred and too narrow. There's nothing he could use as a weapon.

He shouts a few times, leaning against the bars, but no one comes. He fiddles with the combination lock, but it's turned in such a way that he can't see the numbers, even if he could crack the combination.

He yells again, is answered again by silence. He paces the length of the cell like a caged predator, stopping to attempt the combination lock over and over.

Night slips in, and still no one comes as he shivers in the cell and shouts obscenities at whoever's captured him.

The sky gets light and then dark again. He thinks of Scarlett and longing stabs him so acutely that for a moment he can barely breathe. The waiting is breaking him; he wants to howl and beat at the walls with frustration and anger. He is meant to move. He is never meant to stand still, to think, to really feel. But now he does, in the darkest part of the night, beneath a starless sky.

He remembers Ash, his precious heart, his sunrise smile. Imagines him across the vast distance that separates them, leaning over his copy of *War and Peace* with that look of determination he always has when he's reading. He wonders if Ash has missed him, and, for the first time, he truly, deeply misses Ash.

In his pocket, they have left his wallet. He pulls it out and unfolds the piece of paper he keeps there. He brushes a fingertip over Jude's tidy writing. It's not a profound note, just a detail about a job they did, and he isn't sure why he's kept it.

He viciously tears it up and throws the pieces on the ground, where they scatter, stark white against the filthy floor. Then he sits on his mattress, leans his head back against the wall, and thinks of his city, and dreams of home.

Part III

27: One

I DON'T KNOW how long I've been wandering these twisting stone streets, this grimy, graffiti-tagged labyrinth, only that each pathway leads back to the center, to the hollowness of loss, to the raw ache of betrayal. Only that all the doors are boarded up, metal bars in the windows, neon lights jeering: no escape, no escape.

And for a long time, I didn't want to break free. This city is safe, the faceless, indifferent people hurrying past in the rain, no one to fear. No one to love. No one to hate but myself.

But then, as I walked, stepping from corridors of darkness to sallow pools of light beneath yellow streetlamps, I saw her in the distance. Wearing a white dress that clung to the curves of her body, diamonds on her neck and brow, waiting for me. I moved forward and she stepped back, and, like a siren, she lured me through the night. But the apparition didn't last, dissolving into the mist just before the street came to a dead end.

I saw her again and again, luring me farther from the center than I'd ever wandered before, but each time, when I got close, she vanished.

Now, someone steps into my path, blocking the entrance to this alleyway. My own familiar face looks back at me from a distance. My face but not mine.

Ras holds his long knife, turning it to catch the light for a second's sinister gleam. He raises his head to meet my eyes, then glances at the gun in my hand. "You still hate me," he says.

I heft the weapon, studying his features, wondering if I do.

"You hid here like a fucking coward," he continues, "and took every good thing with you. But now, it doesn't matter what you are or what I am. Now we fight. For the last time."

Is this how it's going to be? May the stronger half of my soul win? Which of us would it be? I honestly don't know.

"I'm not afraid of you," I say, and finally, after all these years, it's true.

"You want to punish me. You want to be rid of me." He bares his teeth. "You can fucking try."

"Ras." I cast the gun aside; it slides across the wet ground, far out of my reach. "I don't want to fight."

"You hate me," he says. "You left me."

"I don't hate you." I walk toward him with slow, deliberate steps, my palms open and facing him, to show him I'm not a threat.

"You want to kill me. I'll kill you first." The shadows around him shift restlessly, obscuring his face entirely at moments, casting the angular features into harsh relief at others.

I don't slow my approach, even as he raises the knife with an unsteady hand, and I can see that he is afraid.

Ras never could feel fear.

"I took every good thing for myself," I say. "I'm sorry."

"I'm not." He pushes the knife into my gut and twists it, his jaw set, his eyes the dark green of a deep forest. I laugh softly. He is himself, even at the end.

"I'm going to miss you," I say as he jerks the knife out of the wound. I don't feel any pain, but rather a sense of expansion, of openness, as though it's not blood that flows from me, but my very self.

I step forward, placing my feet where his are resting solidly on the ground; my right onto his left, my left onto his right; and it's like stepping into water, a caress, not a resistance. I hold my breath, and then we breathe together, dissolving into each other, the same inhale, the same exhale, the same beat of the same scarred heart. Until he becomes a part of me and I a part of him. Until his malevolent will becomes instinctive as breathing, easy as love, deliberate as each step I take. It was as though I only had a left hand, and he only a right, and now we have both, his dark and my light, his laughter and my sorrow.

And love. And love. As we merge, I feel his awe at my reckless love for Ash, for Scarlett, for my family. And I feel his wicked, gleeful joy, his love for this life, this world, and I wonder how I ever could have left it. His strength becomes mine, my will becomes his, and everything we are is broken and made whole again.

Then there is no we, no he, nothing in my heart or mind separate from me. I'm no longer Jude, nor am I Ras, but someone new, seeing all the light and dark of the world together, two perspectives, two people, merged.

I OPEN MY eyes slowly, breathing in the frigid air, savoring this first moment of the rest of my life. A soft clicking sound comes from nearby. Elena stands before me, lightly drumming her long fake nails against the concrete wall.

"Hey, baby," she says with a sly, wicked gleam in her eye. "Miss me?"

I try to move, and the rough texture of braided nylon digs into my wrists and ankles. I'm seated in a rickety chair, the metallic back cold against my bare torso, my hands bound behind me and my feet tied to the chair legs.

"Of course I did," I say, keeping my voice neutral and steady. "Didn't you miss me?"

"You know, I really did." She reaches down to pick up one of the knives arrayed on a little table by her side. "We had fun, didn't we, baby?"

She turns the knife so it catches the gleam from the fluorescent light, and I realize just how desperately I want to live. I want to see Scarlett's smile; I want to hold Ash in my arms. I want to hear my mother's laugh and spar with Eli like we used to. I want to walk the streets of my city and feel the rain on my face, the skyscrapers above me shooting up into the thin air of the sky.

I am not going to die here.

I sink into the cold, ruthless clarity that always guided Ras through danger, drawing on his strength and his fearlessness as easily as I breathe.

"Your father..." I say, shifting against the rope lashed around my chest to lean back in the chair, projecting an air of casual assurance. "It was nothing personal."

She shakes her head slowly. "I gave you a chance. All you had to do was tell me Eli fired the gun. Just a few little words and we wouldn't be doing this. But no. You had to go and be a fucking hero."

"So you're just going to kill me?"

"Yeah." She gives me a cold smile. "Eventually."

I remember how Ras learned from her, the confidence he made his own. I want to wear that confidence, to wrap myself in it like a cloak, to arm myself with his strength, and keep close to my heart Jude's tenderness.

Behind my back, I cautiously test the knots holding my wrists. She was never any good at tying knots, and I can feel a little give in the rope, a place where, if I work at it, I might be able to unravel the bindings. I just need to keep her busy until I can get free.

"Lenochka," I say. It was Ras's pet name for her, the diminutive form that implied an affection he always denied. She meant something to him; even through his thick armor of indifference, she mattered. And so she matters to me, because I am him, and every strength of his, and every weakness, is mine.

I look her in the eye and summon as much sincerity as I'm capable of. "Lenochka. I forgive you for this."

Behind my back, I work a single strand free. Progress.

Her eyes widen, and she takes a step back, clutching her knife. "Don't bullshit me, Ras."

"I'm not. You were the first person who saw me for who I really am, the first person who understood me. You taught me so many things. If you're going to kill me today...better you than someone who means nothing to me."

And I mean it, every word, except that I don't intend to die here today. I have too much left to do. Somewhere far away, Scarlett is waiting; Ash is waiting; my city is waiting for me.

Behind me, the rope snags, then tightens, my fingers slipping from the right twist of the knot.

"You killed my father," she says softly. "You spilled the blood of my family. Ras...why couldn't you just tell me it was Eli?"

My fingers scrabble furiously at the knot, but it's getting tighter, not looser. She raises the knife and presses it gently to my chest, not quite breaking the skin, just like she used to do. Only this time, I don't think she'll be holding back.

She pushes the knife forward, blood welling up around the blade, a sharp sting of pain. I force myself to focus on the ropes, the fingers of my left hand trembling as I pick at the nylon cord until it slips too far to the right and I lose the proper angle.

Blood drips off the shining metal as she pulls the blade away and looks me in the eye. I lift my chin and meet her gaze. Behind me, my fingers scrabble for purchase on the knot, barely able to reach it until I realize I can use my right hand—Ras's dominant hand—just as well as my left now. I gently tug at the knot and it starts to slide free. As she raises the knife again, the rope around my hands loosens and falls to the floor.

In one smooth, quick movement, I grab another knife from the little table sitting beside me and swing it forward, driving it into her left eye. She shrieks, stumbling backward, clawing at her face, until her head collides with the cell bars and she slumps to the ground, knocked unconscious.

I untie my legs and stumble free of the chair. I kneel down beside her, pressing my hand to her neck. Her pulse jumps lightly against my fingertips.

"You are going to be so angry with me when you wake up," I whisper to her, and then I call an ambulance from her phone. She'll probably lose that eye, but she'll survive to play this game again another day.

I lean forward and kiss her on the forehead. "Come back to the city," I say. "I'll be waiting for you."

28: Love Like a River

IN THE ENTRYWAY to Scarlett's mansion, Eli puts his hands on her waist and gives her a fond smile, kissing the tip of her nose. She laughs, placing her palms on his chest so she can feel the warmth of his body through his shirt. But her heart is still in Moscow, in that hotel room, hearing Ras say, "I don't love you."

"You know, we could move in together tomorrow," Eli says. "We don't have to wait until we're married."

He's cautiously broached the subject more than once, and, every time, she's quickly changed it. She's not ready to lose her privacy, for him to know how haunted her nights are, how much she drinks in the hours between midnight and sunrise, how often her dreams turn dangerous. All details that she shared effortlessly with Ras and Jude but cannot bring herself to reveal to anyone else.

"My mom needs me here," she says. "Amber needs me. And your parents need you, especially now."

He sighs heavily. "I know, baby. I just wish... I just wish it could be about us for once. Is that selfish?"

"Of course not." She stands on tiptoes to give him a kiss. "Maybe we can do lunch tomorrow."

Eli agrees and says his goodbyes, smart enough to know when he's been dismissed, easy-going enough not to mind.

Upstairs, she stands in front of the full-length mirror in her bedroom, unclasping the elaborate diamond necklace around her neck—one that Ras stole for her in a time that seems so distant it may as well belong to another era. She sets it gently on the dresser and looks back at the mirror.

Ras stands behind her, all in black, silent as a ghost.

She meets his eyes in the mirror, that familiar verdant green. "You came back."

"I missed you."

She wants to look away, knows dimly that she should. He is a riptide, deep and deadly as always, waiting to sweep her away.

She turns, and he stalks toward her like a panther, pushing her roughly against the wall beside the ivory wedding dress hanging on display, waiting for the seamstress to come and alter it.

"You've been busy, haven't you," he says, grabbing the skirt with his fist and jerking, tearing the delicate lace.

"You left me," she replies, her voice growing louder with each word. "I thought you were dead. I mourned you, you son of a bitch."

"You mourned me?" He pins her to the wall, holding her by the shoulder. His hand is warm, firm and unyielding, and a small jolt runs through her to feel his touch. "For how long? How long was it before you started fucking my brother?"

"I love Eli." She can see the words hit him like lashes across the back, his green eyes dark, fierce, intense as always. "He took care of me when you broke my fucking heart."

"You don't have a heart."

"And you don't give a fuck about anyone. Eli loves me. Eli—"

"You are mine." He moves a hand from her shoulder to brush her cheek. "You'll always belong to me."

She lifts her hand, to push him away. To pull him close.

"Say it." His mouth inches from hers, his words desperate. "Say you're mine."

"I'm yours," she whispers.

He presses his lips to hers, to claim her, to beg her, to love her. She meets him with frantic, passionate kisses, like she could fit the thousand endearments she can't say into a few wet moments.

He pulls away, but not far, breathing hard. Surprised as he studies her face. Whereas she had known it would come to this from the moment she heard his voice.

"You should go," she says, thinking for the briefest moment of her betrothed.

"I should." His hands tighten on her waist, and he leans down to kiss her again. She pulls him close. Nothing in her life will eclipse this passion, and nothing, no obligation, no love, no duty, could turn her from it.

In bed, lying beneath him, a soft click sounds, the spring of a shining blade in his hand. He carefully cuts apart her clothes, so he can peel them from her skin. She laughs, helping him open them. His smile is the moment dusk falls and the streetlamps light up as one. The shadows made deeper by the light.

"I love you," he says. The press of his lips—tender enough to break her.

He enters her slowly, reverently, then holds still, their bodies intertwined, letting the perfect moment linger and last.

"Who are you?" she asks, tracing the curve of his ear with a fingertip. He is Ras, and he isn't. He is Jude, and he isn't.

"I'm...I'm both," he says, his voice rough.

She always knew they would merge someday. She wants to ask how, but he thrusts against her, drinking in every movement of her face, every soft gasp, every shudder of pleasure. As an addict might watch the press of a syringe, the spoon, the candle, and the dark bubbling liquid. For all that he might be a prince of the underworld, for each weapon he wields, for every life he's taken, he belongs to her, in this moment and always.

His body shakes against her, moving hard, on the edge but holding back.

"Ras," she says, because the name fits. Because it would be strange to call this man a name that belongs to a boy who died. "Come for me, Ras."

In her thrall as always, he obeys, with a soft groan and an erratic thrust of his hips.

Afterward, he kisses down the length of her body to make love to her again with his fingers and tongue. Then she rides him while he runs a slick hand over her skin and tells her over and over he loves her. They fuck until they're both exhausted, the only words between them murmured endearments, the ecstatic call of a lover's name.

They fall asleep curled together, his head against her breasts, his finger still inside her. Her arms holding him close.

I STAND OUT on Scarlett's balcony as dawn colors the sky pink and she sleeps peacefully in the room behind me. I hold the phone to my ear and let it ring and ring and dial the number again when he doesn't pick up.

"Jesus Christ." Gideon's voice is thick with sleep. "Do you have any fucking idea what time it is?"

"We haven't talked in a year and that's how you say hello?"

He groans. "You couldn't wait a few more hours to call?"

"How is he?"

"I missed you, too, Jude." He sounds more awake now, and annoyed.

"How is he?"

"He's fine. I would have let you know if he wasn't."

I close my eyes and breathe out a long sigh of relief.

"He's doing great, actually," Gideon continues. "He's sober now. Took the money you gave him and went to rehab. He's even got a job. Works as a barista in a little coffee shop in Bayside."

I smile, but the feeling expanding in my chest is as much bitter as sweet. Was it really so good for him to have me gone? Was my absence what it took for him to get the life he always wanted?

"I'm not the only one keeping an eye on him," Gideon says. "Your dad's had someone watching him for the last couple of months. Probably hoping you'd show your face. I don't think Ash is in any danger, but you should be careful."

"I will be," I murmur, heart sinking. I want desperately to see him, to take him in my arms and hold him. That would be enough, just his body pressed against mine and the solid, breathing fact of his existence. But it would put him in danger. "Thank you, Gideon."

"I'll let you know if anything changes. And Jude— welcome back."

"Who was that?" Scarlett asks, standing in the doorway in a red silk robe.

"Gideon Brooks." I step toward her, putting my hands on her waist so I can feel the silk of the robe slip over the hot skin beneath. "He's my father's accountant. He's...watching over someone for me."

"Ash?" she asks.

I raise an eyebrow, surprised she'd know his name and worried about what she thinks now that she knows. "How did you find out about him?"

"Your father told me everything. I really wish you had told me, back then. I would have understood."

"I still love you," I say. "Both of you."

I hope she won't ask me to choose. I don't think I could. I can't keep those loves in separate boxes anymore, they twist and tangle together until I can't imagine one without the other. My love for Ash is bright and warm as a summer's day, the heat of the sun on bare skin, a sky blue and shining and endless. My love for Scarlett is a winter night, the sky hung with stars, the ground blanketed in luminous snow beneath a heavy moon. They are the two halves of my heart, and, without either, I would be incomplete.

"Ash is a good person, isn't he?" she asks, turning from me to look out at the perfectly manicured grounds beneath her balcony.

"Yes," I say. "The best of people."

"I thought so."

She's quiet for a long moment, and, when she finally speaks, her voice is as cold and clear as the striking of a chime, cutting through the morning chill.

"I need you to do something. I need you to do it for Ash and for me. For Eli and for your mother." She presses her hands to the railing and leans forward, her hair blowing in the slight breeze. "I've been laying the plans for months. Everything is ready, Ras. I just need you."

"What for?"

She releases the railing and turns, slowly, deliberately, to face me. "To take over the syndicate. To kill your father and step into his place."

She's deadly serious, her eyes on mine, her expression grave and solemn. She means it, every word.

I take a step back, out of her reach. "This is what you wanted." All the time we spent together, the favors she asked me for, the hits we did, all of it was to lead up to this one moment. "This is what you've always wanted. And Eli won't turn against Vance, so you need me."

"All I wanted was for you to be alive again," she whispers, tears shimmering in her eyes. "You died and it broke my heart. You can't expect me just to tape it back together and love you the way I used to."

"So that's it?" I take another step back until I bump up against the closed glass door. "Now I'm just a means to an end?"

She's silent for a few moments, her eyes on mine, and I can see her thinking, calculating, planning. "I love you. I love you more than I can ever say, but I'd be lying if I said I'm doing this for you. If you don't want to help me, I'll...understand. I won't try to force you into it."

Last night, lying in her arms, I could feel her love. For once, she didn't try to hide it. She used to be desperate for any signs of my affection, and hid her own, as though love was a transaction and she didn't want to give more than she received, for fear of running out. Now, she's different. Maybe my death made her stronger, more confident, more able to give and trust that she will receive in turn. Or maybe it was Eli's love that helped her grow, or maybe it was neither of us, but rather the power she's gained helping my father run the syndicate from the shadows.

She steps toward me, looking up at me with her brown-sugar eyes shining. "You believe me, don't you?"

"Yes." I am a means to an end for her, but that's not all I am. She gives me what love she's capable of giving, and that will always be enough. "But taking over the syndicate isn't as easy as walking into Vance's office and shooting him. Do you have any idea how big it is? How many people we would need to—"

"Of course I do," she says. "I told you, I have a plan."

I believe her, of course. She's smarter than I am, and more ruthless, and if she says it's possible, then it's possible.

There's something strangely compelling about the idea. Before I ran away, everything I did was to succeed in the syndicate so that someday Vance and I would run it together. The contract kills in London and Moscow and across the globe were not as meaningful or satisfying as my work in the Warrens, where people knew me and liked me, where there was a sense of community, of honor among thieves. Where I could walk those dark, dingy streets and feel like I was coming home.

As long as Vance is still at the helm, there will be no place in the syndicate—or in the city—for me.

I tell her I'll do it, and she smiles. If I don't take care of Vance, I'll never be able to see Ash or my mother again. And part of me burns with an anger time and distance have not been able to diminish. I do it for my city, because this is the only way to make the city mine again. But most of all, I do it for her.

"WE NEED TO win over the people on the streets," she says, and we do. Quinn shrieks with surprise when I walk back into her bar, and after she punches me and gives me a tearful hug, she joins our cause immediately, giving me the information I need to get started. She reignites the old rumors about Ras that used to float around the streets of the Warrens and adds some new ones. With a little incentive, the tall tales start to spread.

The man Vance appointed to replace me as supervisor is a tyrant, as coldhearted as I was kind and universally despised. When I kill him, I take his list of contacts—pimps, drug dealers, gun smugglers from the Stacks—and make a lot of new friends.

In exchange for a little cocaine and the promise of my protection, the tabloids publish sensational stories until the name Ras is known across the city. The street kids spray paint my smiley face wherever they go, until I've marked every slum from Bayside to Ghost Town. My father might not know it's me, but he knows someone is coming for him.

"We need to cause trouble for Vance," she says, and we do. Blowing up a warehouse full of drugs—after moving the goods, of course. Strangling his most loyal bodyguard, a man I'd known since I was a child, one I'd never been particularly fond of. Gutting his most proficient drug smuggler, leaving him to bleed out on the bow of a ship after stealing every ounce of the heroin he brought into the city.

I always sign my work—love, Ras. It's to spread notoriety, Scarlett tells me, but I think she also wants to taunt my father, to fuck with his head, to see him brought low. She never says anything, but I can see the anger in her eyes, jagged and sharp as a broken shard of ice when she talks about him.

"We need the suits," she says, and we get them—as much her doing as mine. The syndicate people embezzling from major corporations, rigging bids for construction jobs, bribing public officials, these men and women with their Armani and their Rolexes, have all chafed under Vance's new, relentlessly aggressive regime. Scarlett takes them to three-martini lunches and steakhouse dinners and speaks their language, the language of money. A few are hesitant, but the corpse of the man who refused to work with us—

slumped over his desk, blood running into his keyboard—makes a compelling argument. You're with us or against us, we tell them. There is no third option. All but the dead one switch to our side.

"We need the support of a few lieutenants," she says, and we get it. With a bribe to the lieutenant in charge of drug distribution of a few hundred thousand dollars—pocket change from Scarlett's vast fortune. With a knife fight—and a long but shallow cut along my right arm—to prove to the half-mad lieutenant in charge of gun smuggling that I'm "worthy" of his loyalty. With a few corpses to show the lieutenant in charge of prostitution that I'm not fucking around. And with the lieutenant in charge of information, who I've known since I was little, all it takes is a promise. To take my father's life. Scarlett promises me she has a plan for the other six, who will fall into line once my father is dead.

I don't think about him, don't picture him in his office, pacing by the window, wondering how control of his syndicate is slipping away from him like the tide receding to sea. Wondering who he can trust as I persuade more and more of his most important people to join me.

I tell myself this isn't about him. This is about Scarlett and me and what belongs to us. What we've earned, after months of waging this relentless campaign. What I deserve, after years working for the syndicate. After a lifetime of training.

29: Estate of Unrest

IF JUDE WOULD only come back, everything would right itself. The chaos Vance has been fighting these last two months would be resolved; that elusive, infuriating trickster who calls himself Ras would be no match for the missing son. And yet somehow he has proven a match for Vance, a king whose pawns are rapidly depleting, the chessboard emptying.

Soon. It will all come to a head soon.

He watches from the windows in his office as a thunderstorm casts jagged bolts of lightning at the city below. How could Jude, talented and smart as he was, so thoroughly disappear?

Scarlett hands him a whiskey without asking and stands by his side. The flashes of light throw her features into sharp, almost ghostly, relief.

"I couldn't find anything at the harbor," she says. "I'm sorry."

"Don't worry about it." He's galled but not surprised that Ras has pulled off another heist without a hitch.

"I feel like I'm failing you," she says, a surprisingly earnest note to her voice.

"You're not." He believes this completely. "If there was something to be found, you would've found it."

She nods, her eyes downcast. She's been acting strange lately, prone to long, melancholy silences. And not nearly as efficient or helpful as she usually is. It makes him wonder if

Eli knocked her up, if that's the reason for their sudden engagement and too-soon wedding.

"A storm's coming," he says, staring out the window. "Coming for me."

"For us," she says. And normally she'd be right. She earned her place by his side, the place where Jude should stand, the place that still feels so vacant, despite her strong presence.

"You're gonna sit this one out, sweetheart." Although he knows this might be his last fight, he feels no fear, just a steely resolve for the confrontation to come.

"I want to be by your side."

"I know." He glances over at her, the daughter he never had. "But Ras is gonna come after me when I'm alone." It's exactly what Vance would do if their roles were reversed. "Don't you worry. I'll be ready for him."

She holds her chin high, her gaze regal and steely, wearing an elegance that belongs to a bygone era. "I know you will."

"I want you to stay at the house for the next few days. While Eli's gone, I need to be able to keep an eye on you."

Eli is in Russia, investigating Ras's mysterious past and trying to figure out what the hell happened to Elena Nikitichna, who vanished without a trace. Vance thinks it's a dead end and that they could have had someone less vital take the trip, but Scarlett insisted it be Eli. He's supposed to be there another week, but Vance decides he'll bring his son home earlier, to make sure someone is guarding Scarlett around the clock. Maybe Eli can surprise her. Vance used to do things like that for his wife—flowers, fancy dinners, gifts. Sweet memories turned bitter by time and Nikita's betrayal. He should have done the cheating bastard in himself.

"Vance." Scarlett is turned toward him, her face tilted upward to meet his eyes. "I have to tell you something." Her hands are clenched at her sides, and she takes a deep breath.

"What is it?"

Her eyes dart away from him, and she presses her lips together, as though fighting some internal battle.

"I..." She struggles for words—the first time he's ever seen her speechless. "I want to tell you..." She lets out a long sigh and her fists unclench, as though she's come to some decision. "We all make sacrifices to get what we want. Don't we?"

"Sure," he says, a little worried by the intensity of her gaze.

"You've been like a father to me," she says, her eyes wide and shining. "Whatever you've done, whatever I've done...it's been good to know you."

It feels oddly like a goodbye when she kisses him on the cheek and walks out the door. But he doesn't dwell on it, turning back to his city, under siege by the storm.

30: The Prodigal Son

SCARLETT STANDS ON Eli's balcony, the garden beneath her awash in moonlight. Ras has a single red rose for her; he tucks it into her hair and gives her a kiss.

"It's time," she says with regret and eager breathless anticipation. Eli should still be in Russia for a few more days, and all their plans have fallen into place. There's only one thing left to do. It's time to cut the head off the serpent.

"I know," he says, and, for once, she can't read his expression. "I'm ready."

"I'll draw him out. Tomorrow evening, you can meet us at—"

"No," he says, in a tone too confident to have belonged to Jude and too serene to have been Ras's. As though, in their coming together, the two halves of him made more than the sum of their parts. "It has to be me. Alone."

"He's dangerous," she says uneasily.

He gives a dark, bitter chuckle. "So am I."

"Ras." She reaches for him, but he catches her hand, lifts it, and presses a kiss to the palm like he did the first time they met. And she finds everything she wanted to say falling away from her.

He asked her if this had been her plan all along—seduce the boss's son and use him as a ladder to reach the highest echelons of the syndicate. She doesn't know how to tell him it isn't true, how to say "I love you" the way that he does, with utter, boundless sincerity. But she feels it. She feels it like the wind beneath the wings of a bird in flight when Ras kisses her, like the fond warmth of home and hearth when she wakes up in the mornings to see Eli lying beside her. She loves them both, in her way, or so she thinks she does. Is it really love if she's unwilling to sacrifice her ambition for their happiness? Is it really love if she's unable to choose between them, but rather lets herself lie to Eli to keep him in her arms? After she's killed their father, will they really believe that she ever loved them? And yet, she does. A selfish love. A love like poison, but a love nevertheless.

"He's in the east wing," Ras says. "Wait for an hour, then come down."

"I will." She gives him a kiss and hopes it won't be the last. She's not afraid that he will fail, but once his father is dead on the ground, he might never forgive her for starting this war. "Ras, I—"

"Stop right there." Eli's low voice comes from within the room behind her.

Go, she mouths at Ras, and he swings his legs over the balcony's railing and climbs down into the night before Eli can see his face.

Eli darts past her, leaning over the railing into the darkness, his gun drawn. He lingers there for a moment, then spins and directs a hard glare at Scarlett.

"You're back early," she murmurs.

"I came back to surprise you," he growls. "And this is what I find? Is this why you wanted me to go to Russia in the first place? So you could fuck around behind my back?"

"Eli," she says softly. "It's not what you think."

"It's not?" He slides his gun back into the holster and then his hard hands are on her shoulders, digging his fingertips into the skin left bare by the thin straps of her tank top. "Then what is it?"

"He's a friend. That's all."

Eli shoves her against the wall, the cold stone rough against her back. "Don't fucking lie to me. That was Ras. You said his fucking name. You're not just cheating. You're sleeping with the fucking enemy."

"It's not like that."

His hand closes around her neck, gentle pressure from his fingertips resting heavily on her throat. "You fucking whore. It isn't enough for you to cheat, is it? You've been selling all our secrets. I should fucking kill you right here."

He tightens his fingers, just slightly, his eyes wet and fierce. Moving carefully, she slips his gun out of its holster and wraps her fingers around the grip, pressing it gently against his stomach.

He takes a half step back, looking at her with an expression of stunned betrayal. Then his hand darts between them, and in a smooth, practiced motion that takes only a few seconds to execute, he jerks the gun out of her hand.

"Is that what it's going to be like?" he growls, holding the weapon in a fist so tight his knuckles are pale, the barrel pointed downward.

"You threatened me." Scarlett feels the same kind of betrayal that is written on his face, the ghostly impression of his fingers on her throat still lingering. She always thought Eli would be better than that. Out of all the violent men she knows, she thought he would be different.

"You've been telling him everything, haven't you?" Eli says. "I trusted you. Dad trusted you. And now..."

One hour, she thinks, imagining Ras creeping through the dark mansion, stalking Vance through the shadows. Keep Eli busy for one hour, and they will have won this final battle.

"Let's talk about this," she whimpers, forcing herself to cry. The tears come forth with unsettling ease. "Please, Eli. I can explain everything."

AROUND ME, THE hallway is silent. No soft brushes of footsteps on the dark green carpet, no huff of breath, no rustle of clothing. But a fragment of a second before I strike, he knows I'm there. His body tenses as though from an electric jolt, and I dart back into a dark alcove, knife in my unsteady hand.

"Come out," he says, drawing his gun and pointing it at the shadows that conceal me.

I move into the light and he pales, his mouth half open as he looks me over.

"Jude," he whispers.

"My name is Ras," I say, clenching my fingers tightly around the handle of my knife. I feel the shock and horror and shame on his face as keenly as though it were in my own heart, but I don't let go of my weapon.

"No," he murmurs. "I can't believe that."

I step forward. "Believe it. You made me what I am."

"All this time... It was you all this time?"

"Yes."

He raises his gun. "Don't come any closer. We can talk this out, son."

I ignore him, taking another step forward. "I'm not your son." My hands tremble with rage or pity or sorrow. "Your son is dead."

"Don't," he says, so authoritatively I almost obey. But I force myself to take another step. And another. Until the barrel of his gun is pressed directly into my chest, his hand white-knuckled around the grip. I feel the ghost of another gunshot, thinking of the dull metal of the bullet still lodged in my heart. Did he want me to die? Or did he just mean to take away the man I love?

"Go ahead," I say, fury rising through me like steam. "Shoot me again. I love Ash, and once this is done, I'm going to find him and I'm never going to leave him. So shoot me. Show me how much you love me."

He takes a deep, unsteady breath. "This isn't you, Jude."

"My name is Ras," I say. As steady and assertive as he ever was. I know who I am now, and I'm not afraid.

"Your name is Jude." He carelessly throws his gun aside, a strange peacefulness coming over his face. "I know. I raised you."

My anger dissipates quickly, even as I try to fan its flames. He's speaking so gently, like the father I remember, the one who taught me to shoot and to throw a punch, the one who was always so proud of me. The one who loved me.

"I'm going to kill you," I say, as much to convince myself as him.

"Why is that?" he asks. Calmly, curiously.

"You took my childhood from me," I tell him, in this dark hall in this dark house where I ran military drills every day of my life until I was old enough to leave, where I first killed a living being, where I strove and strove to be what he wanted me to be. "You made me into a monster."

He raises his eyebrows and speaks gently but firmly, imparting a lesson. "Where do you think you would be without me? You wouldn't be here, that's for sure. You wouldn't be on the verge of taking over the syndicate at nineteen years old."

Is he right? He made me what I am—the man who loves the game, the strategy, the hunt, the bloody victories of our tireless coup. Who would I be without his guidance?

"You shot me," I say harshly, trying to rekindle that fury he so easily dispelled. "You tried to kill Ash. You made Scarlett think I was dead."

"You tell me you love that boy. What would he think if he could see you right now? What would your mother think?"

For a moment, I see them, the sorrow in my mother's eyes the night I came back from my first kill, the feel of her fingers as they squeezed mine hard enough to hurt. And Ash with his kind heart—he can never know. If he did...

"They would want me to stop," I whisper.

"I know, son," Vance says with the kind of compassion and understanding I might never find again. "They don't love you, the real you, the way I do. They don't understand you like I do."

He's right. I know this, in a deep-down weary way. To my mother, I'm a wayward son. To Ash, a thug with a secret heart of gold. And to Scarlett—inscrutable, ruthless—I'm a weapon she doesn't have to understand to fire. Only my dad could understand the kind of monster I've become. Only he could see the depths of it and still find something to love.

He puts a hand on my shoulder. "I'm not going to tell you to stop. There's only one thing between you and the glory you've always wanted."

I love him. Even as the part of me that was once Ras howls for vengeance, even as Scarlett's commands echo in my ear, that love flows through me like a hidden current, one that runs so deep I'd almost forgotten it.

Could love be enough?

The dull light glints on the blade of my knife as I raise it with a trembling hand.

He laughs softly but with bitterness absent. "No crime boss lives to a ripe old age. Go ahead. Do what you have to."

I draw a shaky breath. There's no separating my soul here, no dark waters to swallow the light, to drown the love so I don't feel a thing. My shadowed half and my sunlit heart meet and intertwine, tangling together, bleeding into each other.

This is the truth of me, here, my knife, my city, my father.

I press the blade forward.

"Damn, son." Dad coughs once, blood appearing on his lips. Resignation in his eyes but no surprise.

"I'm sorry," I whisper.

He shakes his head. "I love you, Jude." His head slumps forward, then raises again, slowly. "I'm...proud of..."

Two more rattling, bloody breaths, and his body stumbles forward into my arms, heavy in death.

I lay him out on the floor, gently drawing his eyelids closed like heavy curtains in a mourning house. I press one hand to the tall window looking out over my mother's garden and lean on it, laughing. Harsh, broken bursts of laughter that sound almost like sobs.

The torrent swells, then passes, and I calm, looking out over the rosebushes. When I was very little, I cried over a rose I had broken off one of those stems. It was the first thing I ever killed. Eli tried to fix it for me, but when I went back to see it the next day, I learned the truth.

You can't fix a rose.

Out in the garden, I picture a dead rose among the snarl of thorny vines, discarded on the indifferent ground, petals shriveling brown and falling, one by one, away. I wonder if the same rosebush still blossoms down there, missing a beautiful crimson flower.

I SIT THERE, in the dark hall, leaning my back against the wood-paneled wall hung with pastoral landscapes in their fancy frames. I don't know how long I wait, or what I'm waiting for, as clouds slowly cover the stars outside the window and muffle the bright disc of the moon.

After some indeterminate amount of time I hear the soft, careful shuffle of house slippers.

I lean my head back against the paneling and close my eyes. I'm not ready for it when the lights flick on and my mother gasps. She runs toward me, stumbling, and kneels at my side.

"Jude," she whispers, pulling me into her arms. I lean limply against her. "My baby. Scarlett told me you were alive, but I needed to see with my eyes."

"Mom." My voice is choked with emotion, but I hear it distantly, like an echo without a source. "Dad's dead."

"Oh, Jude." She puts her hands on either side of my face. "My baby. My sweet boy. You set me free."

Just past her, my father lies still and lifeless.

"I'm sorry I left," I murmur, resting my head in the crook of her neck. "I'm sorry I didn't tell you."

"Shh." She runs a gentle, soothing hand over my hair. "Is okay. Scarlett explained everything to me. I understand."

One more set of footsteps sounds nearby, the clack of high heels on the wooden floor, and then Scarlett appears at the end of the hallway, Eli behind her, his gun drawn, moving silently as always.

"Dad," he says, and in his voice is the emotion I should be feeling, as he crosses the hall and stumbles to his knees beside the corpse. "Dad," he says again brokenly. And then he looks up and sees me for the first time.

He stands, towering over me, aiming his gun at my head. "You're Ras," he says, low and cold. "Of course you are. I should have seen it coming."

"Eli," Mom says, standing quickly and stepping between us. "Please."

He brushes her aside with a sweep of his free arm, the gun still trained on me. She stumbles and catches herself against the wall, but Eli doesn't even glance at her. "Get up," he says to me. "You're going to dig a fucking grave."

I lean my head back against the wall and look numbly up at him. "You don't have to point a gun at me. I want to do it."

Mom finds us a spot on the grounds, at the base of a weeping willow, and gathers a few shovels from a nearby shed. Eli helps me wrap Vance's corpse in a thick woolen blanket so we can carry my father out into the garden and lay him beside a row of thorny rosebushes nearby, to wait while we dig.

While I break the ground and Eli watches me with a cold, reptilian hatred, Scarlett kneels beside Vance's corpse and kisses his forehead, pressing her hand to his cheek for a second before she takes his gun and everything from his pockets.

"You don't need to watch this," she says, with a hand on Mom's arm. "Let's go back to the house. They'll be okay."

Mom nods. She's starting to turn pale, averting her eyes from the corpse, and she lets Scarlett lead her away.

"You could help me," I say to Eli as I dig.

"Fuck you." His hand rests purposefully on the butt of his gun, in his holster but still clearly a threat. "You faked your own death just so you could come back and take over the syndicate. You killed our dad. How fucking sick is that?"

"That's not what this is." The shovel bites into the soft soil, and I lift it, letting the dirt rain down onto the pile behind me.

"Then what happened? Explain it to me, Jude, because this doesn't make a lot of fucking sense."

"Does it matter?" I just feel weary, like I've been treading water for so long I can't remember standing on dry land. The temptation to simply let myself sink is almost irresistible.

He draws the gun. "It matters."

I drive the shovel into the dirt and turn to him. "Dad shot me in the heart and he couldn't kill me. If you think you can do better, go ahead."

"That's a fucking lie," he growls. "Dad loved you more than anything in the world. And you killed him."

I pick up the shovel again and resume digging. I don't want to have this conversation. Even if he knew what happened, even if he'd been standing in that same room with me, it wouldn't matter. He's made up his mind about me.

I dig in silence until the hole is deep enough, my mind mercifully blank. This isn't what I thought I'd be doing the night Scarlett and I finally won the syndicate, but it seems better to laugh at the absurdity than to cry at the tragedy of my own making.

"Do you have any last words?" Eli asks.

I raise an eyebrow, standing at the edge of the grave. "Are you going to shoot me?"

"Yeah," he says with a grim look in his eye I recognize too well. He only wears it when he's about to do something he knows he'll regret. "So if you've got something to say, you'd better fucking say it now."

I tell him I love him. Not because I hope he'll let me go—he's too far gone for that. But I hope some part of him will hear it all the same.

"Don't fucking lie," he says.

Movement behind him catches my eye, a slender, silent figure, but I keep my gaze focused on his face.

"I'm not," I say. "I always loved you, and I never meant to hurt you."

"You—" He flinches as Scarlett reaches him and jabs a needle into the side of his neck, the horse tranquilizer she uses on the rare occasions when she has to do this kind of work. She catches him as he crumples, staggering beneath his weight, and I help her lower him to the ground. She tosses me a rope and I tie his hands while she takes his gun and tucks it into her waistband, the two of us working as harmoniously and seamlessly as we always do.

"Thank you," I say.

"He'll be out for a while." She glances at my father's corpse. "Let's finish this."

I lower the body into the grave as gently as I can and fill it in while Scarlett watches silently. I wish I could read the expression on her face. Does she feel as wrung out as I do?

She takes my father's favorite gun, the gleaming, intricately inlaid silver pistol, and pushes it into the ground to make a sort of headstone. We stand beside the mound of dirt, and I struggle to think of something to say.

"Here's to you," Scarlett says, Vance's flask in her hand. She drinks and passes it to me. "You black-hearted son of a bitch. May you rot in hell." She huffs a soft laugh. "Someday, we'll see you there." She says it gently, almost tenderly, like a eulogy.

"I'll see you in hell," I repeat, looking down at the mound of dirt. Speaking softly, almost reverently, as though it's a promise, not a curse.

"We'll take down the devil, you and me," she whispers, taking the flask of whiskey from me and kneeling on the grave. "We'll be unstoppable."

She lifts the flask to her lips again, then turns to me, her eyes shimmering in the fading light. "Give me a minute."

I suppose that's my cue to start dragging Eli back to the house. He's heavier than our father, broader and more solidly built, and I'm exhausted from carrying Vance's corpse, digging, and the sheer surreality of this night.

Eli's stirring when Scarlett finds me at the house. I've got him tied securely to a chair in his bedroom.

"What are we going to do with him?" I ask her.

She puts her hand on my cheek and gives me a strained smile. "He's going to leave the city. Or else."

"And if he comes back?"

Her eyes meet mine, serene and confident. "Then we'll be ready."

31: The True Heart

THE TRAIN RIDE from the University in Bayside back to Ash's apartment in Ghost Town takes more than an hour, and tonight, like most nights, Ash is eager to be home. He leans against the window and stares out at the tenements and suspended billboards flying past. Beside him, a girl with giant pink headphones is reading a thick paperback, feet tapping energetically against the floor, and all around them the clouds close in like gray cotton stuffing, filling the sky. The rain, slapping its sparkling droplets against the window, always reminds him of Jude. It brings him back to that too-short spring, Jude stepping into their apartment from the smog and stink of the city, smelling like fresh rain.

He hurries the three blocks from the train station to his apartment, the rain assaulting him, with water and with memories, of how Jude liked to walk the wet streets, pulling him along and laughing, saying how beautiful the city was like this. With Jude, the city was full of wonders; without him, it has become haunted, long nights in a place where the neon lights never go out, where the roar from the freeway never ceases. Without Jude and without the drugs, he's assaulted by the unrelenting bleakness, the poverty, the suffering.

After Jude, it was as though the drugs stopped working. He couldn't slip into the purple benzo twilight where nothing mattered, where he floated indifferently above the world. And the euphoria from the opiates had a flat, dull edge. For a time, Ash wanted to die, but Jude had paid for Ash's life with his own, and Ash could never betray that sacrifice.

Instead, he decided to live. He took the money Jude gave him and used it for rehab, not college, and got sober. A last act of devotion for someone who could never know he'd done it. After he successfully completed the inpatient treatment, he visited Jude's grave to tell him but, instead, stood at the edge of the grave for half an hour, unable to speak. Consumed with guilt for the way he'd run, leaving his lover to die in that shitty apartment with only his bastard father for company. He wishes he could visit Jude's grave more often but knows Jude's father might be there. And after all that Jude sacrificed to save him, he wouldn't put his life in danger again.

He clatters up the exterior staircase to the third floor, fumbles with his keys, and finally gets the door open. He's so glad to be out of the downpour that it takes a moment to register that the lights are already on. A black coat hangs on one of his two rickety chairs, dripping onto the linoleum. Beside it, a dozen roses. He brushes his thumb over one of the red flowers, more curious than afraid. Then he looks up at the man standing in the doorway to his bedroom and drops his keys and backpack to the floor with a jingle and a thud.

He stares across the suddenly vast space between them. He can feel his grip on reality starting to waver, because this green-eyed ghost looks so real. "You're dead."

"I was." Jude walks toward him. There's an easy grace in the way he moves now, fluid and languid as a cat. A confidence to the set of his shoulders, a touch of arrogance in the tilt of his chin. A spark of deviousness in his eyes. Lacking the exuberance of the Jude who grinned and swaggered and made Ash feel both helpless and giddy at the same time, and the quiet intensity of his counterpart. He is both and neither now.

"I thought you were dead," Ash says. "You let me think you were dead. I...that was the worst thing that's ever happened to me."

"I'm sorry," Jude says, and Ash is reminded how much he loves that Jude is a few inches shorter and has to tilt his head upward for a kiss. He is reminded how sincere Jude can be, how he can make promises and truly mean them, how he'd say the sweetest nothings with no trace of humor whatsoever.

"My father is dead," Jude tells him. "He died just a few days ago. I would have come to see you sooner, but I didn't want to lead him here."

"Shit," Ash murmurs. "I'm sorry." Both for Jude's loss and the swell of relief Ash feels now that the man who tried to kill him is gone.

"Don't be. I'm not." Jude picks up the financial aid forms on the table and crumples them up, tossing them in the trash can in the kitchen. "You're not going to need that."

"Jude..."

"The flowers are for you." Jude steps closer, close enough to touch. "I've missed you, Ash."

Ash blinks back tears, vision blurring. "I used to lie in bed and imagine that you were next to me. I would pretend as hard as I could that you were lying there beside me and tell myself that as long as I didn't look over there, you'd be there. But eventually I'd have to look. And you were never there."

Jude pulls him close, and he buries his face in Jude's shoulder. "I'm here now," Jude says.

"Where were you?"

"I wandered, for a while," Jude says. Ash studies the lines of his face, drinking in his presence, his features gaunter now, more angular and sharp. Ash's heart beats a singular rhythm. He's alive. He's alive. He's alive.

"Why didn't you tell me?" Ash whispers. "You could have sent a postcard—Hey Ash, stop mourning. I'm not really dead. Something. Do you know how hard it was to get over you?"

Jude gets very still, meeting his eyes. "Have you gotten over me?"

Ash doesn't answer, torn between the impulse to throw Jude out of his apartment and the yearning to hold him close enough to feel his heart beat.

"I should tell you something else. My name, my...real name, is Ras."

"You're Ras?" Ash takes a step back, thinking of all the rumors he's heard on the streets. Of Jude always saying he'd let Ras take care of any trouble, and the violent implication that went unspoken. "All this time?"

"Yes. All of those terrible things, I'm the one who did them. And I'm not sorry."

Ash considers himself a good person, a moral person. Doesn't everyone? And yet his first impulse is not to think of Ras's victims, but of his own broken heart.

"Why did you lie to me?" he asks. "Did you think I'd leave you?"

"I thought you might."

"I wouldn't." Ash steps closer, enthralled as he's always been by those green eyes, the color of a coiled jungle snake. "I know there's good in you."

Jude puts a hand on the side of Ash's face, solemnly brushing a thumb over his cheekbone. "You are the good in me."

Ash leans his cheek against the warmth of Jude's palm, and when Jude hooks his other hand around his waist and pulls him close for a kiss, he wants to cry because he spent the last year willing to sell his soul to have just one more night like this, and, in the end, it costs him nothing.

32: Queen of the World

VANCE'S OFFICE—OR the office that was once his—shines in the orange glow of the late-afternoon sun, huge and dipping in the west.

Scarlett stands by the window, silhouetted in the light. Looking down at the city below, imagining her syndicate—they may call Ras the boss, but the syndicate is hers; she took it, she earned it—spreading through it like a virus through a vital bloodstream. It's a symbiotic relationship, she thinks. The city and the syndicate, intertwined from the very beginning, from the first quarry workers who decided that crime paid more than backbreaking labor and formed an organization that would endure longer than they could imagine.

The door opens and Ras walks in, giving her a wide, cheerful smile. He was probably with Ash last night—she knows he wouldn't stay away any longer than he had to. She finds it doesn't bother her as much as she expected it to. After all, the love she had for Eli never made her love Ras any less.

He stands behind her at the window, puts his arms around her, and pulls her back against his chest.

"I can't believe we made it," she says, leaning into his warmth. She knew her plan would work, but it still feels unreal to stand here, the victor, the queen.

"We made it," he says, and he sounds as satisfied as she feels. "And we made it really fucking good."

"You did good, boss," she says.

He chuckles, a low, dark sound in her ear. "We both know better than that."

"What do you mean?"

"I mean we both know who's in charge. It's not me."

She turns in his arms, facing him, his hands lingering on her waist. "You're going to have to work on that attitude if you're going to be the syndicate boss."

"Maybe I don't want to be the boss." A sly smile plays on his features. "It's all paperwork and meetings."

"This isn't really the time to have an identity crisis," Scarlett says gently but firmly. "Your lieutenants are going to be here soon." Four of the ten know Ras and have aided his guerrilla campaign. Fear has to be enough to persuade the rest to pledge their loyalty to the new boss.

"You don't know me as well as you think you do," Ras says. There's a slight sharpness to his voice. "Growing up, I never wanted to be the boss. I never even thought about it, because if I was the boss, it would mean my father was dead."

"Oh," she says softly. She feels that grief too—not as keenly as he does. She's not capable of that, but she feels something for the man who was the closest thing to a father she's ever known. A quiet, dignified sadness nestled close to her cold heart.

"I wanted to be Vance's consul," he says. "That was my ambition. Now...I'd be your consul, if you let me."

She blinks at him, startled out of her grief by the offer. "You want me to be the boss?"

"You already are. I just want to make it official."

She has wanted this so desperately it's hard to believe someone could simply give the title away as nonchalantly as he has just done. Does it really mean so little to him? Or is he simply willing to make such a sacrifice because he can see how she wants it?

And then there are other concerns. The lieutenants who are probably already on their way expect to be led by Ras; the people who work on the streets know his name and his reputation. No one knows who she is.

And yet...that could be an advantage. It's harder to cut the head off of a serpent when you don't know where to find it. Ras would still be there, the face of the syndicate and its heart, while she would be the mind, ruthless and untouchable.

It only takes a few seconds for her mind to run through the logistical challenges, weighing her options, constructing solutions, making a final decision.

"Okay," she says, putting her arms around his neck. And then she laughs with the sheer giddy realization that after all she has sacrificed, all she has fought, she's made it here. He is alive, and she is alive, and they've won. "Okay. I'll be the boss."

"Good." He gives her a kiss and lets her go as the first knock on the door sounds, a heavy thump through the wide room.

The lieutenants arrive all at once, which is concerning. It may be a simple coincidence, or it's possible they coordinated this ahead of time. Whatever the reason, the office is soon filled with the ten lieutenants and their bodyguards—most have at least one.

"Where's the boss?" asks Paulie, the barrel-chested, baby-faced man in charge of forgeries and counterfeiting. He's never liked Scarlett, never approved of the presence of a woman in what he obviously believes should be an exclusively men's world.

"Jude?" another man says incredulously, staring at Ras. A bodyguard of one of the lieutenants, someone Scarlett has never met, but of course Ras would know him. Before his death, he knew everybody.

"My name is Ras now," Ras replies, and the room is filled with soft murmurs of surprise and worry, hands dipping low to wait by the butts of guns in hip holsters.

"Where the hell is Vance?" Paulie demands, and the other lieutenants, the six that have not yet come to Scarlett's side, echo his query. The four loyal ones stand quietly, ready to shoot if it comes to that.

"Vance is dead," Scarlett says in a cold, commanding voice that carries easily across the room and ends all conversations.

"Jesus," whispers another lieutenant. "I never thought nobody could take the old bastard down."

Neither did she.

Scarlett allows a moment of silence to linger, and, if she believed in any sort of god, she might have sent out a quiet prayer for Vance. Instead, she thinks back to their first meeting, in this very room, how afraid she was and how she refused to show it. How he looked at her with surprise, but also respect, when she told him she wanted to put a bullet in Chris's brain.

"What happened to him?" someone asks.

"I killed him," Ras says, and every pair of eyes in the room snaps to him, hands lingering near holsters, ready to draw. Scarlett needs to take control of the room and quickly.

"You might think you know this man," she says, gesturing to Ras. "But you don't. This isn't Jude de Haven. This is Ras, and he is every bit the killer you've heard stories about. I've made him my consul."

Everyone is watching her, the air in the room tense and electric with the possibility of violence, but she's not afraid. She's sixty stories in the air, floating above the streets, alive for the first time in eight years, the chaotic potential of the city spilling in from every direction and she owns it all.

This city is mine, she thinks. *And I'm going to build it into something cruel and beautiful.*

"Wait a fuckin' minute," Paulie says, stepping forward from the throng. "You think just 'cause Vance had a hard-on for you, now you're gonna take his place?"

"I am the boss," Scarlett says, raising her hand to silence the buzz of conversation that's just beginning to sound. Vance once shot a man for a similar accusation. "You will show me the same respect you showed him."

"Fuck that." Paulie spits on the carpet. "I'm not taking orders from a fucking cunt."

Scarlett doesn't even need to look at Ras, just drops her hand, and the gunshot sounds before she's completed the motion. He is her weapon of choice, his love for her like an invisible tether, a connection unseen but keenly felt, and together, they are more than they could have ever been apart. The head and the heart; who could stand in their way?

"I don't ever want to hear the words 'I'm not taking orders' ever again," Scarlett says, enunciating clearly and coldly as Paulie careens forward, his head hitting the glass table with a resounding *thunk*, blood pooling on the sheer surface and dripping to the floor. "Do you understand?"

"Yes, ma'am," says one of the loyal lieutenants, and the others follow suit, making noises of agreement and affirmation.

"Good," she says. "Let's get down to business."

33: From Mr. Hyde, with Love

MOM AND I stand together in the greenhouse, the late-afternoon sun heavy and hot on my shoulders. She pulls a pair of gardening gloves over her delicate hands and passes me some shears.

We set off into the garden. Mom stops by the old marble fountain that marks the very center of the estate's sprawling grounds. A cherub posed on a pedestal pours water into a large circular pool. Mom throws a penny into the still, clear water, and it joins the other coins on the bottom, shining copper in the sunlight. She's the only one who ever does that, but over the years, the fountain has built up a large collection.

"What did you wish for?" I ask.

She glances at me. "It won't come true if I say."

We follow the winding stone path until we reach the rosebushes. "What color?" she asks me.

"Red. I have a date."

She leans in to smell one of the flowers, a vibrant crimson blossom. She brushes her fingers over the petals, then carefully reaches for the stem, and I step forward with the shears. The rose falls into her open palm, and she hands it to me so I can strip the thorns off while she searches for the next perfect flower.

"It's funny how you're supposed to bring flowers for women and not men. Why do you think that is?" My heart races as the words leave me, like my innocuous speculation gave away something dangerous.

Mom gently untangles another rose from the bush and holds it out for me to cut. "I think roses from your garden are a good gift for man or for woman. Not a man like your father, but for nice man... I think it's perfect, Jude."

I glance around out of habit, even though, now that my father is dead, I have nothing in this place to fear. It's just Mom and I surrounded by the sweet, fresh smell of roses and, beneath it, the verdant, earthy scent of things growing.

"His name is Ash," I say, and she turns to face me, releasing the rose. "My date. The roses are for him."

"He is good to you?" she asks.

I nod, and she gives me a wide smile. "Good. I want you to be happy."

I feel like all the air has been pressed out of my chest, and I take a deep breath, shaky with relief. "That's it? You're not angry?"

"No. I'm not angry. When you were little boy, I knew you were different and I didn't understand. But I bought books and read and learned about how it is to be gay. I learned that it's part of you. Jude, how can I be angry at you for who you are?"

"You knew?"

She puts her hand on the side of my cheek. "I am your mother. Of course I knew. Your father refused to hear what he didn't want to hear. But I listen to you."

I smile, leaning against her palm, and she grins back.

"Now tell me all about this boy," she says.

ASH STARES DOWN at his Intermediate Russian textbook, the bustle of the coffee shop a comfortable drone around him. He loves the language, but today, the Cyrillic letters swim restlessly before his eyes. The sound of it in his mind as he reads over the words only reminds him of Jude—Ras—who lied to him about not being able to speak Russian, and so much more.

He can still hear their conversation of a few days ago, as clearly as he can hear the barista calling out orders now. Ras's voice, saying, "I'm in love with you both" plays endlessly on a repeat track in his mind. And accompanying it, the image of Jude staggering backward, blood soaking the front of his shirt as he told Ash to run, as he saved Ash's life.

There could be no doubting Jude's love. But Ash doesn't know if he could bring himself to share it.

A bouquet of red roses is set gently on the table before him, and he looks up. Ras is studying him with such fervent longing it's easy to forget that he loves someone else too. Without being invited, he slides into the chair opposite Ash.

"Jude…" he begins, but the name no longer fits the man before him, and he corrects himself. "Ras. You said you were going to give me some time to think."

"I did," Ras says, leaning forward. "It's been three days."

"I know." Ash has counted every one, each long and lonely. "That's not a lot of time to think about what you asked me."

"I missed you."

Ash almost says, "I missed you too," because it would be the truth. But he holds back. Instead, he pulls one of the roses out of the bundle on the table and runs his finger down the stem, over the little bumps where Ras has cut away the thorns. The petals are soft beneath his fingertips, and he begins to pull them off one by one, slowly, as he talks.

"I don't know what you want me to say, Ras."

"Say you'll try it."

Ash sighs, mindlessly plucking the rose, as though he's a little kid saying with every fresh petal, "he loves me; he loves me not."

"If you love me, why did you need her?" Ash asks. "Why wasn't I enough?"

"You were. Of course you were."

Ash picks up the next rose in the bouquet and begins shredding it in the same careful way. Ras watches his hands for a moment, then looks up at his face.

"I don't think you realize how beautiful you are," he says. "You're the guiding light in my life. I don't know what I would do without you."

He loves me, Ash thinks, pulling off a petal. Then the next: *He loves me not.*

"Ash," Ras says quietly. "When I was thirteen, my father told me to kill my cat."

Ash glances at him, startled, but doesn't interrupt the story that spills out like a confession, a story he'd have a hard time believing if it didn't explain so many strange things. Jude was two different people; he remembers that clearly, the one who liked to tie him up and tease him, and the one who liked to make slow, gentle love. One's wicked laugh and sinister grin, and the other's shy smile and sweet soft kisses. And the person he is now, a third entity, tender as Jude, mischievous as Ras. But he never guessed the division was so stark, so well defined.

By the time Ras finishes the story, the table is littered with rose petals, the bare stems piled to one side. Ras picks up one of the petals and presses his thumb into the curve, a restless gesture, and Ash realizes Ras is avoiding his gaze. A hint of insecurity beneath Ras's swagger and charm.

"That makes so much sense," Ash says. "I thought you were just lying to me all the time. Like when you said you couldn't speak Russian. Or how you had all those nice clothes you never wore with me. And you forgot things we did together all the time. Why didn't you tell me?"

"I'm supposed to be strong. I didn't want you to see where I was broken."

"You are strong. You saved my life."

"Come home with me tonight," Ras says, putting his hand on Ash's. "We'll talk more. I'll answer any question you want me to."

Ash hesitates, torn between the sick feeling of betrayal he's been nursing since Ras's admission, and a violent longing welling up from somewhere deep inside him.

"When I thought you were dead, I told myself I'd give anything if it would just bring you back," he whispers.

Ras lifts Ash's hand to his lips and gently kisses the back of it, then holds it between both of his own, and just that little touch, that slight connection between them feels like it's glowing, warm and soft as candlelight.

"We can talk about it. But I'm not promising anything," Ash says, and wonders why it feels like falling as he sweeps the rose petals to the side and closes his textbook, getting up to put it away. But then Ras kisses him, a hand on his hip and no more than a quick press of lips, and the falling feels more like flying, because he knows the Jude he loved is still there, and Jude would never let him hit the ground.

34: To Fall

WHEN ASH WAKES, the other half of the bed is already empty. Dawn is spilling in through the penthouse windows, a red-orange glow to the east sky. His classes at the university don't start until late morning, but it takes time to get there, and he wants to have breakfast with Ras before he leaves.

After he showers and pulls on some clothes, he glances down at the slick black surface of the dresser—severe, angular modern furniture like the rest of the spacious apartment. His collar sits there, curled around a little yellow sticky note that says "I love you," and is signed with a smiley face in black sharpie.

He's fastening it around his neck when Ras appears in the doorway, grinning, shirtless and sweaty from his morning workout. He's not the shy, sweet boy Ash fell in love with, not anymore. He has a gleeful confidence that borders on arrogance, and a sinister aura that clings to him like a shadow, despite his constant cheerfulness.

"You're beautiful," Ras murmurs, giving Ash a kiss and running his finger under the leather of the collar to test the fit.

"Where were you all night?" Ash asks.

"You'd probably rather not know," Ras says, and Ash understands. Every dark thing about Ras gets put into a box, never to be opened, never to be examined.

He did the same mental gymnastics with Jude; only the extent of the things he must ignore has changed. He does it easily, almost subconsciously, because Ras is like an eclipse, his very presence large and exuberant enough to block out the sun. Ash would gladly stay in the shade, just to be around him.

It was easy to fall in love with Ras—with his confidence and charm, his generosity, and the strange appeal of power and violence. But most of all, because he still retains the best of Jude. A boundless capacity for tenderness. A deliberate gentleness. And a startling innocence when it comes to matters of the heart. For all Ras's strength and all his fortune, Ash could break him simply by walking away. He has never been so wanted, so needed. And that, more than anything else, keeps him on Ras's leash. It's the reason he can tolerate Scarlett's presence in their relationship.

He brushes his fingers over the scar on his lover's chest. It's smaller than he thought it would be, little more than the size of the bullet that made it.

"Does this ever hurt?" Ash knows the bullet is still there, buried in a little knot of scar tissue on the surface of Ras's heart. As much a part of him as the memory of the moment it landed.

"Not for a long time," Ras says.

Ash smiles, somewhat reassured, though the heavy guilt still tugs at him; the regrets that haunt him in the darkness cast shadows even in the morning sunlight. Everything that happened to Ras—the bullet, leaving the city, his family's fracturing—could be squarely blamed on Ash. He sometimes wonders how much happier Ras would be if they had never met.

"Hey." Ras must see the dark thoughts churning in Ash's mind because he smiles, gently pressing his thumb to the center of Ash's chin and stealing a kiss. "Don't worry so much. I'm fine."

Ash nods, looking down at the floor.

"You were worth it," Ras says, and gives him another kiss before stalking off to the shower. Ash watches him go, his insecurities scuttling off to their dark corners to creep up on him in the next unguarded moment.

He sits at the kitchen counter, his Russian textbook open in front of him while he waits for Ras to come out and make breakfast. Scarlett lets herself in, her hair wind-tousled but somehow still perfect. Ash isn't attracted to women, but he can still acknowledge her beauty, and, at first, it was hard to believe he wasn't second best, a scruffy alley cat trying to compete with a regal purebred.

It didn't help that she was aloof and cold. But he realized after a while that she was just as insecure about her place in Ras's heart as he was—or maybe more so. Ras hadn't jumped in front of a bullet to save her life; he wasn't marked—scarred—with the tangible evidence of his love for her. And although Ras spends a few nights a week with her, Ash is the one living with him, the one tied to him by a hundred mundane domesticities.

Ash and Scarlett started to meet, just the two of them— her idea. Just to have coffee and talk, never about Ras, but about school and books that they both loved. And even though she is as close as you can come to royalty in this city and he's from the streets, there is a connection there he knows he can trust.

Their relationship isn't perfect—both he and Scarlett struggle with it sometimes—but they make it work. For Ras.

This morning, Scarlett gives him an unguarded smile, sitting at the counter beside him with a cup of coffee. She adds cream and something from the flask she keeps in her purse. Vodka, probably.

They chat about school, where they're both excelling. He has no idea how she finds time to run the syndicate, do her charity work, and take a full course load.

"Good morning," Ras says, greeting each of them with a kiss and a wide smile. He likes it best when the three of them are all together, practically glowing with happiness when he can have both his loves in the same room.

He makes them pancakes, chatting with Scarlett about syndicate business. Ash writes out his Russian homework until a plate of chocolate-chip pancakes is set beside him, an affectionate hand running over his back for a moment before Ras returns to the stove. It feels unreal to sit with the boss of the syndicate, eating breakfast and talking about dinner plans, while her right-hand man covers his pancakes in so much syrup they become an island in the middle of a dark, glistening lake.

Even more unreal is the thought that today, like every day, he will go to campus and spend his day learning things for the sheer joy of it. And then he will come home to someone who loves him in the kind of mad, reckless way he thought could only happen in books. It's an easy thing to forget the darkness that clings to Ras like a subtle second shadow when he brings so much light into Ash's life. It's an easy thing. To fall.

35: The Dark City

I STAND WITH Scarlett on a rooftop near the rendezvous point, watching as she expertly sets up the sniper rifle. I always feel a small twinge of sadness to see her where Eli should be, and although I'm glad she always has my back, I miss my brother desperately.

"I'd rather do this quietly," she says. "Use your knife if you can. But if I see any of them leave the building, I'm going to shoot."

"They won't." There should only be three, one city council member and the two crooked union leaders she's making a deal with. A deal no one cut us in on, a deal no one asked our permission to make. They've been warned but are stupid enough to go ahead with this anyway.

"I know." Scarlett gives me a sly smile. In her black clothes, she blends in with the darkness, as cold as this winter night. As beautiful as a siren, luring me deeper and deeper into the shadows. She's the kind of ruthless that crushes empires, this woman who would spare a murderer if she had nothing to gain by their death but would kill any number of innocents to further her goals. And I'm the weapon in her hand, slicing my bloody path through her enemies. But even as I fight and kill on the streets of the dark city, Jude, as he once was, is still with me, tempering the violence that comes so naturally. I am always in control—even in my darkest, cruelest moments, his rules hold me back. I am violent only when it serves a purpose. And I trust Scarlett to tell me what our purpose is.

In truth, we share the responsibilities of her office evenly; her cunning and my ability to lead people. She couldn't have taken the throne without me and couldn't keep it without my help either.

She glances at her watch. "Go get 'em."

This is a dance I know how to do, a dance I've done as long as I can remember, practicing with Eli when I was little and graduating to real victims as a teenager. The flash of a knife in the dark, the jerk of a head to the side, exposing the artery that pulses with every frantic heartbeat. This sanguine victory—what power could surpass it? In the vicious moment, even love seems a pale, distant second.

But when it's done and I'm flicking my knife, blood spattering in a crimson arc along the floor, Scarlett walks in, and I'm reminded of the power of my other half. A love to drown in just as easily as I might drown this city in blood.

She looks disdainfully down at the corpses. "Nicely done."

I give her a gleeful grin and do a playful bow. She laughs, leading me out into the darkness.

I SIT UP straight, my breath coming in short gasps, and open my eyes to the lights of the city twinkling around me. I'm covered in sweat, shaky and nauseated, hands clenched in fists, clinging to the bedsheets.

A soft sigh comes from beside me, and all the air leaves my chest in a rush of relief that leaves me weak. Ash is on his back, dark curls spread over the pillow, serene in sleep.

I didn't kill him. Of course I didn't. It was a dream, nothing more.

I brush some hair out of his eyes, and even that little touch feels like a miracle—that he's still with me, that he forgave me, that he loves me.

His eyes flutter open and he smiles at me. "Hey, baby." His smile fades as he looks me over. "What's wrong?"

"It's nothing. Go back to sleep."

He looks up at me with sweet, dark eyes. "You have bad dreams."

"They're just dreams." I get out of bed and he follows me, his feet softly scuffing the carpet. He puts his arms around me from behind.

"Baby," he says. "Whatever it is, I can take it. You don't have to hide from me."

I look out through the floor-to-ceiling windows that stretch across the east wall of my penthouse apartment. The city sleeps below us, the little lights glowing like bio-luminescent creatures in a dark ocean.

"I dreamed about my father," I say in a voice that isn't quite my own, detached and impartial, despite the tangled web of emotion inside me.

It's strange to feel such ambiguity, to hold two different emotions in my mind at once. To love someone and loathe him. To fear him and to defeat him. To cherish his life and to take it. But I took it. I took all of this, the streets below, wet from a recent rain, the streetlights reflected in golden puddles.

"In my dream," I say, "my father is dead. But then he opens his eyes. And he asks me a question."

He asks me to count the bodies, to walk the trail of devastation I've left in my wake. To measure my broken mind, the jagged, ugly seam where it healed. To count the pieces of my soul still missing, the scattered shards of glass. He tells me what I already knew: that killing him broke what was left of Jude's heart and that Ras filled the broken places with darkness.

"He reminds me what I lost. And then I look past him, and in the dark hallway is another body. Sometimes it's you. Other times, it's Scarlett or Eli or my mother. As soon as I see it, I know I've killed you too."

Ash takes my hand and gently squeezes.

"He makes me look at you," I say. "At your corpse. And then he always asks me the same thing. He asks me if it was worth it."

"What do you say?"

"I wake up. And then I see you sleeping beside me, and I know that nothing could ever mean more than that."

He smiles. But just past him, there's so much more darkness than light on the streets below us. And the dark city knows the truth, even if Ash believes the lie.

I could have killed Ras, in that moment just before we became one. I could have destroyed the darkness in my heart, the cruelty, the capacity for violence. My father would be alive if I had. Instead, I became the man he always wanted me to be.

He taught me to kill what I loved, so I did. And in my dreams, he lies there, bleeding in the dark hallway, dead but speaking. Asking me if I feel remorse. Asking me if I have any regrets. Asking me if it was worth it.

And I say yes. Every time.

Acknowledgements

This book would not exist without the devotion and care of my friends and family, who stood by me as this story gripped me in a fever that raged for four years. Jason, I love you with an ardor that will never be tamed by time or familiarity. Mom, Dad, Emily, and Max, thank you for supporting this unlikely and often unwieldy endeavor as you faithfully support all my endeavors.

Nikki Belaire, you are my #1 fan and your unwavering support has helped me to keep going in the hardest times. Jeanne Marcella, your wry wit and wisdom carried me through and kept me from making a lot of questionable decisions. David Neilson, your thoughtful council and stalwart support have meant the world to me.

I couldn't have done it without any of you, and I'll always be grateful.

About the Author

Sarah Kay Moll is a wordsmith and an amateur homemaker. She's good with metaphors and bad with coffee stains, both of which result from a writing habit she hasn't been able to quit. She lives a mostly solitary life, and as a result, might never say the right thing at parties. She's passionate about books and has about five hundred on her to-read pile. When she does go out, it's probably to the library, the theater, or the non-profit where she works.

Sarah lives in a beautiful corner of western Oregon where the trees are still changing color at the end of November and the mornings are misty and mysterious. She spends her free time playing video games and catering to her cat's every whim.

Email: skmoll@gmail.com

Facebook: www.facebook.com/SarahKayMoll

Twitter: @skmoll

Website: www.sarahkaymoll.com

Also Available from NineStar Press

Connect with NineStar Press

Website: NineStarPress.com

Facebook: NineStarPress

Facebook Reader Group: NineStarNiche

Twitter: @ninestarpress

Tumblr: NineStarPress